Naked Coffee Guy

Sunset Bay, Book 2

Crissi Langwell

Cover & Interior Design: Crissi Langwell/Canva
Inside Art: Shutterstock
Author Photo: Danielle Kinney

ISBN: 978-1-961240-02-5

Publisher: North Coast Stories
This book is also available in hardcover and ebook.
Please visit the author's website to find out where to purchase this book.

www.crissilangwell.com

NORTH COAST
STORIES

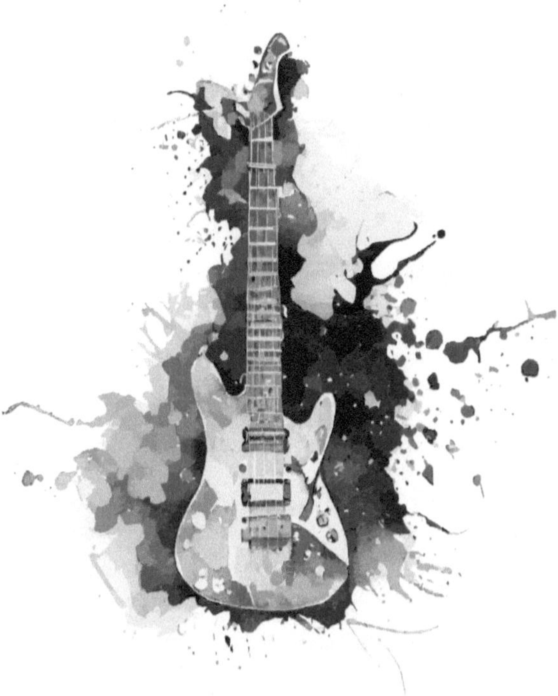

"Sometimes it takes a good fall to really know where you stand." — Hayley Williams

Books by Crissi Langwell

ROMANCE

Masquerade Mistake ~ Sunset Bay 1

Naked Coffee Guy ~ Sunset Bay 2

Savior Complex ~ Sunset Bay 3 (Coming 2024)

For the Birds

Numbered

Come Here, Cupcake

OTHER BOOKS BY CRISSI LANGWELL

Loving the Wind: The Story of Tiger Lily & Peter Pan

The Road to Hope ~ Hope Series 1

Hope at the Crossroads ~ Hope Series 2

Hope for the Broken Girl ~ Hope Series 3

A Symphony of Cicadas ~ Forever After 1

Forever Thirteen ~ Forever After 2

www.crissilangwell.com

Sign up for Crissi Langwell's romance newsletter:

Crissilangwell.com/subscribe

To Summer, my eternal rock kid who was the biggest fan of this book before it was even written

Maren's Kickass Playlist

Ain't It Fun ~ Paramore

Special ~ Garbage

Don't Get Me Wrong ~ Pretenders

West Coast ~ Lana Del Rey

Only Happy When It Rains ~ Garbage

vampire ~ Olivia Rodrigo

This Is Why ~ Paramore

Still Into You ~ Paramore

Watermelon Sugar (cover) ~ Xavier Dunn, Eluera, XD Project

Landslide ~ Fleetwood Mac

The Devil In Me ~ Garrison Starr

Take Me Anywhere ~ Tegan and Sara

Ribs ~ Lorde

Criminal ~ Fiona Apple

Toxic – 2WEI

Burning ~ Yeah Yeah Yeahs

Help I'm Alive ~ Metric

Sunshine Baby ~Japanese House

Stay High ~ Brittany Howard

Maroon ~ Taylor Swift

View full playlist at

crissilangwell.com/sunset-bay/naked-coffee-guy

Table of Contents

Please note:
The novels in the Sunset Bay series feature strong, independent women who have sex, love the word fuck, and face challenging issues. Triggers may include experience with addiction. Each book can be read as a standalone, and all end in a HEA.

Chapter One

Maren

"Baby." He breathes it in my ear, which should have made me hot. But nothing about Brock makes me even lukewarm. He's just a means to an end, a Band-Aid to my non-existent love life, and the reason I don't feel the need to couple up and settle down. He's also kind of my meal ticket, since he manages the apartment I live in. I have a feeling it's why my rent hasn't raised.

Hey, I'm not above securing rent control, even in non-conventional ways. Brock has been eyeing my ass since I moved in, and a couple years ago I finally gave it to him. We're not exclusive. Hell, I have no idea what he does in his own time. But now and then—especially when I'm in a dry spell like my current situation—I text Brock and he comes trotting. Consider it my cure for

California's housing crisis.

He cradles the back of my neck, shifting his weight as he pulls my leg around him. "Fuck, your legs are so long," he murmurs, running his hand over my calf, then my thigh, and over my bare ass before he resumes thrusting into me.

"Less talking, more fucking." I nip his bottom lip, sucking on his lip ring as he groans against my mouth.

"Maren, baby, you make this so hard."

This. Not *me*. I don't slow my pace, because if he's breaking off this casual fling we have going, I at least want to get my rocks off before it happens.

"I hope we can keep this going after you find a new place to live."

That stops me. I still my hips and press my hands on his tattooed chest, my black manicured nails digging slightly into his skin as I fight the urge to carve his heart out.

"What do you mean, find a new place?" I narrow my eyes, daring him to retract his words. He grins, then nuzzles my neck with his nose. It's a move that would normally send shivers up and down my body. Instead, I'm trying to ignore the feelings of repulsion that want to reject his dick that is still hard inside me.

"Consider this your advance notice," he whispers, then rolls his hips as he continues grinding. I wrap my leg around his, grab his forearm, then flip him on his back so that I'm straddling him. His face breaks into a wide grin, his eyes hooded with lust as he licks his lips. "Damn Maren, you're a good fuck."

"What advance notice?" He reaches for me, but I swat his hands away. When he shifts under me, I thrust down to immobilize him. I can see the impatience washing over his expression, but I don't care. "What the fuck are you talking about?"

"Hey, you still have thirty days."

I freeze, letting his words sink in. Thirty days. To find a new place. I can barely afford this place, and I know it's below market rate. How the fuck am I supposed to find a new place in a month?

Then I remember the guy I'm sitting on. Despite this sneak attack, he's still hard. And the way he's snaking his hands over my thighs, he thinks we're still fucking.

"You're evicting me while you're inside me?" I slam my hands against his shoulder, pushing him hard against the mattress as I hoist myself off him. I'm deceivingly strong when I want to be, despite my wiry frame, and I find some satisfaction as he grunts from the move, and even more at the red marks I leave behind. I should have clawed his heart out while I had a chance.

"Baby, you'll be fine. With a body like that, I bet you can find a new place in no time."

"I'm not some fucking whore, Brock."

He grins at this, sitting up in the bed. "Come on, Maren. I'm not calling you a whore. But I'm not dumb, either. Why are we even here? It can't be all the non-existent dates we went on, or the sunset strolls we never took. Maybe it's my charm, my good looks, or the way I make you come every time we fuck."

Not every time, but I'm not taking the time to correct him. Sometimes a girl just needs the guy to finish, and a little fake orgasm speeds things along. Speaking of speeding things along, why is his naked ass still sitting on my bed?

"Do you have a point?"

"Yeah, I have a point. You're fucking me because you think I can keep your rent low. But the truth is, I don't have that kind of power. The owner is just too lazy to raise rents."

He's had no power over my rent. The fact that this new knowledge makes me regret the past few years says a lot.

I drag my eyes over him, trying to find the part of him I find attractive. His broad shoulders. His chiseled jawline. His solid tattooed chest and tree trunk arms. His giant hands that have been all over my body…

Not one thing attracts me, especially not in this moment.

I snatch his shirt and pants off the floor and throw them at him. "Get dressed and get out. Lose my number,

Brock." Then I turn on my heel and head for the shower, not even waiting for him to leave.

He's gone by the time I get out. Not even a goodbye. Sure, this was nothing but a casual fling. And sure, I was using him. But his absence without a fight feels like a rejection.

"No, him kicking you out of your apartment is a rejection," I mutter as I towel dry my hair. Fuck, I can be so stupid.

I've never done well with rejection. Correction. In my adult life, I have not had to deal with rejection. It's why I don't do relationships, and why I always break things off while things still feel hot and heavy. I'd rather leave them wanting more than be left behind with a broken heart.

My heart isn't breaking now, but my security is because I'm one month away from being homeless. Again.

I glance at the clock and groan. 3:23 a.m. Letting that fucktard come over when I had to work the early shift was a stupid idea. One I was going to regret later today, for sure. The coffee shop I work at is called Insomniacs, and at this late hour—or early—the name is more than ironic.

I have a decision to make. Go to bed now and get an

hour and a half of sleep before my alarm goes off, or power through and sleep when my shift is over. I choose the latter, slipping on a pair of yoga pants and an oversized sweater. Then I grab my guitar and settle onto the funky orange couch I once scored when a neighbor moved out. The walls are thin, so I can't go ham. But I strum lightly, smoothing out the kinks to a new song I've been working on.

This is the magic that soothes my soul, the thing that makes me forget every single event from my past and all the stress of my present. When I feel like all the dominoes are about to fall, all I need to do is pull out my guitar and lose myself in the music.

But this time is different. My fingers fumble over the strings, the notes sounding tinny within the four walls of my tiny living room. It's not much, but it's mine. Or *was* mine. Even with the funky smell I can't seem to find, and the dark spots on the walls that I think might be growing. Even with the foul-smelling water I can't drink and the wall heater that gives me a headache every time I use it.

I earned this place. I kept myself afloat without the help of anyone. I turned my whole entire life around and found myself a home, supporting myself while most kids were going to college on their parents' dime.

Yet, this is where it got me—evicted without a safety net to land in.

I look at the poster-covered walls that surround me,

absorbing the images of Shirley Manson, Hayley Williams, and Chrissie Hynde, trying to soak up the courage I desperately need through osmosis. It's what I do when I'm on stage. I call on my idols like some New Age crystal-toting hippie calling on their angels. It's their persona I put on, like putting on my favorite shirt. It's what keeps me from getting too shy about performing in public and keeps me from hiding away. When I stand behind that microphone with my guitar strapped to my body, I am Shirley, daring the crowd to fuck with me as I glare at them through kohl-lined eyes. I am Hayley, singing the anthem of a generation, my fist in the air. And in the times when I'm alone with my lyrics, trying to find the words to feelings I wish I had, I am Chrissie, the songwriter who probably wrote the best love song of all eternity when she wrote "Don't Get Me Wrong."

I'm hardly into love songs now. All I can think about is that fucktard who came in here and stuck his dick in me only to tell me I needed to find a new place to live.

Fuck him.

What I need is a new song. I play a few chords, trying to loosen some lyrics from my angry brain in an attempt to move beyond the foul mood that asshole put me in, but each strum of the guitar sounds like *fuck you*—which is both juvenile and cathartic.

So I go with it.

Fuck you, you fucking loser.
You piece of shit, you two-bit poser.
Fuck you, you think you're cute.
Don't act surprised when I give you the boot.
You had your chance, you fucking poodle.
I'm tired of your dangling noodle
Grab your things, it's time to go
You're not my prince, I'm not your hoe.

I burst out laughing, even though I'm still mad at that asshole and this impossible situation he's put me in. Okay, maybe not him. It's really the guy who owns this building. But Brock is the messenger, and a shitty one at that. I mean, he had his dick in me when he broke the news. Who does that?

And the song is shit, I definitely can't play it anywhere. At least not at the venues I usually perform at. I think of my friend Claire and her seven-year-old son Finn, who are almost always at my shows when I perform at Hillside, especially now that Claire's fiancé Ethan owns the outdoor bar venue. Whenever I put the word *fuck* in my lyrics, she can tell me exactly how many times I sang it because Finn sang them with me.

I fucking love that kid.

And I fucking hate this situation.

And, glancing at the clock, it's time to start getting ready for the longest shift ever at Insomniacs. At least it might help get my mind off the mess I'm in.

Chapter Two

Maren

Every person in Sunset Bay needs their coffee this morning, and apparently they've all come to Insomniacs to get it. I haven't had a chance to breathe since the shop opened. To top it off, my coworker Nina chose today of all days to be late. Okay, fine…she chooses every day to be late. But it's closing in on eight, and she still hasn't walked through the front doors. In Nina time, this is actually late. And until she shows up, it's just me and my useless manager, Susan. Seriously, the woman is blind to the fact that I'm drowning out here while she takes up space at one of the tables, coming up with next month's schedule.

Susan, we don't need a new schedule. We need you to get off your lazy ass and make some coffee.

But I can't say anything because I need this job. Now more than ever, since a breach in employment will not look good to any new landlord, nor will it help me secure the deposit I can't afford.

"I'd like a triple shot latte with chocolate syrup and extra foam," the customer facing me orders.

Fun fact. A latte with chocolate is…drum roll please…a mocha. But try to correct a customer, and you'll find yourself on the other end of an argument you never wanted to enter in the first place.

And extra foam? On a mocha? Whatever dude.

"Anything else?" I key in his latte as a mocha and try to ignore the growing line behind him.

That's when Nina bursts through the front doors.

"I'm here! Let the party begin!"

Nina uses her hair as a canvas, and today is no exception. Yesterday it was faded pink, but today her long locks are mermaid green with blue highlights. To finish the look, she's wearing shimmering green and blue eyeshadow, and her long nails are painted a vibrant blue. As annoyed as I am with her, I'm also impressed. I love fashion, but my color palette is usually in the black range. Nina wears colors loud and proud.

"You're late, Nina," Susan says, not bothering to even look up.

"Sorry, there were extenuating circumstances." The

smirky side-eye Nina gives me is a prelude to whatever wild story she's about to unfold. Last week it was about the date she went on with a guy who failed to mention he was still in high school. She only found out when his mom tracked his phone and showed up at the movie theater they were making out in, then lectured him about going out on a school night while Nina made her escape. The week before, Nina escaped out the second-story window of a guy who forgot to mention he was married before his wife came barreling up the stairs.

Ten out of ten, her wild story was about a guy.

"So there's this guy," she begins, as she takes over the cash register and I move to the espresso machine. I roll my eyes, but keep my ears perked, even over the whoosh of the steam wand and the cadence of chatter throughout the shop. "He's new to the neighborhood, but holy hell, is he making an impact." She goes on with the story even as she helps the next customer, a mousy middle-aged woman who looks like she'd rather be praying than listening about Nina's smoke show neighbor.

"The guy has a literal eight-pack. I mean, I've read about eight-packs in that blue alien book series. You know, the one with the barbed peni—"

"Nina." I shoot an apologetic look at the woman in front of my coworker.

"Right. That will be $8.50," Nina says, twirling the screen so the flustered customer can finish her transaction. "So, every morning this guy walks around our neighborhood, shirtless and barefoot, carrying nothing but a cup of coffee." Nina holds the back of her hand up to her forehead, pretending to swoon. The next customer is standing there, waiting to give his order, but seems more invested in the story than the lady before him had been.

"Every morning?" I ask.

"Yeah, every morning? Even if it's raining?" the customer asks.

Nina shoots the guy an annoyed look. "This is California. When was the last time it rained?" But then she grins. "And yes, every morning. So far, without fail. The guy has the whole neighborhood wrapped around his finger, including me."

"Nina, less chit chat, please," Susan murmurs out the side of her mouth while taking inventory of the pastries. "Maren, when you put in the pastry order this afternoon, double the amount of morning buns. Those ones are going too fast."

Just the mention of pastries reminds my stomach that it hasn't consumed any food yet. I get through the next hour of drink orders, and when it seems like the morning rush has died down, I take my break.

With my almond milk latte and the last morning bun, I snag a table and pull out my phone, scrolling Craigslist for an apartment in my price range. It's a quick process.

"Shit," I mutter, scanning the rents that far exceed anything my meager paycheck will allow. I've been so spoiled with my low rent that I forgot the reality of housing costs in California. Even renting a room in someone's house will cost more than I was paying for my entire apartment.

I'm not an emotional person. I don't cry at the drop of a hat. When I come close, it usually comes out in anger. But this is a whole new experience of feeling hopeless. I don't have any family to help, or a savings account that will pad my income until I figure out a better solution. I don't have the education for a better paying job, and I just so happen to live in one of the most expensive tourist traps in SoCal because I never thought to move someplace more affordable. Partly because I lucked out on this apartment, but also because this is my home—always has been. Plus, there's Claire and my favorite kid, Finn. My best friend and I have been through too much for me to up and leave.

Even though I don't want to do it, I think Claire is my only hope in this situation.

I step outside the shop and call her. She picks up on the third ring.

"Hey," she says, and I note the breathlessness in her voice.

"Did I catch you at a bad time?" I ask, hating how

weak I sound right now. But I *feel* weak. I've made it my mission to never need anyone, and right now, I'm tearing out the backbone of that resolve.

"No, not at all." She laughs then, and I hear muffled sounds. "Ethan, give me a second."

Fuck. I *was* interrupting.

"I'll call back," I say.

"No, it's fine. We just got Finn off to school and are cleaning the kitchen. I could use the distraction. What's up, everything okay?"

"Everything's fine," I lied. "Why would anything be wrong?"

"Because you never call me. Usually you just show up, bearing gifts of coffee and pastries. Which, by the way, I miss. You haven't stopped by in a while."

She's right. Ever since Ethan proposed, our friendship has taken a backseat. She's been wrapped up in wedding plans and family stuff, and I've been holding back to respect the process.

Plus, I hate to admit it, I'm a little jealous. For years I've had my friend all to myself. But now, she's preparing to make this complete life change by getting married and shit, and I'm still single Maren—working a dead-end coffee job, entertaining casual flings and cutting them off when they appear to be heading toward seriousness.

But now that I see how happy Claire is and how her

life seems to be heading into this whole new realm of adulthood, I can't help but feel a twinge of regret. I'm twenty-six years old and about to be homeless for fuck's sake.

"I'll drop by tomorrow morning," I promise, all the while trying to figure out a way to ask Claire if I can crash on her couch without completely destroying my thread of an ego.

"Ooh, can you bring me one of those morning buns? I'm obsessed."

"You and the rest of Sunset Bay," I say, the taste still lingering in my mouth. These buns really are pure deliciousness, kind of like cinnamon rolls but not gooey at all. They're actually crispy, fried cinnamon pastries with hardened sugar on top. We just started serving them and run out every day.

"Is that Maren? Tell her to bring two. I'm starving," Ethan says in the background.

"You just ate breakfast, sparky," she laughs. "And she's coming tomorrow, not today."

He says something I can't hear, and when Claire giggles, I know it wasn't meant for my ears. It's also apparent that if I move in, I'll be taking a front row seat to their lovefest. As much as I love my friend, I think I'd rather live in my car than be an intrusion—or a witness.

"My break's about over, but yeah, I'll bring morning buns for all of us. We already sold out and it's not even nine o'clock."

We end the call and I stay where I'm standing for a moment, wondering what the fuck I'm going to do. I should have said something. It's not like I have any other choices.

"You still have a month or so to figure this out," I reassure myself. But I don't feel reassured. I feel scared.

There are a few minutes left of my break, so I take the time to scroll through Instagram. But, as usual, my scroll turns into a pseudo stalking session when I open my search history and touch the name at the top of the list.

Lydia Huerta.

It's been years since I've seen my little sister. The last time, she'd been hiding behind my father as I begged my parents to take me back. I'd been out for a month at that point and wasting away from both the drugs and lack of food.

In a way, I understand why they wouldn't let me back in their home. Lydia was nine, and I was a strung out seventeen-year-old with a death wish, ready to take down everyone with her.

I wouldn't let me in, either.

I still don't forgive my parents.

Looking at my sister's photos, I can see she's happy and surrounded by friends. She's now the same age I was when I was kicked out, but her story couldn't be more different. We look a lot alike, from her dark hair and pale Latina skin to her wide eyes the color of espresso. Just like our mother. What's different, though, are the deep dimples in each cheek, a feature she models in every single one of her smiling photos. You don't even have to know her to see that she's kind and lovable. And it makes my heart ache that I'm not in her life.

In her latest photo, she's clad in her green and gold track uniform, the colors of the high school I used to go to. She's surrounded by friends, all sweaty and smiling. It's apparent they've just finished a run—another difference between us. The only reason I would be running is if something were chasing me, and even then, I'd be weighing the pros and cons of breaking a sweat versus being maimed.

If I came home, would Lydia know me?

I close out of her account quickly and head back to the shop. It's not going to happen. I am not crawling back to my parents' house just because I'm in a bind. They didn't help me when I hit rock bottom, and they haven't reached out to me since…even though I still live in the same town and have worked at the same job for years. I'm not hard to find, and they've never tried to find me. I mean, I work in the most popular coffee shop in Sunset Bay, and they have never walked through those doors. Coincidence? I think not.

I step back inside Insomniacs, noting how Nina is leaning against the counter, chatting with Jess, her roommate for the past several years. A glance at the coffee station, and it's like an espresso bomb went off. There are coffee grounds all over the workstation, dirty towels on the counter and floor, and unwashed frothing pitchers hanging off to the side. Susan is nowhere to be found, which means I have to be the one to manage my messy coworker.

Or just do it myself.

Which I do, because I don't have the energy for a confrontation—which is so unlike me because I'm all about confrontation. But this whole house thing is throwing me for a loop, and I realize at some point I'm going to have to get over myself and ask for help.

The question is, who's the lucky person I get to inconvenience?

"Well, that was interesting," Nina says, joining me as I finish cleaning the bar. "My roommate just told me she's moving out, effective immediately."

I stop what I'm doing, and face her, not believing what I'm hearing.

"What do you mean?" I ask. "Like, in the time you've been at work, she's moved all her stuff out?"

"Well, not exactly," Nina says. "I guess she's been chipping away at this for the past week and I just haven't noticed. She says it's because I'm a slob and always stealing her stuff." She shrugs, then reaches across me to grab her coffee from under the counter. Of course it has no lid, and it sloshes on the shelf and across the floor. Nina doesn't notice, though. "I think she was just looking for an excuse to move in with her boyfriend."

"You think so?" I ask, wiping up the spill. I'm only half in this conversation. The other half of me is thinking about how to insert myself as a prospective roommate. Even though Nina really is a slob. Even though, as I've just noticed, she's wearing the exact same shade of lipstick that I am, which most likely means she went in my purse while I was on break.

Even though Nina is difficult and half the time I don't like her, and if I live with her, I will be around her—All. The. Time.

"It's fine, though. Really. I have nowhere to put most of my clothes, and they're all over my living room while I reorganize my closet. But with Jess gone, I don't need to reorganize anything because I can just use her room as my closet."

I snap out of my thoughts and re-enter the conversation, unsure if I heard her correctly.

"Wait. You're willing to take on Jess's portion of rent just so you can have a closet? How much did she pay, anyway?"

"$700 a month."

I widen my eyes. That's less than what I'm paying now, and just a fraction of what I've seen on the market. I've been to Nina's place. It's a huge, beautiful Victorian, albeit a mess. But there's room to move in there, even with her shit everywhere.

"How much is it to rent the whole place?" I ask.

She shakes her head. "Nothing. It's my grandma's house. I inherited it when she died, and it was fully paid off. I only have to pay property taxes and utilities, and this job and Jess's rent more than cover that. Well, now, just this job since Jess it out." She shakes her head. "Regardless, I'll be fine. But you're a good friend for worrying."

Chapter Three

Maren

I never did ask Nina to give up her dream closet in exchange for me living with her. It's like the old Maren has died, and this new Maren is weak as shit. Seriously, I can't figure out what's wrong with me.

Actually, I can—I'm triggered. All of this brings me back to those days I had to survive on the street, all because my parents wouldn't take me back. When I'd go days at a time without eating. When I'd spend sleepless nights in my car. When the only thing that could take the edge off was a bottle of whiskey I'd swiped from a store and the Xannies in my pocket.

And now I'm here, facing the same situation—but sober—and I can't for the life of me put myself in a position to asking for help.

Because what if they say no?

I hate that this is even an issue, that something so small is keeping me from asking for help. I just don't know how to get past it.

I climb the stairs to my apartment, and that's when I see it. The envelope taped to my door. Looking down the line, I see I'm not the only one. We all have envelopes, and I know exactly what's in each one.

With shaky fingers, I take the envelope inside and lock the door behind me. I tear into it and pull out the letter, hoping for at least more time. Nope, it's still thirty days. That asshole Brock must have known about this for a while, and he only told me about it this morning.

Fuck that guy.

I look around the apartment. At my various plants around the room. At the modest couch and the simple kitchen. At how clean everything is and in its place. At my idols looking down at me from the walls.

"I guess it's really over," I say to Shirley, Hayley, and Chrissie. My guitar sits in the corner, and I instinctively move toward it so I can partake in a little musical therapy. But inside, there's this ache that won't go away, that needs something stronger than guitar strings to carry me through.

Which is why, an hour later, I find myself at Torches, a rooftop bar overlooking the city side of Sunset Bay, a glass of red wine in my hand and a million stars overhead as the ocean crashes in the distance. I see none of it, only the wine.

So far, I haven't had a sip. I know once I do, I'll give up seven years of sobriety—years I struggled through to make it to this day. But everything feels so stupid right now. Like, why was any of it worth it if I was just going to lose it all in the end? I've had to fight my whole life for everything. Nothing has come easy. I've watched kids I went to school with go out and make something of themselves and afford lives beyond anything I could imagine, all while I'm stuck making coffee for the elite masses of Sunset Bay.

My dreams don't even require much. A simple life funded by my music, with enough money so I can quit my day job. If I hadn't been kicked out, I would have been happy living in my small apartment forever.

Everything I touch turns to shit, though. I'm still playing the same venues to the same people. I'm still serving up coffee. And in thirty days, I will be living in my car because I can't ask my best friend to crash on her couch, I can't go back to my parents, and I can't ask Nina to give up her closet.

I lift the wine to my lips, the earthy scent traveling straight through my nose. Why I chose wine, I don't know. It had never been my drink of choice before. This is more Claire's style, not mine. I guess I didn't want something I'd go back to again. Tomorrow, I'll return to sober life. Today? I drink.

But I never get the chance. Someone bumps me from behind and wine sloshes down the front of my shirt. Today, of all days, I'm wearing white instead of my usual black. Now it's a deep shade of maroon, splattered across me like a gunshot wound.

"Watch it, asshole." I whip around to tear the offender a new one, but nothing prepares me for the man in front of me. And when I say man, I mean that all my life I've been surrounded by boys, and they don't even come close to the specimen I'm facing. He has long, wavy dark-blonde hair pulled back into a ponytail, deep blue eyes, and his Viking-like beard is trimmed close on the sides and long in the front, reaching to the top of his solid chest. I mean, add some dirt and a few weapons, and he could be sailing off to pillage and plunder.

Holy hell, the things this man could do to me.

And he's tall! I stand 5'11" in my four-inch heels, and he towers over me like I'm a sapling and he's a redwood, his broad shoulders blocking my view of the rest of the room. He's doing things to my insides by just standing there, his eyes sweeping over me as if they alone could undress me.

"Sorry 'bout that. Can I get you another?" he asks.

He doesn't look sorry. He looks like he could devour

me. I'm losing myself in his hooded eyes, swimming in the deepest blue of them while my fingers tingle, wanting to run my hands though his beard and then tug until his lips are on mine. Then his question registers and I realize I've been standing there like a shell-shocked lunatic, staring at him while he waits for me to respond. Even more, I realize my own lusty feelings are muddying my perception. This guy probably isn't into me. I just want him to be.

What the fuck is wrong with me?

"No, I don't drink," I stammer, feeling my cheeks go red as he glances at the stain. "I mean, I haven't for years. Tonight is just…" I look to the floor, noting some droplets of wine that have dried on my boots. "It's just been a bad day, and I almost made a terrible mistake."

He places his hand on my shoulder, and I am both thrilled and appalled that he is this close to me, touching me. Does he not know the effect he has on me? On anyone in this room? Is there even a room around us? What is life?

He studies me for a moment, and I find myself studying him right back. He feels familiar to me, even though I've never seen him before in my life. But I'm comfortable in his presence, in a way I've never felt with any man before. Like we knew each other in a past life. I note a question in his eyes, and I wonder if he's feeling the same way. But then his face breaks into a wide smile.

Fuck me, that smile. If I thought he was gorgeous before, now I just want to wrap myself around him.

"I'm Mac," he says.

Mac. Such a simple name for someone who's suddenly bigger than the sky.

"Maren," I return.

He nods, his hand remaining on my shoulder as he looks me in the eyes. And when I say looking, I mean no one has looked at me this way. Not a single person. It's like he can see inside me, see my thoughts and feelings as if they were items to be treasured.

"Maren," he repeats, and my name in his mouth makes me feel a little weak-kneed.

This is not normal. I'm the queen of casual, usually the pursuer, and never one to swoon over anyone. And here I am, swooning.

He removes his hand from my shoulder, then tugs at the back of his neck. For a moment, I see the struggle in his face, like he's in two different places in me. Then his eyes return to mine, and his face softens.

"Well, Maren. I'm having a bad day too. I came here to forget, but then I ran into you. I don't think it was a mistake, and neither was your decision to be here."

"I almost fucked up my sobriety."

"But you didn't," he points out. "There aren't mistakes, there are choices. Today, both of us came here because of a choice. Just like years ago, you made a choice to not drink, and today you made that same choice."

"I think you made it for me." I breathe out a sarcastic laugh, waving my hands over my shirt. "If I weren't wearing this drink, I'd probably be three sheets to the wind by now."

He shrugs. "Maybe. But the Universe has a funny way of stepping in when we feel our weakest."

I snort at this, breaking the spell as I step away. The Universe steps in? Is that why I'm getting kicked out of my apartment?

"You're sweet," I say, "but also a little naïve if you think there are magical forces looking out for my best interest. If what you're saying is true, I'd love to speak with this Universe and tell it to mind its own business, because my life is a mess."

"Fair," he says, but I note the amusement in his eyes. This guy is talking about the Universe and divine intervention, and he thinks I'm the one without a clue. "Can I get you a drink to replace the one I spilt on you?" he asks, then adds, "I'm getting myself a soda water with a lime and a splash of tonic. Would you like one, too?"

"I'd love one."

We end up talking all night in a private lounge area, even as the temperature drops and the people around us get more wasted by the hour. Even as my glass of soda water with a splash of tonic—delicious, by the way—stays empty in my hand. Even as he takes my glass and sets it aside, then smoothly slides his hand over mine and doesn't let go. I'm half in the conversation and half absorbed by the warmth of his hand and how it covers mine completely. I've never felt safer or more understood in my life.

We talk about everything and nothing. I share that my favorite band in the whole world is Paramore, I could eat sushi every day of my life and never grow sick of it, and I haven't seen my parents or sister since I was a teenager. He tells me he was vegan for a few years until he broke his meat fast with a cheeseburger, that the only movie that has ever made him cry was *Gladiator*, how his parents died in a car accident when he was young, and how he was in the foster system for years until he finally ran away. Then he found Benji.

"He was old when he took me in," Mac says, "but so was I. Fifteen, three years away from reaching adulthood, and not a clue about how to be an adult. And this old man saw something in this angry teen and decided to give me a home."

He smiles, but it's tinged with something somber. Suddenly it's clear why Mac believes in the Universe. But choices?

"You say there aren't mistakes, only choices. But

what about your parents? I'm sure it wasn't your choice to never know them."

"True," he says, "and I was angry about that for a long time. But Benji taught me that sometimes the choice is what we do with circumstances, and how we'll move forward. My reality was that I spent years in the system, which meant shuffling from house to house, not all of them great. Then I lived on the streets, fighting my way to survival. My choice was to let that become my identity and remain angry, or to take what I'd learned from those years and change my present and future." Mac squeezes my hand. "I chose the latter, and it's a choice I have to make every day to keep from letting the demons win."

Despite the way my mind is cringing at all the woo-woo stuff about the Universe and company, my heart is becoming a believer.

I could remain bitter about my parents turning their back on me when I needed them most. I could chalk up my current eviction crisis as more proof that my life is fucked and that's just the way it will always be. I could stay in this dark place, white knuckle my addiction, give up control, and sabotage the seven years of sobriety under my belt.

Or, I could make the choice to move forward and figure out what to do with my circumstances.

And suddenly, I feel a million pounds lighter. I don't have a solution to my problem yet, but I do have choices.

I just need to let go of my ego and ask for help. It's so simple that I laugh, tilting my head up toward the stars, and I swear the sky is so brilliant it's maroon.

"Something just happened, didn't it?" Mac murmurs. Then, before I can answer, he's unlacing my boots.

"Uh, Mac?"

"Maren, do you trust me?"

Trust him? I barely know him. And yet, when I look into his eyes and see the intensity of his expression and feel the way he sees me—truly sees me—I know my answer.

"Yes," I whisper.

He removes one boot and then my sock, his hand lingering on the sole of my naked foot before he sets it on the cold ground of the rooftop bar. He does the same to the other, his eyes on mine the whole time. Never has anything felt more erotic, more tantalizing, more intense.

He takes his own shoes and socks off, then stands. He holds out his hand, and I place mine in it, allowing him to pull me to my feet.

I'm struck by how things have changed in a matter of moments. How I came here to forget, to step off the treadmill by undoing everything I worked so hard to achieve. But now I'm here, all my senses absorbing the intoxicating scent of this man, my mouth watering as my eyes glance off his lips, my body straining to move closer to him, my fingers aching to feel the silky cotton of his shirt, the solid smoothness of his chest, and the thick roughness of his beard.

"We're standing on holy ground," Mac says, looking down at me as he moves closer, resting a cautious hand at my hip. He raises an eyebrow, almost like he's asking permission. I nod, just slightly, and his hand tightens. It's subtle, but the message passed between us is loud and clear. This man could own me, but only if I let him.

Mac sways slightly, his firm hand moving to my back, guiding me to move with him, dancing with no shoes under a burgundy sky.

"To hold on to an experience, I like to get as close to the earth as I can, no barriers." He looks down at our feet, and I do too.

"But we're on the rooftop of a seven-story building," I remind him, looking back into his blue eyes.

He smiles, then nods in agreement. "Yes, but by taking off our shoes, we're asking the earth to meet us where we are. And for what I'm about to do, I want the earth as my witness."

I brace my bare feet on the cool surface of the rooftop, feeling his feet slide around mine as he comes even closer. He rests his hand behind my neck, his fingers curling into my hair as I tilt my head toward his.

"Can I…"

But he doesn't finish the question because his mouth is on mine, hands in my hair as he draws me in.

And me? I'm consumed. It's apparent I have never been kissed before, because it's never felt like this. Mac kisses me with fire, pouring lava into my veins, burning me sweetly as I slowly turn to ash. The whole world disappears, and it's just us and the earth under the building, rising to meet our feet.

His mouth lifts from mine, and he cups my face, his thumb brushing over the lips he just kissed. And even though I've just met him, and there's so much I don't know about him yet, I am thoroughly aware that I am now ruined for anyone else.

"I'm a selfish man," he whispers, still holding my face. "I just had to be a part of whatever you experienced."

"Mac, you *are* an experience," I laugh. But inside, I'm dying. Deceased. Obliterated. How the fuck did I breathe before this man?

He looks at his watch—a Salvatore Ferragamo that I know costs close to $2,000 because Nina told me about some guy she dated who flashed his money through unaffordable fashion, including expensive timepieces.

It brings me back to reality.

Despite the fact that I'm still reeling from that kiss, from our connection, and every single way Mac makes me feel, I realize I still don't know him. The fact that he's wearing a watch that costs more than my soon-to-be defunct rent proves that we're from vastly different worlds. I take a split-second to gather information about this former runaway foster kid based on his attire, and notice for the first time that he's dressed in a suit that probably costs five times the watch on his wrist.

This guy is way out of my league, and I'm a fool to think I belong in his world.

"It's getting late," Mac says, snapping me out of my thoughts, "but I don't want this night to end. Can I get you another soda water? Maybe something to eat? Or we could go back to my place where it's a little warmer than a rooftop bar."

I know what he's suggesting—and oh goddess, do I want to take him up on this offer. If he looks this good in a suit, I can only imagine what he looks like without the expensive threads. If he's dressed like this, his place is probably unlike any home I've ever entered.

Yes, I'm embarrassed that he probably makes seven figures while I scrimp on the groceries to survive the month. But honestly, that's not what matters or what I even care about. I never have cared about wealth, and in this moment, I realize I still don't.

What I care about is the fact that I've finally met a man I can relate with on a human level.

I'm all about a good fuck. Relationships? No. But a

good, meaningless fling can be a great thing. No strings attached. No messy feelings. No promises, no rules. Sure, I've come close to caring about the guys I've been with, but never enough to want something permanent.

This is different, though. As much as I want to see what's under that ten-thousand-dollar suit, I'm also craving more of the connection we've shared. For the first time, I'm thinking about what tomorrow will bring. In just a short amount of time, Mac has not only stimulated my body, but he's stimulated my mind. He's made me curious about the future, and if I go back to his place, it's possible the fire we've started will burn out before anything can come of this.

I want something to come of this.

"Let's stay here," I say, and immediately recognize the flash of disappointment. But it's gone as quickly as it came, and he smiles as he stands.

"Then let me get you a refill," he says, leaning down to kiss my cheek. He lingers, and I feel the whisper of his beard against my skin as I inhale his intoxicating scent—a blend of leather and pine that sends a ripple straight to my core. Fuck me, this man is going to tear me apart. And damn, if I don't want him to.

"I'm going to use the bathroom, meet me back here," I order. I move to retrieve my shoes, but he pulls me close again, our bodies fitting like they are each other's missing piece. I feel small pressed against his solid chest, like he could shatter me with just the tip of his finger. He looks down at me, then shakes his head.

"Maren, what the fuck am I going to do with you?" he murmurs, then brushes his lips against mine. Then he's gone, disappearing into the crowd while my body chills at the absence of his heat.

Fuck me.

According to Mac's $2,000 watch, it's nearly two in the morning, and after not sleeping at all last night, I'm starting to feel it. Boots on and now in the bathroom, I take a look at my face in the mirror and realize I look it, too. I don't have to work tomorrow, so at least I can sleep in before my pastry date with Claire. Wait till she hears about Mac.

I glance again in the mirror, looking past the dark shadows forming under my eyes to see what Mac sees. A white shirt with a burgundy stain across the front that I'm just pretending looks natural. Makeup slightly smeared, but still effective at adding drama to my dark eyes and pale skin. Long black hair, a little messy but free of frizz. Lips still holding a light scarlet stain.

Not bad, Maren. Not my best, but not my worst.

I duck into a stall to do my business when someone else enters the shared bathroom. By the volume of their voices, I'd say they should probably be cut off.

"I don't think he came here with her, but he was

definitely into her," one of the girls says. I can see them through the crack of the door, both dressed in tiny skirts and high heels. I keep quiet, unsure if they know someone else is in here.

"It probably means nothing. Women throw themselves at him all the time. You still have a shot at him."

"Shut up," the first girl laughs. "I like my guys with a little less money, thank you very much."

"You're joking, right?"

Yes, dumbass, she's joking.

"Yes, Courtney, I'm joking. He's just been occupied with that chick who apparently can't hold her liquor. Did you see the wine stain all over her shirt?"

Well, shit. They're talking about Mac and me. I'm definitely not exiting this stall now.

"Obviously you have a better shot than she does, Brittany. Just slip your number to him when she's not looking. He'll call, I know it."

"I don't know," Brittany says. She's fixing her lipstick, then turns to her friend who is now out of view. "But it would be a shame to use these perfect lips on anyone but Mac Dermot. By the way, did you hear he's been selling off properties right and left? The guy is probably getting ready to buy an island or something. The latest was that huge apartment complex over on

Beale Street."

My heart drops at the mention of the street I live on. Of my apartment building I was just kicked out of.

"I mean, his face is plastered on that billboard across town, of course he'd be the agent who sold it. I bet his commission was huge."

So that's where I've seen his face before.

I breathe a sigh of relief, knowing he's not the owner. He's just the agent. But still, just knowing he had a hand in yanking the home out from under me changes everything.

"That place isn't bad," Courtney says. "I once knew someone who lived there, said it was the only place in town with reasonable rent. But I guess Mac Dermot sold it to someone who plans to tear the place down and make it a parking lot."

That fucker. I feel like a fool. This whole night, I've been falling for the man who just sabotaged my whole life. While he was talking to me about choices and moving forward and holy ground, he was celebrating a big fat commission—with the money he got for the Beale Street apartment. He probably has enough for a dozen Salvatore Ferragamo watches to wear on his fancy yacht. And in a month, while I'm packing up to leave my house, he probably won't even remember who I am.

I flush, then leave the stall, entering the sudden hush of the girls who have paused their preening to stare wide-eyed at me. I wash my hands, check my makeup, and give each of them a pointed look.

"He's all yours," I tell them, then exit the restroom, leaving their audible gasps in my wake.

I don't confront him. I don't even want to speak to him. As far as I'm concerned, Mac Dermot can rot in hell.

Chapter Four

Mac

She's gone when I come back to where I left her. I hold her drink in my hand, staring at the spot she should have been.

"Hey."

I don't turn at the sultry voice. It's not Maren, I know it. And when this woman's hand snakes up my bicep, it takes all I have to not jerk away from her touch. But I do turn when she takes the drink from my hand. Of course, she's blonde. Smoking body, evidenced by the blouse that cuts to her navel and the skintight skirt that feels like a suggestion rather than actual clothing. Flawless face with high arched eyebrows. A trendy tattoo of a bird on the inside of her wrist. The kind of girl who would eagerly warm my bed if I took her home.

She wraps her pouty lips around the straw, her blue eyes locked on mine as she sips. Then she grimaces and pushes the drink back at me.

"What is this?" Her face puckers in offense, as if she's forgotten she's trying to seduce me.

"Not your drink." I turn to leave, but she grabs my arm again. This time I do shake her off.

"If it's for that lush you were with, she took off. I think she left with some other guy." She shrugs, then moves closer to me. "But I'm here. I'm Brittany."

"And I'm leaving," I say, pushing past her. I half expect her to follow, but don't look back to find out. I ditch the drinks on a table, then head for the exit.

I know Maren didn't leave with anyone. I shouldn't be confident about this, but I am.

And it makes me feel like shit, because she *should* have left with someone else. The last thing she needs is to be with someone like me.

So maybe it's a good thing she took off.

My car is parked in a nearby garage, a black Jaguar sedan with sleek lines and unmatched power; a newer version of a car I once saw when I was just a paycheck to a family with three other fosters. I can still remember the hunger ache in my belly, the way my pants hung loose at the waist but hit at my shins, and how that slinky car wormed its way into my appetite like a cheeseburger and a strawberry milkshake. I wanted that car—more than I wanted to escape the slap of the belt that left welts on my skin, more than I wanted to ease my unquenchable hunger as my foster parents squandered each paycheck on useless junk delivered to the house every day, and almost as much as I craved just one person I could trust.

I knew if I had that car, everything else would fall in place. And here I am. Driving the car. Living the life. Free to make my own choices.

Or am I? The mere thought makes me laugh out loud as I press the key fob, the Jaguar's lights bouncing off the concrete walls. Even though it's been a few years, it still feels like I'm playing a massive game of pretend. Fancy car. Fancy clothes. A watch that costs more than I used to make in a whole year.

I slide onto the leather seats, inhale the still new smell, and think of the way Maren felt in my arms. The lilac scent of her shampoo, and the hint of honeysuckle on her lips. How she didn't pull away when I took off her shoes, pulled her to her feet, and kissed her sweet mouth.

How she didn't recognize me, probably doesn't even remember me, and may even forget me by the time she wakes up tomorrow. But I'll remember, and I'll probably continue thinking of her, just as I have over the past few years.

But I won't contact her. I was too chicken shit to say anything when we first met, and I lost that right before the ink dried on the documents that secured the sale of those apartments.

She's better off without me.

I pull out of the garage, taking the coastal highway that leads to my home in King's Cove, the highest point of Sunset Bay. The gates slowly open and I pass through, my eyes on the rearview mirror as they close behind me, then back to the winding road until I reach my home on a cliff. It's like a metaphor for my life. I'm new money, in a way. Thanks to Benji, I've been around it for the past twenty years, but I'm not used to having it line my pockets. Not used to the women who throw themselves at me. All it took was a decision to try something different, one hell of a lucky break, and a resolve to make it or die trying, and I suddenly have more money than I know what to do with.

This wasn't just handed to me, though. I worked my ass off for this. I grew my brokerage from the ground up, though in a relatively short time. I made the moves that helped us surpass our competitors.

But I'm not an idiot, I couldn't have done this without using Benji's name—and I can't help feeling like all I have to do is sneeze and it will all go away.

Fucking imposter.

The lights are all on, illuminated against the black

exterior that blends in with the dark night sky. It's all windows, which would make the home like a fishbowl if I had any neighbors close by. But I chose this home for the privacy, my closest neighbor about a mile from my door. I also chose it for the endless view of the ocean that makes up my entire backyard. A view I'll never grow tired of. If this all goes away tomorrow, that's what I'll miss the most.

But I won't stay here tonight. I haven't been home in weeks, though the clean smell through the open door lets me know the housekeepers have been, keeping the vacant home free of dust because that's what they're paid to do. Even though no one is here to enjoy it.

I drop the bag of laundry near the front door, knowing it will be dry-cleaned and hanging in my closet by the end of tomorrow. Then I take the stairs two at a time until I reach the large room that makes up the entire second floor. I pass the Florida King bed on the way to the closet, opening the double doors and stepping inside to racks of suits, shoes lining the shelves, and an armoire with a few dozen watches, a wide variety of luxury silk ties, cufflinks, and twenty-seven different pairs of sunglasses.

I pack a few suits in a garment bag I've laid across my bed, then grab a few more pairs of shoes.

I know this drill, how to pack in the least amount of time possible. I spent years doing this very thing, though back then I didn't have much to pack. Now it feels like a joke to have my hands brushing against linen, silk, and mohair fabrics, and my eyes wandering over Bentley and Cartier aviators.

My ten-year-old self would shit a brick.

I take what I can carry, laying it flat in the trunk of my Jaguar. Then I travel the winding road back into Sunset Bay, toward the freeway that serves as the vein of our coastal town, until I reach a house I'm more than familiar with.

Benji's home. And for the time being, my home too.

I sit in my car out front, peering at the place I grew up. The house is too large for a dying man. But he refused to go to the hospital. There are dozens of untouched rooms, though they were like that long before the cancer diagnosis. Now they're cleaned each week by the housekeeper I hired, only to collect dust and be cleaned once again.

The only rooms that are used now is the living room, set up with a hospital bed and a fold-out luxury couch for the overnight nurse, and my own small bedroom in the back of the house. The one I lived in starting at age fifteen. The only room in this house I consider mine.

The place I'll sleep tonight while dozens of families over on Beale Street wonder what the hell they'll do in just a month's time.

The dash camera says it's just past four in the morning, but I haven't been sleeping much the past few weeks anyways. Now that the deed is done, the ink dry, the contract all in place, I wonder if sleep will come easy again.

Has it ever?

In a few hours I'll be driving to the office, so I don't even bother to cover the Jaguar. I pull my clothes from the trunk and walk the short pathway to the house between two mounds of dry grass—the casualty from years of neglect. My key slides into the lock and I turn it noiselessly, just in case everyone is sleeping. But once I reach the living room, a small light in the corner lets me know Hattie is awake.

The nurse glances up from her book, then slips a bookmark in as she rises to her feet. Her grey hair frames a slender face lined with age, even more pronounced by the early hour. I'd worry about her all-nighters; except she's been doing this for decades; says she prefers overnights to days because it keeps her off her feet.

"How is he?" I ask, then look to the sleeping figure in the bed that takes up a corner of the room. Benji's chest rises and falls, a small groan escaping his lips with each breath, and the monitor next to him beeping in time with his heart.

At this point, Benji is just to be kept comfortable. He's not on Hospice, because to do so would take away some of our end-of-life choices, and I want control over the way his last moments are lived. This includes the nursing staff, a team of five nurses who care for Benji on rotation. It's been a few months, and we're all on first name basis—Hattie, Anna, Shane, Amber, and Bill. All of them have been amazing with my benefactor, treating him with the utmost care, even on his most difficult days. But Hattie, with her motherly care and tireless spirit, is undeniably my favorite.

"Anna was here before me, and she said he slept most of the afternoon and evening," Hattie says. "When I got here, he ate a little at dinner but not much. He had a slight fever upon evening, but nothing too serious."

I lower my garment bag on the couch, then cross the room. I feel his forehead, and he stirs slightly but remains asleep. It's damp, but cool to the touch, as if his fever just broke.

"Did you catch any sleep?" I ask her. She shakes her head. Hattie never sleeps on her shifts, even though I wish she would.

"But I got to the part where the government plot was revealed, and the heroine is kicking some serious ass," she says, picking up her novel, a book named *Numbered.* I'm not much into reading, but kickass heroines remind me of a certain raven-haired vixen who left me tonight without a word.

She's better off.

I retreat to my room, turning on the monitor next to me. Hattie is here, but it makes me feel better to keep tabs on Benji in case anything changes. Through the monitor, I can hear the slow rock of Hattie's chair, the steady beep of the electrocardiogram, and Benji's slow breathing.

He has weeks at most. Maybe a month. And once he'd dead, his sins will remain on my shoulders. But I've kept his secrets because I owe him that much. I clean the messes he's left behind, praying it's enough penance for whatever awaits him after this life. Praying it will save me too, because Lord knows I've enough sins of my own.

I pause for one more moment, listening to the regular symphony of the home. When I'm finally convinced it's no different than any other night, I close my eyes and hope to get at least two hours of sleep before my day begins again.

Chapter Five

Maren

One month later

Everything looks unfamiliar when I wake up. The sun is coming in from the wrong side of the room, my feet hang off the wrong side of the bed. I pat the space beside me before opening my eyes, grateful to find it empty.

Then it all comes back to me. I'm at Nina's house, in the smallest room in existence, and here for the unforeseeable future.

I'd stayed in my apartment up until the very last minute, relishing my solitude until the day all tenants were to vacate the premises. Plus, it helped Nina get used to the idea before I moved in. She hadn't been thrilled about giving up the room that was supposed to be her closet, but of all my possibilities for my next home, she was the best choice.

With a bunch of asterisks, that is. I mean, she is Nina. But having a sloppy roommate who occasionally steals my stuff is better than being homeless.

And I'll never be that again.

I'm still sore from yesterday's move. I've never been one for exercise beyond a brisk walk, so carrying box after box down the stairs was a workout I was not conditioned for. Thank goodness for Claire's boyfriend. Ethan and his buddies took care of the heavy stuff while Claire and I handled the lighter fare. Nina was working at Insomniacs while we moved, but she probably wouldn't have helped anyway.

My treasured orange couch and dining room table were donated to a non-profit for the shelterless. Hopefully they would be a welcome addition to someone's much-needed home. I donated most of my clothes too, since the closet in my new room is behind a single door. Pots and pans, dishes and silverware, cooking utensils…all gone. Nina said they weren't necessary, since her grandmother's house had all these things.

I couldn't keep them if I wanted to. Between her grandmother's old furniture and Nina's clothes and belongings covering every surface, there just wasn't space. And the room I'm in now? It's large enough for me, a bed, a few favorite outfits, and all my guitars lined up on the wall.

I feel kind of like I did the first day I moved into my apartment. I don't have the same awe at having my own place…because I don't…but I definitely have the same amount of things to my name—practically zero.

As for Mac? I think of him every day. Mostly to think of all the ways I could unalive him, or maybe just give him a violent case of Montezuma's revenge. I hope he's miserable in his mansion, haunted by all the "choices" he's made that have ruined innocent people's lives.

But in quiet times, I remember the way he kissed me. How he looked at me. How he felt pressed against my body. Sometimes when I'm alone at night, my swirling fingers undoing the ache in my core, I think I can even smell him.

I haven't dated since that night. It's only been a month, so I'm hardly a saint. But in the past, I at least had Brock to fill that space, and no thank you.

It's more than that though, and I can't deny it. The connection we shared was something I'd never experienced before, and now I'm unsure I'll ever feel it again. That's what hurts the most. I let my guard down with him. I saw someone I trusted. And just when I entertained the idea of this going beyond that night, of maybe even being something that had lasting power, I learned that I never really knew him at all.

I obviously can't trust myself around guys. So, for now, I'm swearing off all men and focusing on me.

Also focusing on how I can make Nina's house feel more like a home, because goddamn, that girl has clutter.

I roll out of bed, stretching my aching muscles before padding down the hall to the kitchen. Nina's dirty dishes are all over the sink, and I push them aside as I search for the coffee pot. Eventually I locate it in one of the cabinets, along with a canister of coffee. I pour a generous amount of grounds in the filter, fill it with water, then flip the switch and wait until I'm holding a steaming cup of coffee in my hand. I look in the fridge and see that Nina prefers dairy to my usual almond milk. I decide a creamy cup is worth the stuffy nose the dairy will give me, and finally enjoy my first sip.

Heaven.

I look out the window of my new neighborhood, each sip breathing new life into my tired body, when I notice someone outside in the dim morning light. I peer closer, my eyes widening at the sight of his bare feet and naked chest. Oh goddess, this is Naked Coffee Guy! Nina has been talking about this guy all month long, so much that I feel like I'm seeing a celebrity. From far away, I can make out the dark shading of tattoos that snake up his arms and splay across his chest. He moves with purpose, no sign of discomfort as each bare foot lands on the rough asphalt. As he approaches the front of our house, I can see the steam rising off the top of his cup of coffee, which he sips periodically as he walks. But now that he's closer, his features become clearer. Specifically, his long beard.

A beard I've run my hands through, have dreamed about for a month. A beard that's been the star player in so many of my late-night solo fantasies.

Holy fuck. It's Mac.

It hasn't even been a full day in this neighborhood, and he's here, wrecking my sense of home. Yet, as horrified as I feel about his intrusion, my core flutters with excitement, as if she's finally going to get some.

"Down, girl," I mutter. But I can't look away. The muscles in his chest flex with each step, and his perfect washboard abs are like a ladder down to the bulge filling out his loose shorts. His arms are massive, and I can just imagine what it would feel like to run my hands along the hills and valleys of his biceps while he leans over me, lifting my legs, thrusting…

"Oh, I see you've met Naked Coffee Guy," Nina says, peering past me. I jump back, surprised at her cat-like entrance. "I thought I'd missed the show."

We both watch him stroll past our house, hiding behind the curtains anytime it looks like he'll peer over at the kitchen window. I note the movement of curtains at the house across the street, and same with the one down the way. The guy obviously has a fanbase. For a moment, I forget myself, feeling a bit of haughty pride that I've kissed this Viking god, and they all *wish* they had.

Then the final details of that night slam into me, and I feel angry all over again. I push away from the window, offering Nina the better view of Mac's backside retreating down the street.

"He's all right," I say, and Nina whirls around, a look of shock on her face.

"Maren, I'm beginning to think you hate men as a species. That man is not just *all right.* He's fine as fuck. You wish you could nab a hottie like that instead of wasting your time on guys who manage your rent, then kick you out of your home."

I snort into my coffee, and she grins like she's said something funny. I know she's referring to Brock, but she has no idea how ironic her words are. I obviously have a type. I like men who screw me financially, not just literally.

I know I can't tell Nina about Mac, especially since I now know he's our hot neighbor. But I can tell Claire. And I do when I'm at Claire's house after my barista shift, an hour before Finn is supposed to come home, which gives us free rein to talk openly.

"He's Naked Coffee Guy?" Her eyes widen, and I can tell she believes this is good news, even though she knows he's a dipshit.

I'd told Claire about Mac early on, once I'd secured a place at Nina's house. I knew once Claire found out my lease was ending, she'd offer me a place in her home. And sure enough, she was ready to pack up her craft room and give it to me. While living with Claire and her family would be infinitely more fun than living with Nina, I couldn't put her out like that. Claire was a highly sought-after book swag artist, and that craft room was her livelihood.

While she finally accepted the fact that I "chose" Nina over her, she couldn't get over that magical night I'd shared with Mac—even though he'd fooled me into thinking he was some insightful, down-to-earth charmer. Oh, he was charming all right.

"You see? It's fate, Maren." She takes a bite of the pastry I brought her, this time a Danish with sweet cream in the middle. "Wow, that's good. I'd have to buy looser pants if I were surrounded by these all day."

Ethan strolls in and nabs the pastry from her hands before she can take another bite, then takes his own huge bite.

"Hey!" Claire tries to grab it back, but laughs as he pulls it out of reach. See, that's the difference between

Claire and me. She laughs when someone messes with her food. I'd stab them with a fork.

"Here, you can have his," I say, mock glaring at Ethan. He shrugs, then grins, his mouth full of Danish as we protest the grossness. He's all sweaty after his workout, and leans his soaked chest against Claire as he kisses her.

"Ew," she squeals, but I can tell she likes it. Reason #433 why I can't move in here. I'd have to see their cuteness every day while I'm doing my best to swear off men.

Even though the man I'm swearing off is now about to be my every morning eye candy.

But I'm happy for my friends and their serendipitous love story. They met for the first time the night Claire graduated high school. I'd been in the thick of my addiction at that point, and the terrible friend that I was, I abandoned her at a party where she knew no one while I got high in one of the bathrooms with some forgettable guy. I still feel twinges of guilt over that, but if I hadn't, she wouldn't have met Ethan. Then she wouldn't have gotten knocked up and had Finn, who I swear is only the best kid in the world. Thing is, Ethan never knew since they didn't speak after that one night. It had been a masquerade party, and they both played into the whole mystery thing by never revealing their faces, let alone their names. It was both weird and romantic.

The good news is, I redeemed past Maren's mistakes by introducing Ethan and Claire just last year. Ethan is Nina's cousin, and she had the brilliant idea to set him up with someone dependable and kind—in her words, *boring*—since the women he usually chose were more beauty than brains. But Claire is both beautiful and brilliant, and she had also chosen to live the spinster life rather than subject her son to a revolving door of men. Like Claire's mother had done to her.

Neither one of us knew that Ethan was Finn's real father. Now, they're this disgustingly happy family…and I couldn't be happier for them.

Except right now, when they're being super cute and in love, and I'm still nursing a sober girl hangover thanks to my dilemma and new nemesis—super star real estate agent Mac Dermot. Even just the sight of his mug on the freeway billboard makes me want to gag.

Okay, maybe it makes me lust a little too.

"So, how are you going to handle Naked Coffee Guy?" Claire asks when she finally comes up for air.

"Wait, I obviously missed something." Ethan makes himself even more comfortable at the table.

"Don't you have work?" I ask him.

"When you own the bar, you make your own hours." He smirks, kicking back, waiting for me to fill him in.

"He's this guy who walks around shirtless and

without shoes every morning in Nina's neighborhood, carrying his cup of coffee," Claire shared. "He's also the same guy that Maren almost banged the first time she met him."

"No, I didn't almost bang him," I corrected her. "I was actually making plans to *not* bang him in hopes of a second date when the bomb was dropped."

Claire tilts her head at me. "I don't know, though. It's not like he knew he'd just sold your home."

I know this. I mean, the guy was probably just doing his job. But it doesn't change my living situation. Knowing he had a hand in the sale, I want nothing to do with it.

"It doesn't matter. This was the only rent controlled place in all of Sunset Bay, and no other rents even came close. He had a hand in selling this place with practically no notice, leaving us all to scramble for a place to live."

"But at least you have Nina, right?" Ethan asks. I shoot him a glare as he feigns innocence with a shrug. "All right, Nina is difficult, but she's also very thoughtful and kind. You only know her as coworker Nina. Wait till you get to know my cousin on a more personal level. I swear you two will be best friends before you know it."

"No she won't. That spot is mine," Claire says, shoving his arm. He laughs, then gets up.

"And that's my cue to get ready for work." He leans down and kisses Claire's cheek, then leans down and does the same to me while I roll my eyes. "See you tonight?" he asks me.

I nod, giving him a cheesy thumbs up. I have a gig tonight at Hillside, one of my favorite places to perform. One, it's fun to work at a place where you know the ownership, and two, it's where I got my start performing live. I now have a small following of fans that frequent Ethan's outdoor bar, ensuring my Hillside performances always have people singing along.

Finn's school bus pulls up, and we watch as Ethan forgoes getting ready as he trots outside. He runs to his son and throws him over his shoulder while the kid struggles. I've never seen so much joy on Finn's face in all the years I've known him.

"He really loves his dad, doesn't he," I murmur. Claire looks at me and smiles, her eyes a little misty. She laughs, wiping away the moisture before any tear has a chance to fall.

"Sorry, I'm such a sap. But yes, sometimes I have to check to see if I'm awake because I can't believe how happy I am. Then there's this small part of me that tells me to be cautious, because nothing this good can last forever."

"That's bullshit," I say, and I wrap an arm around her shoulders. She leans her head against me. "You and Ethan were always supposed to meet." And I mean it as

I say it, but I hide the part that feels a little wistful.

Where is *my* someone?

"What kind of coffee do you think Naked Coffee Guy drinks?" Claire muses, then winks at me. It's almost like she's reading my mind. I nudge her just as Finn follows Ethan into the house, ensuring I have to choose my words carefully. Claire knows I judge guys on the type of coffee they drink because it also gives me a clue to what kind of lover they are. Too milked down, and they probably left their backbone at their mother's house. Strong and dark, and I may not see the light of day for weeks, if you know what I mean. And no coffee at all? Probably a douche. Case in point…Brock woke up every morning with a Red Bull.

"Be good, ladies," Ethan warns with a wink before heading to the shower. He obviously heard Claire's question.

"Auntie Maren," Finn says, throwing himself at my waist as I brushed away any thoughts of…coffee. Claire grins at me over Finn's head, and I stick my tongue out at her.

"I brought you something sweet at the kitchen table," I say, and Finn releases me and scrambles for his seat, tearing into the bag to find the last Danish.

"After homework," Claire says, snatching it just before he takes a bite.

"Aw, Mom!" he whines.

"Yeah, you're no fun, Claire Bear."

Finn grins a toothless smile but relents and gets his homework out.

"So, any coffee guesses?" Claire hisses, pulling me from the kitchen so we're out of earshot.

"Probably a vanilla milk," I guess, and Claire laughs, shaking her head.

"Come on. I remember the way you talked about this guy, even when you were your angriest. He's got to be a dark roast kind of guy. I mean, how did he look walking your neighborhood this morning?"

Like fucking Thor. Just thinking about him, and I'm feeling squirmy and well aware of my month-long drought.

"He's a straight up espresso," I tell her.

Chapter Six

Maren

Hillside is packed as I perform for the outdoor venue. It usually takes me about five songs to warm up to the crowd, and tonight is no different. I see a few regular faces singing along as I play, which never fails to make me feel like a real rock star.

I like playing for small crowds. There's an intimacy here that I know I'd never get playing a stadium. Don't get me wrong, I'd love to experience the difference. Whenever I get a gig, a small part of me hopes there's a producer in the audience, looking for their next big talent. I often think of Jewel, a singer-songwriter who was living in her car and playing bars and coffee shops to a local following—just like me—before a record label discovered her.

I'm not playing these gigs with the sole purpose of being discovered. I love performing. I feel the most like myself when I have a guitar strapped to my chest, a microphone in front of me, and I'm singing lyrics I wrote because of a feeling. And to hear the crowd sing my words back to me? The adrenaline is unlike any drug I'd taken in the past. But because it's a small crowd, it feels safe, like I'm among friends.

To focus on bigger stardom would take away from the magic of these events, from all the ways these gigs fill my spirit. I'm determined to be present at every performance, connecting with the crowd on a personal level rather than trying to see what I can get out of it. Of course, I still send out demos to agents and producers with the hopes of getting picked up. But on stage, I offer the crowd all of me, no barriers as I reveal my soul. It's not only empowering, but it's also when I'm my most vulnerable.

Which is why it feels like a gut punch when I see Mac in the crowd—and he isn't alone.

I stumble over my words as he stares straight at me, seeming to ignore the girl talking to him. I collect myself and continue with the song I'm singing. But instead of singing to the crowd, it becomes a conversation between Mac and me. His eyes haven't left mine, and despite the wide range of emotions I've had over him this past month, I can't look away either. Seeing him in person is different than hating him from afar. I can't tell myself one-sided stories anymore. Instead, I'm faced with the undeniable realization that this man has an effect on me like no other, that if he just said the word, I'd be putty in his hands.

Maren, he sold your home to a demolition company.

And just like that, I shut it off. The feelings. The pull. Every way he's drawing me in by just keeping his eyes trained on me. I end the song I'm singing, then grin at the crowd as everyone cheers.

"This next song is a little rough, but one I came up with on the fly about a month ago when I met someone who ended up being different than I expected."

I dare a glance at Mac, disappointed to see him now facing the girl he's with, his eyes off me.

Use it, Maren.

"I call this one 'Dance with the Devil,'" I say, strumming a few chords. I glare in Mac's direction, even though he's still not looking at the stage. Then I channel my feelings into the song.

Your charm is what I noticed first
The way you made my cold heart burst
Your sapphire eyes, your cunning smile
The taste of your lips, like honey cursed

I had my doubts, you made me believe

I never knew worship 'til I was on my knees
I tried to resist, but your hands in my hair
Felt something like heaven in a coastal breeze

You said we're standing on holy ground
You took off my shoes as you set my crown
You wanted the earth to meet our feet
But as we danced, you dragged me down.

Because dancing with you is to dance with the devil
Your kingdom is built with the hearts that you break
You said you wanted the earth as your witness
Did it witness your lies from each promise you make?

I drank your poison, but I made my escape.

I look toward Mac the whole time I'm singing, who has finally stopped talking with that chick. At first, he seems pissed when he realizes the song is about him. But then his face relaxes into a grin, which only infuriates me more. When I'm done, he gives me a standing ovation—the icing on the cake.

"I'm going to take ten, so use this time to grab a drink from the bar or order dessert. And don't forget to tip the staff, they work hard to get you all drunk." The crowd laughs as I leave the stage. I can feel Mac's eyes on me as

I make a beeline for the bar, and I can't help wondering if his girlfriend notices how much attention he's giving me.

"The usual?" Ethan asks from behind the bar. I love that even though he owns the place, he also works alongside his staff.

"Sure," I say just as he places a soda water with a lime and a splash of tonic.

"I'll have what she's having," a voice says behind me, and I groan without turning around. Ethan looks at me and gives a silent head tilt. *Is that him?* I nod ever so slightly, and he does his best to bite back a smile.

"Here you go, bud," Ethan says. "On the house."

"Traitor," I mouth, though I know for a fact that Ethan doesn't charge anyone for soda water. Still, he should have charged Mac a premium price just on principal alone. If his face is really on a billboard, I'm sure he can afford a measly soda water.

It's obvious Mac isn't going to leave, so I finally turn around only to find him too close to be a mere acquaintance. I'm pinned between him and the bar, his arm resting beside me as he leans in, forcing me to look up at him. His scent is intoxicating, a hint of cedar that goes straight through me, channeling my core in ways that make my breath feel shallow. Everything about him is electrifying, and I'm implicitly aroused. *Get a grip, Maren.*

"Interesting song lyrics." He challenges me with his icy blue eyes and consuming stare. I sip my soda, trying to will my beating heart to calm the fuck down.

"I like to sing from the heart," I finally bite out, hoping the edge in my voice hides the hammering in my chest.

"About anyone I know?"

I lick my lips, meeting his electric gaze with a bit of my own ice. "No one worth remembering," I say.

"You wrote a whole damn song about him. That doesn't sound like anyone you've forgotten."

I don't answer. I'm not even sure what to say. I want him to know just how much I hate him, but I don't want him to know I spend every day thinking about him. And now that I know his nearly naked morning stroll leads right by my kitchen window, I'm not sure I can shake him…or that I want to.

He moves closer, his warm breath invading my breathing space. My whole body betrays me as I inhale his woodsy scent, imagining myself claimed within his massive arms.

"You left," he growls, and this time his blue eyes are full of fire. This is different from the man I met at Torches. And still, the possessive way he's leaning toward me has me remembering the urgency of his kiss, the invitation to come home with him, and all the things he could have done to me had I accepted. I gulp, forgetting myself as I glance at his lower lip, swollen and ready for the taking above his perfectly groomed beard. But then the reason I hate him slams my memories.

Did you hear he's been selling off properties right and left?

I push my hands against his chest, forcing him to take a step back so I can move out from under him.

"I had somewhere to be," I counter, then turn to walk away. He grips my arm and forces me back in front of him. Miraculously, my drink stays in its glass. I glance over at Ethan, who's busy with another customer. I know if he saw the way Mac was caging me in, he'd be around the bar in an instant. I kind of want to see that. But also, I kind of feel excited at the idea of Mac dominating me.

Cool it, Maren. This is your drought speaking.

"Get your hands off me," I hiss, turning back to Mac and yanking myself out of his grip. "Won't your girlfriend get mad seeing you with me?"

"She wouldn't even be here tonight if you hadn't ditched me." His gaze darkens, his hands clenched as he leans against the bar. "Look, you're obviously mad about something. You wrote a whole goddamn song about me. Mind telling me the sins I've committed?"

I stare at him, wondering if he's for real. I mean, of course he has no idea that he took my home. But does he really sleep easy at night, knowing how many families he displaced just for a stupid commission?

I want to tell him everything, to put him in his place as I shed some light on how his arrogant business moves have dire consequences for the people underneath his feet. That his so-called holy ground is just a battlefield of the bodies he's stepped on along the way.

But I can't.

He probably has no idea what it's like to wonder if today's the day the streets will kill him. He said he was a former runaway, but it's obvious that past is long forgotten because his world and mine are in completely different galaxies. If I tell him why I'm angry with him, I'll also have to explain the sad state of my paycheck, and how this pathetic wage is still a giant step up from where I once was. And while I should be proud of how far I've come, I suddenly feel small and insignificant as I stand here in front of him, fighting the urge to shrink under his watchful eyes.

"It's nothing. The song is nothing. You've done nothing."

"Then why did you leave that night without any kind of explanation, or even your number?"

I fiddle with my straw, hating how even in this moment, I can't help but notice the way his jeans are slung low on his hips so casually, just waiting for my hand to find what's underneath. No suit this time, but I find the jeans that much more enticing.

"I just had somewhere else to be."

"At two in the morning?"

I shrug. "Yeah. Ever heard of bed?"

It's a double entendre, and I find some satisfaction at the way he licks that lower lip. I'm teasing him, I know it. But in the process, I'm teasing myself. Mac Dermot is not someone that belongs in my bed, let alone my world.

"Look, I tried to let you off easy," I say, twirling my straw in my glass. "I realized too late that I really wasn't interested. I'm sure you're not used to hearing those words, but it's true. We're just too different, and I figured it was easier to walk away than to string you along for the rest of the night."

I start to leave again, and again he stops me. But this time his mouth is on mine, and fuck if I'm not kissing him back. It's like all my reasons on why this is a bad idea completely evaporate, and I'm left breathing him in like air, clutching him closer, savoring the taste of his tongue dancing with mine. It doesn't even matter that we're at a bar in a public space, that people are expecting me back on stage, or that we're here creating a scene that could catch this bar on fire.

He breaks away and I gasp for air, unsure how I'll ever breathe again if he's not there to breathe for me.

"Not interested?" he says. Then he walks away.

He. Mother. Fucking. Walks. Away.

"Holy hell," I whisper, then quickly look around.

There are a few amused glances around me, but no one calls me out. Even Ethan shoots a thumbs up, which receives a dirty glare from me in return. He's supposed to be on my side. Mac is the enemy.

And the enemy sure knows how to kiss me stupid.

After collecting myself, I make my way back to stage, welcomed by a few hoots and hollers from those who saw the *show* at the bar. My face reddens, and while I'm dying inside, I wave them off as if what they saw was no big deal. Even though it was everything. Even though my insides are tied up in knots over the complicated feelings I have.

I begin the set with a slowed down version of "Watermelon Sugar" by Harry Styles. It was already on my setlist, and the crowd is obviously eating it up. But I can't help regretting the choice as the words' meaning flows through my mind and out my mouth. It's a fun and flirty song, but the core of it is about the female orgasm. It's a terrible choice for a song after receiving a kiss like the one Mac gave me.

As if I'm drawn to him, my eyes find Mac again. He hasn't left but is standing there getting berated by the blonde chick he showed up with. She's giving it to him hard while he just stands there, taking it. Finally, she throws her drink in his face before leaving.

I'm thrilled on more levels than I can count. I want

Mac to suffer. I also want him free and single, even if I can't touch him with a ten-foot pole. But then I see a few people whispering around the little scene he caused—the second one of the night—and then looking at me, I realize I'm being taken down with him.

They think *I'm* the homewrecker.

Don't get me wrong—I am not one to worry about petty gossip or what people think of me. But this kind of drama could hurt my smalltime music career. Short of attempting to save face by telling the crowd everything, I instead abandon my setlist and go with a song I wrote years ago, but with lyrics that ironically fit the current situation:

When you say these things to me
You make me want to believe
But your mouth tells two different tales
What do you mean, what do you mean, what do you mean?

I look at Mac the whole time I'm singing, aware of the shift in the crowd around him. Now, instead of looking at me, they are looking at him. A murmur of awareness rises up to greet me, and I know they know the song is about him.

Even more, I know *he* knows.

He stands there alone, his hands in his pockets as I continue the song. But this time, I change the lyrics completely so that there's no doubt who I'm singing to.

You're not a man who's used to hearing no.
Because when you kissed me, I tried to tell you so.
Wearing her drink looks so damn good on you
Joke's on you, bud, because you've lost me too.

It's a total bitch move on my part, and I'm trying to wrap my callous heart around it without letting my conscience penetrate my soul. But then Mac smiles, and fuck if it doesn't go straight through me, even as I keep my poker face on while finishing the song.

The crowd erupts in applause, plus some laughter from those in the know. And Mac? He tilts his head at me as if I've won this round—as if there's a round to be won—then he turns and leaves. From the lack of satisfaction I feel, I think he's the one who actually won.

And I can't help wondering if I'll ever run into him again.

Chapter Seven

Maren

I mean, of course I'll run into him again. He's my goddamn neighbor. Which obviously means I have to move.

I realize this as I stand at the window, watching him on his daily near-nude stroll around the block, unaware he has a fanbase.

Literally. I saw it on Nextdoor, a whole entire thread dedicated solely to Mac Dermot. Plus the TikTok video of him that went viral last week. I practically lost my shit over that one. Then Nina and I watched roughly 800 of the two million views it had already amassed.

Thing is, no one knows his name. Or who he is. Or anything about him at all.

No one, but me.

And now, as I hide behind the curtain clutching my own coffee while watching his muscles ripple under the rays of the just-rising sun, I contemplate other places I could live. Seattle, maybe? They have an epic coffee scene. Maybe someplace in the Midwest where I could afford a house three times the size of this one for the price of my old apartment.

But I don't want to move. I mean, yes, eventually. Nina's clutter is no joke, and I'm not the kind of person to clean up after others, so it would be nice to move into my own place again. But for now, this is home. It's the only way I can continue living in Sunset Bay and work at Insomniacs, both of which I actually love. And it allows me to be near Claire's family, which is most important of all.

So I'm just going to have to learn to live in the same neighborhood as that hunky Viking dipshit. Looking at his ass as he continues his stroll beyond our house, I can see it will be hard (all puns intended) but manageable.

Oh, and he can never know I live here.

"Enjoying the show, I see?" Nina says, snickering as she joins me at the window.

"Fuck, that man," I breathe.

"Trust me, we all want to." Nina laughs, while my cheeks feel flush at how close I came to fulfilling that desire. "Want to ride to work together since we're working the same shift?"

I take in her robe and messy unwashed green hair. We have to be there in fifteen minutes, and she needs at least forty-five.

"Nah, I'm about to leave in five. I'll meet you there."

She shrugs as she opens the fridge. Then she stands there, contemplating the food. Did I say forty-five minutes? I'll be lucky if she shows up in an hour.

As I exit the house, I look up and down the street before leaving the safety of the open front porch. Mac is probably on the other side of the neighborhood by now, but I can't be too careful. This is going to get old really quick, I know it.

I slip into my Honda unnoticed, then pull away from the curb. I go the opposite direction he did, even though it's the long way to work. Two turns and I'm almost out of the neighborhood, sight unseen.

Then I see him. Or rather, I almost run him over.

He's crossing the road as I make my next turn, and I have to slam on my brakes to avoid hitting him. Mac's hand thumps the blue hood of my car as a reflex, and the impact leaves a dent in its wake. My eyes are like saucers as his meet mine, and I see his expression transition from shocked anger to slow recognition. His bare tatted chest expands as he takes a deep breath—maybe to say something, maybe to yell—and I have a split second to decide what to do. Apologize and clear the air about the reasons I hate him, which haven't stopped me from thinking about the way he kissed me, and how I want to do it again. Or escape and pretend he never saw me at all.

I do the latter.

I back the car up and pull around him, hightailing it to the main road that leads to work, my heart pounding the whole way. All the while, the image of his chest up close is seared in my mind, and I'm just as breathless by that mind souvenir as I am about the fact that I almost killed him. By the time I've reached the parking lot, I've called myself every form of the word *idiot* that I can think of, then include a few Spanish words my father was fond of saying in my presence. *Estúpida. Imbécil. Tonta. Idiota.* I bang my hand on the steering wheel, wishing I'd taken Nina up on her offer. Sure, we'd both be late and Susan would blow a gasket. My job might even be in jeopardy since it's apparent Susan likes Nina more, even if my roommate is a flake. But if I'd gone with Nina, Mac probably wouldn't have seen me.

It's barely been a day since I learned I live in the same neighborhood as the Viking, and I've already failed to keep my living quarters unknown. I'd be a terrible secret agent. My only consolation is that he doesn't know the exact house I live in, and I plan to keep it that way.

True to my prediction, Nina strolls in exactly one

hour after she was supposed to clock in. Susan tells her she's late—again—and Nina offers a thin excuse of an unexplained emergency that I know has everything to do with the new shade of blue hair she's sporting. I'm actually impressed she had time for the hue exchange, though experience has taught me to never underestimate Nina. She may suck as a barista and is disorganized as fuck, but when it comes to fashion, she's nothing but focused. Her robin's egg hair isn't vastly different from the mermaid hair she had when I left this morning, but the green undertones make the blue a beautiful shade of turquoise.

"Nice hair," I murmur.

"Nice chest," she says in return. I look down, checking to see if there's been a nip slip. When I see nothing, I start to ask what she's talking about, but she's not even looking at me. She nods at the door, and my stomach drops.

So do I—literally to my knees—hiding behind the counter.

"Take the register," I squeak, then crawl to the coffee station where the machines are tall enough to hide me.

Because Mac Dermot, with his piercing blue eyes and sexy as fuck beard, is in the building. Fully clothed in his white button-up shirt and panty-soaking slacks. But here.

Nina somehow composes herself as Mac approaches the register, but I know she recognizes him by the way she fidgets with the hem of her super short skirt. When he turns to see the pastry choices, she looks at me and mouths "Oh my god," her eyes wide as cinnamon rolls. At least her freakout is distracting her from my own, because I am ready to plummet through the floor.

"I'll take a morning bun and a black eye coffee, no cream," he says.

A black eye coffee. I freeze, absorbing the reality of his coffee order. A black eye is a coffee with two strong shots of espresso. If my calculations are correct, his coffee order would make him the kind of lover who would take me in the…

"Buns, Maren. Can you check in the back to see if we have more morning buns?" The look on Nina's face makes it apparent she's been trying to get my attention for a while. Worse, I see Mac craning his neck, then relaxing into a full grin when he takes in my shocked face.

"Ah, the girl with the killer car," he says, then rubs the hand that landed on my hood for emphasis. But damn if the motion doesn't have a double entendre, because I'm suddenly thinking of other things he could be rubbing, which makes me even more flustered than when I received his coffee order. It doesn't help that his shirt sleeves are rolled up his forearms, revealing his muscular tan arms covered in tattoos. It's the kind of look that makes me think he's about to get down to business.

I want to be that business.

"Maren?"

Morning buns. Right.

"On it," I squeak to Nina, then flee to the back. We never have extra morning buns, but today must be Mac Dermot's lucky day because there's the second box I ordered. I bring the whole box out and shove it into Nina's arms, purposely avoiding Mac's face as I scurry back to my coffee station to fill his drink order.

Why am I flustered? I hate this man. He stole my home.

But fuck me, he looks so good dressed for work. I've seen him so many times half naked, which by the way, I'm not complaining about. But something about his business attire is inspiring a whole new set of fantasies I never knew I had. My eyes trace the outline of his chiseled chest. His tatted arms make me want to run my hands over them as I feel the curve of his muscles, and the way his body tapers down into those slacks that skim the slope of his ass…

I hate him. I hate him. I hate him.

I place the drink on the bar, about to call his name, when his fingers brush over mine. I look up just as he takes the drink, his blue eyes fixed on mine.

"Take a break," he murmurs. Then he turns, exiting the shop as I stand there frozen in place.

"That was Naked Coffee Guy, wasn't it?" Nina hisses

beside me, snapping me out of my stupor. I offer an awkward laugh, hiding the fact that my whole entire body is a heartbeat, and I cannot seem to form two thoughts, let alone words.

"Looks a lot different with clothes on," I finally bite out. "I need a break, take over?"

I don't wait for her answer when I disappear into the back room. I pause for a moment, trying to muster up a reason to not go outside. But nothing is strong enough to keep me from opening the staff door and slipping into the back alley. The door has barely closed behind me when Mac has me up against the wall, his body pressed to mine. One hand holds his hot coffee while the other is at my neck, lightly pressing as he cups my face.

"Maren," he breathes, then he consumes me with a kiss. All reason is lost as my mouth searches his, the heat of his body setting me on fire. In spite of everything this man is, I have never wanted anyone more than I want Mac Dermot. I tell him this without words, my hands clutching his shirt, glancing off his flushed skin underneath. His mouth breaks from mine as he hisses, then he presses even more forcefully against me.

"I want you," he says in between kisses. I can't even respond, I'm so ready to devour him. If he took me right here, I'd let him.

He pulls away but keeps me in place against the wall.

I whimper under his stare, internally begging him to keep going. Instead, he brushes the back of his hand over the side of my face. Just that one tender motion has me closing my eyes against the sting of tears, which I manage to keep at bay.

I'm shaken by the sudden emotion he pulls from me, and I push him off as I pull myself together. "Why are you here?" I ask.

"I could ask the same of you this morning. Why were you in my neighborhood? Are you stalking me?"

"Your ego is really something, isn't it?" I straighten my skirt before fixing my hair. "Can you fit in small rooms with a head that big?"

He smirks at that, then looks me up and down in a way that makes me feel utterly naked. "Baby, if you think my head is big, you should see my other parts."

"Please," I scoff. But fuck if I don't mean *pleeease*, as in, *I'm ready when you are.* "I'm only on a ten, so if you're done mauling me, I need to get back to work. And Mac? Don't come again."

I turn to leave, but he grasps my wrist. Loosely. In a way that would allow me to slip from his hand if I wanted to. I don't want to.

"Why are you resisting this?" he asks, "Resisting me?"

I could tell him. He has no idea he had a part in my sudden housing situation. But he had to have known his quick sale left dozens of families scrambling for a home. Everything about him is everything I can't stand. He's made of money. His life is built on destroying people like me. He's upper class while I'm one lost paycheck from ruin.

I could also tell him that when he brushed his hand across my cheek, he touched a part of me inside that no man has ever cared to touch. That there are things about me that no one has ever seen, not even Claire. I just know Mac could be the one to break down my walls.

"I can't," I admit.

"Can't what? Can't do us?"

Can't resist you.

"I just can't," I say. I turn back to him but pull my hand from his. "Look, my life is complicated right now. You are just enough chaos to turn my world upside down, and I can't handle a relationship and all that goes with it."

He pauses, and it's long enough that the window to leave is wide open. But I don't leave. Damn if I don't stay, hoping he'll say the words that will make all the complications go away.

"What if we don't have a relationship," he says slowly. He moves toward me in a way that has me backing up. I hit the wall and he leans in, his finger tracing my bare arm, leaving goosebumps in its trail.

"And?" I close my eyes as he comes close, gasping as I feel his hot breath at my neck.

"And we keep this casual," he murmurs, his lips brushing my skin with each word. "No dating. No meeting each other's family. No public displays of non-sexual affection."

I smirk at this. He's basically saying holding hands is off, but humping in an alleyway is fair game.

"Then what would it be?" I ask, even though I see exactly where this is going.

"Sex," he says, then clamps his teeth on my throat, making me gasp at the pleasure mixed with pain. Making me want this, even though I know it will break me in the end.

There is no casual with Mac Dermot. This is clearer than the hold he has on me, and the way his hand clutching my thigh makes me want more. I will always want more with him. Pretending we can keep this just about sex is a fool's errand, and yet, denying him is impossible. So there's only one answer I can give.

"Yes," I breathe.

Chapter Eight

Mac

Fucking dumbass. That's what I am. I unlock my car and throw my keys on the dash, hitting the palm of my hand against the steering wheel. The final strike hits the horn, and I roar into the emptiness of my car at my assfoolery. I shouldn't have come. But Maren is like a drug and I'm in desperate need of rehab, and fuck if I didn't just suggest an arrangement that will make me OD.

It's obvious I can't escape her. I finally take out that chick who's been hounding me for a date, and Maren is the one singing on stage. Then she almost runs me over this morning in my own goddamn neighborhood. And now? At the coffee shop?

Okay, that one was planned. I saw her blue Honda in the parking lot with a dent mark in the hood around the same size as my hand, and I knew she was in there. I also knew that if I didn't get another taste of her sassy mouth, I was going to go mental.

The jury is still out on that one though, because after that kiss, I can't even see straight.

I told her I'd text her when and where to meet me. I could tell she was uncomfortable that I held the cards. I get the feeling Maren doesn't like being told what to do. But she wants me, maybe as much as I want her. The way she kissed me back. Every time. I knew it the first time I saw her. I knew she'd set me on fire and burn me to the ground.

And I'm here for the inferno.

But I shouldn't be. Because the thing about Maren is that she's too good for me. Beyond her cool exterior, beyond the armor that keeps everyone at arm's length, she's so full of goddamn heart, so brutally honest with everyone. And I'm a lying sack of shit.

I should tell her everything, come clean now so that she'll save us both and just walk away.

My phone vibrates in my pocket, and I sigh when I see the number light up on the car dash. No name, but I recognize the number from the dozens of times I've taken this call before.

"Yeah."

"Dermot. Jay Abbot here. I was hoping we could go over some of those missing details before we head to print."

I grip the phone so hard, it could break in my hand.

"Listen, dipshit. We had a deal. This doesn't print until the old man's dead. You hear me?" This fucking reporter has been hounding my ass for weeks now, ever since he got wind of some of Benji's rapid sales along with the debt. When Abbot learned Benji was at death's door, the guy was practically salivating.

Benji has fucked over a lot of people. There will be plenty of people who are waiting to dance on his grave. But his name is still worth something in this region, and while he's alive, I'm the keeper of his reputation. All this hotshot reporter sees is a chance to elevate his name with a breaking news story. But Benji isn't a news story, he's the reason I'm still alive.

"Relax," Abbot says, but I hear the nervousness in his voice, "I don't mean now."

"No, you mean when he's dead. Have a betting pool going there, Abbot? Any guesses for when the old man keels over?"

Abbot clears his throat and mumbles an apology.

"Look," I continue, "I'll get you the rest of the information once Benji has passed, not a minute sooner. I can't have you breaking this story while Benji is still alive."

"But you'll call, right?"

I can hear the desperation in his voice. I wonder how old Abbot is, how long he's been reporting. Is this his first break? Does he have an editor riding his cock for this story?

I don't really care about him. If he loses his job over this, fuck it. Not my problem. Who I care about are all the people who will never be paid back for what Benji has done to them.

I don't want to do this. If I could, I'd let Benji's sins die with him. I couldn't give two shits about this fucking story.

But for them? This is the least I can do.

"I'll call."

I hang up, toss my phone on the passenger seat, then peel away from the curb.

The phone rings again, and I'm about to send it to voicemail but stop when I see the name on the dash. It's not Abbot like I thought, but Benji. I push the button to answer.

"Hey."

Benji's breathing is labored, and it takes him a moment to say anything.

"This woman…" He wheezes, and I wait for his fit to stop, "she's stealing…my food. She gives me…shit. Rancid shit."

I sigh, realizing it's going to be one of those days. I hear muffled talking in the background, and I know it's

Anna, today's day nurse.

"That's terrible, Benji. Want to put Anna on the phone for me?"

"Who the hell…is Anna," he forces out.

"Your nurse. That woman. Can you put her on please?"

He has another coughing fit, and I feel my body tensing up. Benji has his lucid moments, but they're getting further apart. Every time he slips into the shadows of his mind, I wonder if he'll come back from it.

"Who…is this?" he finally rasps.

"Benji, can you put Anna on the phone." I bark the words, regretting my choice to leave the phone within his reach. But Benji isn't a prisoner, despite the soft foods diet he's on since he chokes on anything larger than a grape. There's so little he can do on his own anymore, and using the phone is one of them. Which makes me feel terrible when I hear more muffled noises, and then Benji yelling in the background.

"Sorry about that." It's not Anna like I expected, but Hattie.

"What are you doing there? Where's Anna?"

I hear the yelling in the background grow fainter, and I know Hattie has moved to a separate area from him.

"Anna's little boy is sick, and she asked if I could stay on."

"But you worked all night," I say, as if she needs reminding. "Aren't you exhausted?"

"I'll grab a nap when he's sleeping. It's fine."

I can still somewhat hear Benji yelling from the other room. "It sounds like today's been difficult."

"He woke up in a mood and has been calling me an intruder all day."

Hattie is a saint for what she puts up with. Generally, she's great at helping Benji re-center when he gets confused. She's been with Benji long enough that he usually recognizes her, though occasionally he forgets. This time, he seems more agitated than normal. His time is running out, and I'm not sure if I'm ready. At the same time, I know things will be easier once Benji does pass. A lot of problems will be solved, which makes me feel like an ass because we're talking about the man who took me in at a time when no one wanted me.

"I have a few things to wrap up at the office, then I can come home and let you go early." I mentally go over my list of appointments today, thinking of which ones I can cancel.

"Nonsense, Mr. Dermot. Benji is fine, he's just agitated. His afternoon nap might reset him. Besides, he's my only patient, and I have nowhere else to be. I might as well stay here for the job you overpay me for."

I chuckle at this. She's telling the truth. I give each nurse more than they make a year for a job that probably won't outlast the month. But peace of mind, knowing he's well cared for, is priceless.

"When's the last time you stayed at your own house, or even had a night of fun?" she continues. I rub the back of my neck, stalling to answer as I pull into my parking spot at the office. There was a time when I thought having your own parking spot meant you'd made in life. Facing the sign in front of my car with my name on it, it's ironic that it's just the least of the privileges I've gained in this fortunate life. Behind me is a whole office of agents who work under my license, and a staff who answers to me. It's a far cry from the fifteen-year-old thief I used to be, now that I'm more than twice that age.

"It's been a while," I admit, answering Hattie's question.

"It's been never, since you hired me," she pointed out. "You need a break, Mr. Dermot."

I laugh. "Me? You're there more waking hours than I am."

"It's my job, sir."

"And I owe this man my life," I counter. She sighs, but I can practically hear Hattie smiling through the phone.

"With all due respect, Benji wouldn't want you burning out at both ends just for his sake," she says.

She's wrong, of course. Benji was a hardnosed

motherfucker who expected everyone who worked for him to give more than they got. He may have taken me under his wing as my guardian, but make no mistake, I was also his employee. I worked from the moment I woke up to the time I went to bed. I earned my meals and his respect, neither of which came easy. Burnout was a foreign concept to this man.

"Don't come home, Mr. Dermot. Go to your house and recharge, or go out and do something fun. Lord knows you need it."

"But Benji. He's being—"

"He's fine, and so am I. It's you I'm worried about. In the past month, I have not seen you rest for a moment."

I want to argue with her, to pull rank and let her know that I'm the boss, and what I say goes. But that's not how things are with Hattie, or any of the nurses who seem to be watching out for me just as much as they care for Benji. I might sign Hattie's paychecks, but she's quickly stationed herself as the one in charge, at least in a motherly kind of way. It's been so long since I've had a mother, I can't help but bend when she insists.

Besides, I have a sweet little brunette who has made a deal with the devil, and I plan to cash in. Tonight could be the perfect night.

"You'll call me if he gives you trouble. And if…" If his heart stops beating.

"I'll call," she promises, "Now, I don't expect to see you again until tomorrow."

After we hang up, I grab my briefcase and set the alarm on my car. I'm greeted as soon as I walk through the double doors, and my assistant Tara jumps up from her desk with a notebook. Immediately, she starts going over what I've missed since this morning. I'm barely listening to her, my mind distracted as I think about tonight's possibilities.

"Tara," I interrupt. She stops her roll as we stand outside my office.

"Yes, Mr. Dermot?" Her eyes are wide, and I realize not for the first time, how eager she is to please me. She's a sweet girl, and admittedly hot as fuck in her pencil skirt and long hair wrapped in a bun, but I don't fraternize at work.

"Make a reservation at the Seafarer Hotel for tonight. Get the largest room they have."

Tara's breath hitches, and I don't miss the moment her eyes move from excitement to understanding and then to disappointment.

"Yes, sir. Right away."

Chapter Nine

Maren

Casual is the kiss of death. I know this. I've done it way too many times.

Brock, my loser apartment manager-slash-fling, wasn't even the worst of them, though he was the skeeziest. The worst was Damon, the British guy who didn't even like coffee. No, this guy drank tea with milk—which would have been a hard pass, except that I loved his accent and could have listened to him talk for hours. So I gave him a chance, and then he showed me just what those British guys like to do on the other side of the pond.

Let's just say that when Damon said he liked eating peaches, he was not talking about the fruit. My no-relationship rule went out the window as I entertained a global love affair with a lifetime supply of mind-shattering orgasms.

Unfortunately, there would be no his-and-hers luggage in my near future as Damon took my no-relationship rule seriously. When it came time for him to leave, he did so without a second glance—my texts left on read, my calls unanswered, and no access to his social profiles, cluing me in that I'd been blocked.

It was rejection times ten and a perfect example of why I don't do relationships.

Which is why it took me by surprise when I found myself considering a relationship with Mac that first night I met him, and why I'm now nervous about this casual arrangement I've agreed to.

I also didn't expect for him to cash in so soon. After that damn kiss in the alley, I could barely think, let alone add some sense to this crazy situation. He left before I could offer any kind of argument. But when he texted me this afternoon, telling me when and where to meet him tonight, I texted back with a few hard stop ground rules.

1. It would be a secret from everyone. That meant no PDA (sexual and non-sexual), no dates, no telling anyone. Nothing.

2. It would be on neutral ground and coming out of *his* pocket.

I mean, the guy stole my home out from under me. Plus, the watch in his wrist alone tells me he can afford it. He owes this much to me.

In theory, I should be able to treat Mac like any other shag (as Damon referred to it), but I also know that Mac isn't like any of the other guys. Despite the fact that I hate this man, I can't deny the hold he has on me. I *want* him, just as bad as he wants me. My mind may have a list of reasons to stay away. My heart might be building a fortress to keep him out. But my body? It's already screaming his name, and he's hardly touched me.

Hardly. My lips still feel bruised, the memory of his kiss tattooed all over my mouth. I had to go back to work like that, my core aching as I counted down the minutes to clock out. And now, here I am sitting in the parking lot of the Seafarer Hotel, my sweaty hands gripping the steering wheel as I summon the courage to get to the room, my legs clenched together in anticipation for what's to come.

NCG: Coming?

The single word text from Mac makes me bite my lip.

Me: Not yet.
NCG: You will be.

Fuck me. I can't with this man. I look up at the tall hotel building, then I take a deep breath.

"This is just a fuck, Maren," I remind myself, "nothing more." Another deep breath, and I unbuckle my seatbelt, grab my overnight bag, and head for the stairs.

Me: Here

I text as the elevator approaches his floor, then I walk the hallway, inhaling the clean scent as I take in the art lining the walls between rooms. When I reach the number he gave me, I lift my hand to knock but see that the door is ajar, resting on the latch to keep it from closing. I nudge it slightly.

"Mac?" I wait a beat, then push it all the way open. I'm not sure what I expected, but it isn't this. The only places I've ever stayed at were seedy motels that looked straight out of the 1970s that probably hadn't been cleaned since then either. This place is breathtaking and a little overwhelming. From where I stand in the doorway, I can see straight to the windows that overlook the ocean. The moon is shining bright, illuminating the rippling water, creating an ethereal glow that complements the soft glow in the room. To my left is the bathroom, which is about the size of my bedroom. There's a giant soaking tub that's separate from a massive glass shower, and double sinks under a wide mirror framed by a dozen lights.

"Wait till you see the bed."

I jump at the sound of Mac's voice. He catches me as the door closes behind us, then his mouth is on mine, his hands in my hair, my back against the wall as I drop my bag and grip his shirt just to keep myself steady.

I didn't know how this would go, but it wasn't exactly like this. Even though I am melting under Mac's touch and the way he's claimed me with just a kiss—a fucking hot as hell kiss, a kiss that is going straight from my head to between my thighs, making me feel swoony and weak.

But this isn't my usual way of doing things. I'm usually the one in charge, the one who makes the moves, the one on top. The rooftop bar, the alleyway kiss…so far I've let Mac be alpha, giving him way more control than I've ever given anyone in my life. It's time to turn this ship around.

I plant my feet and pivot, catching him by surprise so that it's now his back against the wall, and I'm more in control. I bite his lip lightly, tugging at it between my teeth as I start unbuckling his pants. I like that Mac started without light conversation or any kind of mood lightening experience. But now it's my rules.

He catches my hands in his and tears them from his body, moving so quickly that I'm surprised when I'm on my back on the bed, my hands pinned above my head, his legs straddling my hips so that I can't move.

"Wait." The word escapes my lips before I can stop it. He stops immediately, loosening his hold. I could slip my wrists from under his hands, but I leave them where they are, breathing heavy. I got my way, he stopped. But I can't help feeling like I lost something in the process.

"What do you want?" He licks his lips, his hands remaining loose in their hold.

I don't speak. I can't. How do you even say it out loud, that you want to be the director of this unfolding scene? I've never had to say anything before. I'm starting to think I never chose a man who would even think to question me if I took charge.

Mac is not that man. But damnit if I don't try again.

I wriggle out from under him, moving him so that he's on his back and I'm on top. He catches my hands again before I can even move to undress him, and I can't bite back my groan of my frustration.

"What. Do. You. Want." He repeats each word slowly, his eyes burning into mine in a way that leaves me feeling naked, even though not one stitch of clothing has been removed.

"I want…" I breathe hard out of my nose, wrenching my wrists from his grip. He just lies there, a slow smirk spreading over his face. I'm still straddling him, and I can feel him growing hard under me. The bastard is actually turned on by our battle of wills.

I leap off him but he's quicker, grabbing me by the waist and sitting me on the bed. He towers over me, his hands on each side of my hips. I hold my ground, refusing to budge even as his face draws closer.

"You like to call the shots, don't you?" His eyes gleam as they hold mine, and my breath comes out in short pants at his proximity. I bite my lip, fighting the intense urge to just let him have his way with me. "Say it, Maren."

It's his way of swinging the pendulum in his direction. I know this, but I answer him anyway.

"I want to be in control."

"No."

The word shocks me. I stare at him, waiting for him to take it back and give me the reins. But he doesn't.

"I am not a man who is told what to do, in bed or out, and if that makes you uncomfortable, you should walk out that door right now."

"And what if I stay?" I bite back. I should leave. I have the freedom to leave. And yet, I stay where I am, his face inches from mine. He's close enough to kiss. Close enough to slap. "If I stay, what say do I have?"

"If you stay, you're agreeing to this. You're agreeing to submit."

I bristle, averting my eyes. He takes my chin and moves it so that I'm looking at him again.

"You don't like that word, do you?"

I shake my head. I try to move my head again, but his grip is firm.

"Do you have any idea how much power you actually have when you submit?"

The question catches me off guard. When I think of submission, I think of dependency. I think of all the times I've been let down in life when I've depended on anyone. The word *submit* is dangerous to me. It's not one of power, it's one of weakness.

But I can't say this to Mac. I'm willing to fuck him; I'm not willing to let him in my head by knowing any of my secrets.

I get up from the bed, and this time he steps aside to allow me to pass. I don't leave, and I wonder if that surprises him. Instead, I move to the windows, watching the waves crash under the moonlight.

"What are you thinking?"

I sigh at his question, then slowly turn around. I lean against the window, the cool glass seeping through the thin fabric of my jacket.

"This is new for me," I admit. "Not the casual sex, that's all I ever do anymore. But the roles. I don't…" I pause, trying to find the right words for what I'm feeling, because I'm not even sure I know. "Just like you, I don't like being told what to do," I finally say.

He nods, moves toward me and takes my hand. This

time I don't fight back. I let him lead me to the bed, and he sits next to me.

"What if I *ask* you instead?"

I look at him, eyebrow arched, trying to decipher what he means.

"I won't tell you what to do," he explains. "But I'll ask for your permission."

"Demonstrate." The word wavers off my lips as I try to make sense of the rules my body is begging me to obey.

"Can I…" His words fall away as he lifts his hand. "Can I touch your cheek?"

His hand hovers over my skin, and I can feel the heat from his body, making me tingle. I nod, then draw in a breath as his finger lights on my cheek, brushing my hair away from my face.

"Can I touch your mouth?"

I nod and he traces the outline of my lips with the soft half-moon of his fingernail. I part my lips, and his finger finds the tip of my tongue. I hold his gaze, falling into the ocean in his eyes as I draw his finger into my mouth. It's his turn to inhale, and when he regains his finger, he traces a wet line down my chin toward my neck.

"Can I move my hand lower?"

I nod again, closing my eyes as his finger leaves a tingling trail in its wake. He traces my jaw, his hand lightly circling my neck in a way that makes me want to beg for more.

Beg? I don't beg. And yet, here I am, impatient for his next question.

"Can I undress you?"

I keep my eyes closed, my hands gripping the blanket under me as I whisper, "Yes." I squirm where I'm sitting as he moves to kneel in front of me, sliding my jacket down one arm, then the other, the fabric trailing across my skin. Then he slides off my shoes and socks, pausing to caress the arch before pressing his thumbs into the balls of my foot. I've worn heels for so long, they hardly affect me, and yet his hands massaging my feet make me never want to wear shoes again. He finds aches I never knew existed, kneading them between his expert fingers until I'm moaning.

And I'm still wearing all my clothes.

He makes quick work of that situation, however, his eyes asking the questions now before he removes each article of clothing. A breathless *yes* to each as my answer. My shirt? *Yes*, and he takes his time with each button before exposing my lacy black bra underneath. My skirt? *Yes*, and he has me stand before him as he unzips it and lets it fall to the ground. I remain in my lingerie, full of lace and barely there, while his eyes skim over my body.

"Jesus, Maren," he breathes and falls again to his knees.

As if he's the one submitting. As if I'm in control. But

I'm starting to understand the rules to this game, and I don't move as his hands find my hips. I long to see him undressed, to see the hardened body that exists under his white shirt and black slacks, to run my hands along the tattoo I saw on this morning's coffee stroll that's now hidden under his businessman attire.

I let him take control instead. My stillness is my permission as he slides my panties down my hips, his hands gripping the lacy material until his knuckles turn white. As if it's taking all his restraint to not rip me apart. And fuck if I don't want him to rip me apart.

He stops, studying my sex with enough intensity that, I swear, I'll burst into flames. My core aches, especially when he takes a finger and traces it with a soft outline. I release a moan, my pleas on the tip of my tongue.

"Can I…"

"Yes, please. Don't stop," I beg.

With a growl, he has me on my back and my legs spread. He dips his face between my thighs, lapping the wetness I can feel puddling underneath me. I anchor myself by clutching the blankets as I throw my head back, crying out as he feasts.

"Fuck, Mac. Please." I don't even know what I'm begging for. What he's doing is blowing my mind. But I want more. The orgasm builds, and I don't hold back as it shudders through me. Gripping his hair, I hold him in place as he sucks on my clit, as he slips a finger inside me, as he draws out every drop, leaving me spent on the bed.

Mac rises from his knees, wiping his glistening grin with the back of his hand. The finger that was inside me is now in his mouth, and I groan again, sure that I could come just from watching him enjoy my taste.

He crawls over my body, his tongue bathing me in the process as he licks the salt from my skin. I can feel his mouth even after it's left my body, and I arch my back to receive more of him. He takes the moment to unclasp my bra, leaving me completely naked while he remains clothed. His mouth finds my nipple and draws lazy circles around it before grazing his teeth over the nerve-filled peak. The contrast of pleasure and pain sends ripples through my body, especially when his fingers slip inside me. He alternates pumping his hand with the delicious pressure of his mouth clamped on my breast, and it takes no time to get me writhing again.

"Mac," I moan, needing more. More. More.

"Ask me," he commands, his mouth on mine, my taste all over him. I am lightheaded and unable to form a sentence, let alone two words. But somehow, I manage.

"Will you fuck me?"

"Yes."

His clothes are off faster than I can recover, his cock sheathed with a condom as he crawls back over me. He stops and neither of us move, our gaze locked in on each other, our chests rising with each heavy breath. Then he plunges inside me. I gasp, locking my legs around him as he moves with purpose, a mission. Each thrust is made with precision and calculation, tearing me apart from the inside out as I let him have control.

I submit.

He slows, and when I open my eyes, I see he's watching me. His beard brushes over my breasts, sending electric shocks over each peaking nipple. I snake my hand over the smooth valley in the center of his chest until my fingers find the dark blonde curls on his chin. Tugging, I pull his mouth to mine, and he answers me with a sensual kiss, his tongue seeking instead of demanding. Exploring instead of forging ahead. It becomes a dance—our mouths tangled, our hands memorizing the nuances of the other's body. I run my hands through the wavy hair on his head, loosened now from the ponytail it was in. His locks fall around me, our hips moving in time, and he grips my thigh as he drives into me deeper.

"Mac," I breathe, as he kisses my throat, "I want to feel you come."

It's the closest thing to a command. But when he lifts his head, a small smirk at the corner of his mouth, I see no sign of an argument. He raises his body, one hand going for the headboard as the other grips my thigh. Then he fucks me hard, plunging into me like he's aiming for the ground. I cry out, the feel of him deeper than anything I've ever experienced. And yet, I want more. With Mac, I will always want more. I meet him with each thrust, driving him deeper still, no longer asking, but demanding with my movements.

"Maren," he groans, and I feel him swell inside me. Then he's the one moaning into my neck just as another orgasm rips through me. The bed is annihilated, the blankets all over the floor. His hands find my tangled hair, becoming my pillow as I fall back on the mattress. Our bodies are slick with sweat, and I give in to my urges and lick the salty moisture from his shoulders, his arms, the tattoos on his chest. He's spent, but I can't get enough of him. I straddle him, the energy inside me pulsating into another quick orgasm almost as soon as I slide him back inside me. I ride the wave, his hands gripping my hips as he remains hard inside me, thrusting with every move I make until my orgasm fades into oblivion.

When it's over, I collapse on top of him, my body shaking as I come back to reality. He slides his hand around my waist as I listen to the thrum of his heart. Just moments ago, I felt like I could rip trees from the ground by the root. Now, I feel as weak as a kitten, held in place by the security of his arms wrapped around me.

I should go, but I physically can't move.

And so I stay, our breath slowing to an identical

cadence as I slip in and out of sleep. I'm vaguely aware when he finally slides me to the mattress, covering me with the blanket. I'm half in a dream when he positions himself behind me, his body conforming to mine, his arm pulling me until I'm flush against his chest. And when I fall into sleep, I *fall.*

When I open my eyes again, the first signs of dawn are reflected on the ripples in the ocean outside our hotel room. Mac's body has left mine, his arm under his head as he faces away from me. I watch the soft rise and fall of his shoulders with each breath. I study the tangles in his wheat-colored hair, longing to work them with my fingers before letting him take me once again.

He took *me*, I did not take him. And while vulnerability wraps around me like a cloak, I am surprised that I don't hate the feeling.

I should. This man took away my independence the day he sold my apartment without even caring who it affected.

But the way he broke down so many of my walls…

No.

I can use him for his body, for the way he moves me, for the way he has me screaming his name. I can use him for the money he owes me for selling my home. I can fuck him just as soundly as he fucked me over.

But my heart stays out of it. Because this is just a fuck.

I keep telling myself that as I gather my clothes, my eyes searching the still dark room for every piece of my black clothing. It's like trying to find a guitar pick in a junk drawer. But I finally do, dressing as I watch the slowly brightening sky, Mac's deep breathing the soundtrack of the room.

Then I slip out of the hotel room and into the early dawn.

I stand at Nina's kitchen window later that morning, coffee in hand, scanning the street even though I know there won't be any sightings of a near naked man doing his daily coffee stroll. My lips still feel swollen, and muscles I didn't even know I had are now screaming with every move. It's a luscious reminder of everything that happened last night, and as much as I'm trying to keep my cool, I'm fighting the smile that keeps rising to my lips.

I can't with Mac. We're from different worlds. He makes himself rich by selling off people's homes.

But the things he did, the words he said…

Can I undress you?

Never have four words been so fucking delicious to my ears, let alone my body. If this is casual, I have been doing it wrong all my life.

And if I'm not careful, I'm going to fall for the Viking.

"How's Ragnar?" Nina asks, grabbing a mug from the cabinet.

"Who?"

"You know, the Viking."

My eyes widen, and I feel the heat in my cheeks. *How did she know?*

Then Nina peers out the window and I realize she's talking about Naked Coffee Guy—same man, different context. She has no idea I was with him last night.

"He's a no show," I say, pulling away from the window.

"Really?" She keeps looking, as if I'm lying to her. "He's been doing the same thing every day for a month. I wonder where he could be."

In bed, smelling like me. I sip my coffee to keep from grinning at the thought. Honestly, I haven't stopped thinking of him since I closed the hotel door behind me. The way he took me. His mouth on every part of my body. How his beard felt trailing across my skin. How he was capable of tearing me in two and mending me together, just by thrusting inside me, over and over and...

"What's wrong with you?" Nina asks, looking closer at me.

"Nothing," I stammer, slamming my mind shut as I pour another cup of coffee, "What's wrong with you?"

Nina stares at me for a moment, her stony face

studying me. Then she nods.

"There you are. You were starting to look happy for a second, which is so unlike you."

I shoot her a look. "I'm happy. I'm just not thrilled about losing my own apartment." I glance at Nina's clothes forming a mountain on the couch, and her dishes from last night glued to the coffee table. I'm not happy about that, either. But I figured I'd give it some time before nagging her about it. After all, she's saving my ass from being homeless.

Because of Mac.

How can I lust after the same person I hate? This feels complicated, and I don't know if I like it or not.

Chapter Ten

Mac

The room still smells like her. An intoxicating mixture of lilac and sex. It's in the blankets, the air, and the empty spot of the bed next to me.

I felt her get up when she left. Felt her eyes wander over me as she lingered by the bed. For a moment I wondered if she'd stay. I thought about rolling over and letting her know I was awake, and then asking her to come back to bed.

But I didn't. I kept my eyes closed, my breathing even. If she stays or goes, it needs to be her choice.

Just like when I undressed her. Touched her. Fucked her.

I told her I was the one in control, but the reality is, she was. Just like she's controlled my life since the first time I laid eyes on her.

Years ago.

Okay, controlled is maybe too strong of a word, but she definitely affected it. I watched as she lugged a guitar case bigger than the small bag that presumably carried everything she owned on her way to #17 on the second floor of the Beale Street Apartments, and it was like being broadsided by a 2x4. It wasn't so much that she was hot, though her beauty was unmatched by anyone I ever saw. Her ivory skin, eyes the color of coffee, dark hair with fringe bangs that framed her face, and those perfect rosebud lips, not to mention the slinky nature of her slender body—I could have stared at her for hours, like she was a piece of art.

It was more than that, though. It was the way she carried herself, with a brush of wide-eyed insecurity masked by complete confidence. It was the tender way she carried that guitar, as if she were carrying a small child. Most of all, it was that look of wisdom just beyond the mysterious darkness of her eyes, like she had experienced some serious trauma but still came out the other side.

That's what penetrated me the most. I recognized that look immediately.

Like calls to like. In her, I felt a kindred soul.

This was all without speaking to her, because she

walked by me without even seeing me at all. I was a smooth-faced scrawny guy, completely different than I am now; thanks to a few dedicated years at the gym and a serious break from my razor, I'm now around 100 pounds heavier than I was back then, and my blonde beard now reaches to my chest. Even I have a hard time believing we're the same person, that scrawny kid and me, so it doesn't surprise me that Maren has no idea who I am.

She moved into that apartment, owning nothing but her clothes and guitar. I know because the first day I came in there to check a faulty light switch—I wasn't an electrician, but one of Benji's buddies once gave me a crash course—I saw no couch, no table, not even a bed.

And here's where things got weird.

I was always a shy kid, especially when it came to girls. It wasn't any easier when I was in my twenties. I wanted to help Maren out because I knew what it felt like to have nothing. I also knew how important it was to be independent and earn your way, and I had a feeling Maren's pride was attached to this.

So I started searching for things she could use. Many were used, like the funky orange couch that was left behind in one of the units. It was in great shape, and I had it professionally cleaned. I also went to garage sales and collected pretty dishes, an almost complete silverware set, a dining room table, and a few other items

I thought she might need. I even bought a brand-new mattress set with a bed frame, using a whole month's salary to get it.

I should have just told her that I'd found all this stuff for her. But by then, I'd pretty much amassed a household of belongings. I realized how it might look, that she'd know I was interested in her. Maybe she'd think this was creepy and weird. Maybe she'd tell me she wasn't interested.

So I did the next best thing, I set it all up in one of the vacant apartments, making it seem like someone had used all these things. Then I slid a typed note under her door, letting her know that the tenant in #4 had moved out and left a bunch of things that were free for the taking. I gave it the feel that management was sending the notice to every tenant. But in reality, Maren was the only one who got that letter.

When I checked back later, apartment #4 was cleaned out. A few months later, when I was fixing her plumbing, there she was on her second-hand orange couch, strumming her treasured guitar, surrounded by the things I got for her—and she didn't even know.

Was I a total wimp for not being completely outright? Sure. Did she finally have a fully furnished apartment? Yup. So, job well done. Even that orange couch looked amazing in her apartment, but probably because it was

Maren sitting on it.

It took years for me to finally get to a place where I knew I had to talk with her. At least to get to know her better beyond the tenant-maintenance relationship we shared, which was putting it generously. She barely acknowledged me except for a slight head nod when she came home from work—if she saw me.

As for me, I always saw her. I couldn't take my eyes off her. I finally reached a point where if I didn't make my intentions known, I was going to explode.

But when I finally mustered the courage to walk up to her apartment, Brock was coming out.

Brock. The weasel who knew exactly how to get under my skin practically since the first day we met. And there he was, walking out of Maren's apartment like he owned the place.

"Hey," he'd said, the smirk on his face telling me everything I didn't want to know.

He got to her first. I'd waited too long.

It doesn't bother me that she was with Brock. At least, not in a way that I feel any kind of ownership about what she does with her body, or who she does it with. What bothers me is that Brock had no idea what he had when he had it. He treated her like he treated any of the chicks he fucked, as if she were just a good time and not an incredible human being.

And I'll be damned if I treat her the same way.

I told her this was casual. I acted like this was just a fuck. It was the only way to ease her mind when her distrust was written all over her gorgeous body. She wants me. She also isn't ready to lower her walls.

So I'll give her my version of casual, but then I'll break down every single one of her goddamn walls, brick by brick, until there's no mistaking that we belong to each other.

I leave the hotel and head straight for the office, checking in with today's nurse, Bill, on the way. Benji has been fine, he assures me. He even seems more alert than the notes indicate from the day before.

"That's great," I say, though each change has me on edge. I can find a negative spin to every update, even this one. I'd heard once that just before dying, some people snap out of their confusion and appear completely lucid. Is Benji just having a good day? Or is he on the brink of death? Once I've hung up the phone, I consider turning my car around and heading to Benji's house.

"No," I say out loud. If Bill says Benji is having a good day, we'll leave it at that. My natural impulse is always to jump when Benji says. But I have my own life to attend to, including the job that's paying both our bills.

"Mr. Dermot, Stephen McPatrick called while you

were out, said it was urgent," Tara says as she trots alongside me to my office. Fun fact, Stephen McPatrick uses the word "urgent" as if he earns a paycheck each time. He's a mortgage broker who works with high-end buyers, and tagging his call as urgent is his way of pushing his current transaction to the top of the list. Another fun fact, I do not play into these kind games, regardless of the money on the table. Everyone can wait their turn, and if they get pushy about it, they may move a few rungs down the ladder of importance.

"Who else?" I ask.

My receptionist names off a few others, including one young couple who are ready to purchase their own home. I've talked with James and Anita a few times, and know they are using every cent they have for their first big purchase together. I've already decided to eat the transaction fees, including those of the seller's agent. It's not a lot, but will save them a few thousand dollars that will help them furnish the place they're in.

"If Mr. McPatrick calls again, tell him I'm in a meeting but will respond as soon as I'm out," I say, knowing my "meeting" may take all day. We reach my office, and she lingers for a moment, then glances over my rumpled suit—yesterday's clothes.

"Long night," I say, and she raises her eyebrows.

"Glad it worked out," she says, not even pretending to misunderstand my meaning or the fact that she's, in fact, *not* glad it worked out, as she turns and heads back downstairs to the reception area.

Luckily, I have a few pressed suits in my office, along with my own private shower. Though, to be honest, washing Maren from my body is the last thing I want to do.

Work ends up taking me past the dinner hour. I pick at a steak salad I bought several hours earlier, the leaves already wilting under the dressing. The stacks of paperwork in front of me seem to have grown since I got here, despite closing a few transactions in the past few hours. I could stay all night and probably still have a ton left to do, which is a great argument to pack it in for the night.

I make a quick stop at the store, then find my way to Benji's house. What I really want to do is drive this whole city and find Maren. I want to text her another command to meet me again, to recreate what happened last night. The guilt over this desire is intense. I haven't seen Benji since yesterday morning, and our last phone conversation was worrisome. Anything could have happened while I was gone, yet I'm already thinking of how I'll ditch him so I can get laid.

I force Maren out of my mind, even though I swear I can still smell her all around me. By the time I'm bounding the steps to Benji's house, Maren occupies just a small corner of my mind. Enough that I can focus on the person in front of me.

Benji is sitting up when I enter the room. His eyes land on mine, but I might as well be the help with the lack of acknowledgment. I could blame it on his usual confusion, but a look at his face shows that he's completely alert. Besides, this is his usual face upon greeting me. That, and some kind of order that—

"Did you pick up a pint of butter pecan?" he asks.

"Yes," I say, waving the bag of ice cream. "Hi Anna," I say to the nurse on shift. While Hattie is my clear favorite, Anna is a close second just because she manages to make the concept of dying a fun event. It's not actually fun, but with Anna, you couldn't tell. The girl is a young mom just out of nursing school, and for some reason she thought end-of-life care was the way to go. "What time is your shift change?"

"Tonight's an all-nighter," she says, though she shows no signs of regret. Her phone is in her lap, paused on a show that she and Benji have been watching together. I haven't paid much attention, but I see now that it's *The Bachelor*. The Benji I know wouldn't stand for that crap in his house. In all 4,500 square feet of this home, he has just one television in the theater room, which he only allowed for educational shows and occasionally the news. Now he's sneaking peeks at the phone, as if he can't wait for Anna to continue the show.

"I'll spoon us up some ice cream," I say, but Anna jumps up and takes the bag from my hands.

"I got it. Benji's been asking for you." She's gone before I can argue, before I can tell her to pick out the pecans, though I know she's already on top of it.

"Hi Benji," I say, taking Anna's seat and scooting it so we can see each other's faces.

"Don't '*hi*' me," Benji barks, "Who's Jay Abbott?"

Fuck. I'm going to kill that damn reporter.

"Not sure," I lie, "Why?"

"He had questions about that apartment complex. I told him he could kiss my ass, then I hung up the phone."

I'm irritated that this is the first I'm hearing of this. But I also didn't hire these nurses as babysitters or to monitor anything other than Benji's health.

"Did he say anything else? Did you?" I ask. I'm trying not to look too eager, fixing my face into an expression of boredom, but inside I'm seething. Benji has no idea about the article. I've worked too hard to make the last moments of his time here on earth stress free. And yet, here he is, his beady eyes narrowed as he studies me.

"Nothing else," he says, "I figured you'd know. You seem to know everything, don't you?"

Ah, there it is. Just the tone in his voice tells me where his mind is—the day I quit the apartments to start working real estate full time. Back then, it was a betrayal. I'd grown up believing Benji was raising me to walk in his footsteps, to gain the kind of wealth he'd amassed for himself. But all he really wanted was cheap labor in just one of the ways he cut corners. I thought he'd understand when I strove for bigger and better things. Instead, he decided I was abandoning the family business in favor of a flashy hobby.

Well, that flashy hobby turned into the very thing that is keeping both of us afloat.

"I got ice cream!" Anna sings, juggling three bowls as she comes into the room.

I look toward Benji, who seems to have forgotten our whole discussion, his eyes glued to the bowl. I didn't even get a chance to defend my character. But would it have mattered? He didn't listen before, and he won't remember now.

I take my bowl, and Anna takes turns spooning ice cream into Benji's mouth before enjoying a bite from her own bowl. She turns on *The Bachelor*, and I try not to roll my eyes out of my head as Benji leans over, accepting spoonfuls of ice cream as he waits to see which girls will get a rose.

When I'm at Benji's house, I try to help the nurses as much as possible. They don't really need my help, since Benji is no longer able to leave the bed. But I *want* to help. I feel it's my duty, since I'm the closest he has to a son.

Well, except for my foster brother, but I'd rather leave him out of it. For me, this is my way of saying thank you for all the years he gave me a safe place to stay. So when Benji needs a bath, I'm there with the tub of water and a sponge. When he needs to be turned, I help roll him to his side and scoot him to the middle of the bed. He's probably a hundred pounds by now, just skin and bones in his hospital bed that sits in the middle of the living room—just a fraction of the larger-than-life man he once was, and not nearly as terrifying. And yet, I still jump at his command. I'm three times his size with all my faculties, and his word continues to be the last.

Tonight, I help Anna change his gown, adding it to the pile of laundry I'll do before bed. I try not to stare at the knobs of his spine protruding along the seam of his back, or how his hips jut out at the edges. At this stage, there's no longer a need to fatten him up. Instead of caloric protein shakes and supplements, he now eats what he wants, when he wants, which isn't often. But ice cream? There's always a pint in the freezer.

Benji is lights out almost as soon as his head hits the pillow. The old man can barely stay awake for more than an hour at a time. I wish Anna a goodnight as she makes up a bed on the couch, then I throw the laundry in the washer before retiring to my bedroom in the back of the house.

Here's the thing about this room: it was supposed to be a staff room, along with the room my foster brother stayed in. Both were simple with nothing more than a bed and a dresser. Never once did I think to make it something more, no posters or other art on the walls, no colorful bedspread, no books or games, or anything that might give people a clue to who I was.

Maybe it was because I wasn't even sure who I was. I'd spent so many years shuffled from house to house, constantly on the defense that I didn't have any energy left for trivial things, like interests.

Even now at thirty-five, I struggle with an answer on what I do for fun.

Cover my benefactor's ass. Sell off his belongings to pay his debt. Be the fall guy for all the mistakes he's made. Make sure he dies with honor.

So fun.

Well, there's one thing I do, something I've kept up since I was fifteen years old; I wake up early every day, go for a run, then end it with a barefoot walk so I can feel close to everything.

It started when Benji took a trip to Tunisia while I stayed behind with the security guards as my babysitters. When he came back, it was with all these mystical ideas he'd learned from the people he was staying with. The irony was that his teachings were all about love, an idea Benji was apparently drawn to, but unable to actually show. Not to me, and not to anyone I'd ever seen him around.

But one of the things he taught me was that when an emotion runs deep, the best thing you can do is take off your shoes to be closer to the energy of the world, allowing the true holiness of the moment to flow free.

So every morning, I have held on to this ritual. It's the one thing that ensures there's a portion of the day when the Universe and I are one.

And tomorrow, I'll need it.

I kneel down on the floor and retrieve the metal box hidden under my bed. I trust everyone who comes in and out of this house, but I also know the pull of temptation.

It's a combination lock, and I quickly spin the numbers until it unlocks. Inside is a small jewelry box. My hands have a slight tremor as I open it. I take in the diamonds and blue sapphires, it's such a small thing to be this precious.

I close the case, then return it to the metal box before scrambling the combination and hiding it back under my bed. Pulling out my phone, I quickly book a table at Breakers, a cocktail lounge, with a note to seat us in the back. Then I scroll to my text messages.

Mac: I made reservations at Breakers tomorrow night. Meet me there at 7 p.m.

The read receipt indicates she's read the message, then the moving dots as she types.

Amanda: I'll be there in red.

Chapter Eleven

Maren

As soon as my eyes open in my darkened room, I'm up. I slide my feet into slippers, wrap a robe around my shoulders, and rush to the kitchen to put a pot of coffee on, my eyes scanning the street outside the entire time.

It's been twenty-four hours since I last saw Mac, and I can still feel the way his body felt on mine, how his hands felt as they tugged my hair and gripped my back, how luscious it was to be filled by his—

"Dang girl, you run a marathon before your first cup of coffee?"

"Uh, why?" I study the pot as if willing it to go faster, as if this was my main concern for the day.

"Because you're all flushed and out of breath. Has Naked Coffee Guy shown up yet?"

"Hm?" I say it as if I haven't been looking for him. "Oh, not sure. What time does he usually pass by?"

5:07 a.m. every day. Unless he's sleeping next to me in a hotel room.

"Oh, there he is!"

I lose my cool and dart to the window, staring at his rippling abs as he holds his coffee, completely oblivious that he has an audience. I glance at Nina, and instantly feel annoyance that she's also watching him—as if he belongs to me.

He doesn't. But I know what he feels like in bed, and she does not. I have more rights to him than anyone else.

Real nice, Maren. I force myself to leave the window, grabbing a cup of coffee even as I know he's still within view, if I only looked. I pour a cup for Nina too.

"Come on, we're going to be late for work."

I'm distracted my entire shift, checking my phone every few minutes, and watching the door as if Mac will walk through it. If what we're doing is casual, I'm failing in every sense because I can't stop thinking about him. Is he thinking of me, too? Or is this a game to him?

More than anything, I hate that I'm being reduced to feeling this crazy. I've left guys for acting this possessive, and now I'm the one extending my claws, ready to sink them into Mac and claim him as mine forever.

I know I made him promise he couldn't tell anyone, but I can't keep this in any longer without going completely insane. So, once my shift ends, I head straight for Claire's house and walk in the door unannounced.

I find Claire in her studio, headphones on as she leans over the current craft she's working on. Right now, she's creating tiny books that fit on a keychain, and I recognize Nicole Shannon's most popular series, including the book that's set to release next month.

"Don't tell me you've already read *Fated Hate*." I pick up one of the tiny books and look at it, realizing I'm one of the first to see the cover. Nicole Shannon has been teasing the cover reveal on her Instagram for weeks, and there it is, in all its bare-chested glory.

Claire removes her headphones and grins.

"I read it twice, it's so good," she says. I'm tempted to ask her to borrow it, but I know Claire honors the trust of the authors she works with, and even signs contracts promising not to share books before their release. I know that even if Claire weren't legally bound by NDAs, she would still take it seriously. So I don't even bother asking…even though I'm dying to read this book.

"Hey, what if I accidentally agreed to a fling with an awful person, except that he's not so awful when it's just the two of us, and he's kind of ruined me for any other guy, and now it's making me forget all the reasons I hate him even though I truly hate this person?"

Claire tilts her head at me, then pulls up a chair to sit. I do the same, then bury my head in my hands. "I don't know what to do, Claire. I've never felt this crazy."

"Have you talked with him about it?" she asks gently, resting her hand on my arm. I lift my head and sigh.

"I can't. The whole purpose of being casual is to not have the relationship talk, and we only started this last night."

Claire looked closer at me. "Wait. You're not talking about Brock?"

"Ew, no. I would never catch feelings for that creep."

"Then who?" But as soon as she asks, her face takes on a look of understanding. "Oh my god, you didn't."

"I did." I hide my face again.

"I'm just putting this out there because I hope to god it's true, but are you talking about Naked Coffee Guy?"

I bury my head again as she squeals.

"Maren, that's brilliant! I can't believe you're fighting this."

"You know why I can't fall for him, Claire. Ugh, this was such a mistake."

"No, it wasn't. I want to hear everything, but not yet. Finn is coming home any minute, and we need to leave the house so you can give me every single dirty detail."

I groan, but Claire is already out the door, informing Ethan he's on dad duty while we enjoy a girl's night out.

An hour later we're sitting in Breakers, taking up space at a high-top while she sips a chocolate martini and I nurse a Diet Coke. Claire's mouth is a permanent "O" as I describe everything that's happened since Mac pushed me up against the alley wall outside Insomniacs to the moment I walked out of the hotel room. But I left out the control part, because well, Claire wouldn't understand. Ethan is her one and only love, including sex. I hardly know what their sex life is like, nor do I want to. I can't discuss mine with her either, and I'm not sure I want to see the level of shocked Claire would be if I talked about how dominant I usually am in the bedroom. So I can't talk about last night's role reversal without a lot of explaining.

"And he hasn't called or texted?"

I shake my head. "Casual, remember? It would break the rules."

"You're already breaking the rules by telling me," Claire points out. "So you should text him. if he responds right away, then you have your answer."

I shoot a look at her. "Did you forget the part where I hate him?" Not to mention, he made it clear who was in charge here, and it wasn't me.

Why was I agreeing to this? Oh yeah, because the man's presence alone makes me breathless, let alone the way he fucks me.

"Did you forget the part where he gave you multiple orgasms in one night, and how that's just a precursor to how things could be?"

I bark out a laugh. "Damn, Claire, you're starting to sound like me."

"And you're starting to sound like *me*. Where did Maren go? Because my best friend would be at Naked Coffee Guy's house right now, telling him to shut up and put out, regardless of some petty bullshit."

Okay, so maybe Claire did understand my weird control kink.

"Being homeless isn't petty, Claire." I'm lucky it didn't get that far, this time. I remember all too well what it was like to live in my car, worried I'd be found by some rapist or something. And while Sunset Bay has mild weather most of the year, it gets cold at night just like any place. When you're skin and bones, nighttime feels like the worst.

"Maren, I know that, and I know you have experiences I'm grateful I've never had." Claire holds my hand. She's known me through everything. Of course she can see where my mind has gone. "But those were the old days, things are different now. You could have stayed with me, and you know that. While Nina's not a golden ray of sunshine, at least she has a room you can rent. I know this isn't your ideal situation, and you've had to give up a lot because of it, but what if all of this happened for a reason?"

This is so classic Claire, the eternal optimist. But it also reminds me of what Mac said that first day I met him, about enduring terrible things and choosing how to react to them.

My choice was to let that become my identity and remain angry, or to take what I'd learned from those years and change my present and future…I chose the latter, and it's a choice I have to make every day to keep from letting the demons win.

I hold grudges, wearing them like they're expensive jewelry. The day my parents turned their backs on me, I swore I'd never return. It was a protection of sorts, to keep me from feeling that vulnerable again.

Now I'm doing it with Mac. I know this. Yes, the choice he made affected me and dozens of others. I've done a lot of scrambling in the wake of losing my home.

But now I have a choice. Do I hold this against him forever, and let this taint our obvious connection? Or do I let it go and open myself to the full potential of what we could be?

"He doesn't even know why I hate him." I stare at my phone on the table, wishing it would light up with a text from him. I need to know I'm not alone in feeling this way.

"*Do* you hate him?" Claire asks.

I look up, ready to answer yes, because *of course* I hate

him. But I pause just long enough to doubt my feelings. I hate what happened. I hate that I now live in a tiny room in a messy house with the most flaky and thoughtless person I know.

I hate that Mac played a part in the reason I had to leave my apartment. But do I hate *him*?

"I don't," I admit. "I'm angry with him, but I don't hate him. I can admit that maybe I shouldn't even be angry with him because he was just doing his job and still has no idea that it affected me." And even though it makes no sense at all, I get the feeling if I stop reminding myself that Mac is just a fuck, I could end up falling for him.

How would it feel to fall completely? To just trust that this is the Universe speaking, as Mac told me that first night. What if I let down my guard and made the first move toward something that looked nothing like casual?

I pick up my phone, hesitating for just a moment to look at Claire for moral support.

"Do it," she dared.

With a grin, I unlock the phone and consider what to send. In the past, I would have just texted *Hey*, then wait for the guy to do all the talking. It was a way to keep the upper hand without revealing my cards. But now that I think about it, it wasn't a power play at all. So right now, I'm going to go out on a limb and just say what I'm thinking, to shape the path we're on, and to let him be the one to react.

I know we said we'd keep things casual. But Mac, nothing between us feels casual. I'd normally enter the day after without so much as a thought to the night before, but the other night was different. You're different. I have not stopped thinking about you. Am I alone in this? Because I haven't heard from you for two days, and I'm kind of freaking out. Which is why I have to tell you this, because if you're not feeling the same, we need to call this off. I can't risk falling any deeper than I already am.

I pause, re-reading what I wrote. Claire is over my shoulder, reading along.

"Except for the part where you're practically begging him to end this, this is really good," she says. At the same time, I'm realizing just how touchy-feely the text is.

I can't send this. What was I even thinking? I quickly delete the whole thing and hear Claire's audible gasp as I do.

"Maren, what the hell?"

I shake my head, the phone like a burning ember in my hand. I still want to reach out to him, but I am not about to spill my whole heart to him. So I do what I should have done to begin with.

Me: Hey.

"Way to open up there, Huerta."

I glance up as Claire rolls her eyes, but then I look back at my phone, waiting to see what happens.

Underneath the text, the word *delivered* changes to *read.*

"Look," I say, pointing to it. I place the phone in the center of the table so we both can wait for his response.

And wait.

We stare at that phone for at least five minutes, and nothing happens. No three dots to show he's texting me back. No text at all. Just silence in a moment that feels more naked than his bare chest on an early morning coffee walk.

I look up at Claire and offer a tight smile. "And that's why I'm not going to barf my feelings out to him."

"He's probably not answering because there is literally no way to respond to *hey*."

"Um…he could text *hey* back," I point out, and she rolls her eyes.

"Whatever. Just because he's not texting back right away, it doesn't mean anything."

But I know it does. I know because if he texted me, I'd…

Well, I'd wait a bit so I didn't seem overly eager, even though I would have read it right away.

"Okay, fine. It doesn't mean anything, at least not

yet." I pick up my phone and slip it in my purse. "But if he hasn't texted me back by tomorrow, I'll have my answer."

"He will," Claire says, slipping the waitress her credit card as she waves off the few dollars I'm holding out to her. "You had a $2 soda, I got this."

We leave the bar and head for her car when I realize I left my jacket on the back of my chair.

"Warm up the car, I'll be quick," I say, then jog back to Breakers before she can answer.

A couple are sitting at the table we were at, my jacket nowhere to be seen. I ask the waitress behind the bar if she's seen it.

"Oh yeah, I stuck it in the back in case you returned. Hold on, I'll get it."

I look around while I wait, and a familiar face catches me off guard in the back of the bar. It's Mac, and he's not alone. My heart drops as I fully register the scene in front of me. Mac is dressed similarly to what he wore last night—a white shirt open at the top and black slacks. I can't see the woman's face, but judging from her salon blonde hair and expensive red dress with a side slit, I'd say she's pretty much gorgeous. Mac is smiling, talking with animated hands, and it seems like our *casual* affair is the furthest thing from his mind.

We never said we couldn't see other people. In fact,

in the rules of being casual, it's a given that we're free agents.

So why does this hurt so bad?

"Here's your jacket," the waitress says, interrupting me from my creepy stalking. I turn and take it from her, inwardly telling myself to walk away and forget I even saw Mac.

But I can't. I swivel back in their direction, watching to see just how serious this is.

The answer is immediate. He's holding a jewelry box open and she's leaning over it, her hand at her chest like she's breathless from what she's seeing.

Then Mac looks up, his eyes finding mine. And even from across the room, I can see he realizes he's been caught. Is that even the right phrase? Because he doesn't belong to me, and I don't belong to him.

I turn and run, pushing my way through the crowded bar as I hear him calling my name. But I won't stop, because I never want to see Mac Dermot again. Fuck men, and all the ways they never measure up.

Chapter Twelve

Mac

"Maren, wait!"

I take off after her, realizing how this must look. I think I can catch her, but I underestimate how fast she can run. Those long legs take off down the street like she's a goddamn deer, and I have to pound the pavement to finally reach her. I grab her arm and she yelps into the night, struggling to free herself from me. But my hold is tight. I swing her against the building and cage her in so she can't escape, my face inches from hers. I note the tears in her eyes, which surprises me. It also kills me. I know Maren isn't one for crying. I know she hates that I am seeing her this way, even though she has no idea what she just saw. I hate that, even though she's wrong, I'm to blame for those tears.

"Get off me," she growls, pushing at me. Maren is not weak, but her efforts are fruitless because I don't budge. I know that if I do, she'll take off again, and I'm tired of chasing her.

She eventually stills, probably realizing she doesn't have a chance against me. I take the moment to run my thumb over her cheek, catching the tear that's brimming her eyes. Maren turns her head, squeezing her eyes shut. But I notice the smallest shift in her breath, how she inhales, how her face softens and a small groan escapes her lips. I can't help it. I press my body into hers, feeling her soft curves fall into every hard inch of my body.

"I can explain," I murmur into her hair, brushing my nose against her ear.

She shakes her head, her eyes still squeezed shut. "You don't have to explain anything, we're free to see other people."

I cup her face with firm fingers, turning her head, waiting until she finally opens her eyes and looks at me.

"No, we aren't. I'll consider this casual, if that's what you want. But I am not and will not see anyone else as long as you're sharing my bed, and I expect the same from you." I study her, seeing how she will take this. When she tries to turn away again, I tighten my hold on her face. "Just the thought of some other man touching you is enough to drive me insane."

"So you can imagine what I'm feeling right now," she

spits out. Her eyes shoot daggers at me, daring me to argue. "I'm not fucking stupid. You've obviously made your choice, so let me go so I can forget I ever knew you."

She starts to fight me again, but I press firmly against her and crush my mouth on hers, stealing her breath. She resists for only a moment, but soon she's clutching my shirt, kissing me back, and fuck me, I wish I could take her right here. She makes me ravenous, the way my mouth can't get enough of her. The way my hips grind against hers, and how she meets me with each thrust. I want to wrap her long legs around me, feel her cunt throb on my dick, and taste every goddamn inch of her.

Even as mad as she is, she demands my attention through just a kiss, her mouth searching mine for so many things we've left unsaid. I shouldn't feel this possessive. And yet, as her arms snake around my body, her face tilted to mine as I drink her in, it's hard to believe we don't already belong to each other.

Her phone vibrates against me from her purse, and this time I let her break away from me as we both pant to catch our breaths.

"It's Claire," she explains, not even looking at her phone. "She's waiting for me, and probably thinks I've been mauled."

"Tell her to leave without you," I order.

"But she's my ride."

"You have a ride." I fish her still ringing phone from the purse, hit the button, and hand it to her.

"H-hello?"

Her dark eyes stay on me, even as she talks to her friend. A flash from last night infiltrates my mind. The way she looked lying naked on my bed, completely at my mercy, when she finally let go and opened herself to me. The sweet taste of her when I dipped my head between her legs, a nectar I can almost taste now. I inhale sharply, taking her lilac scent with me.

"Go ahead without me," she continues into the phone, her gaze remaining on me. I can see the hesitancy in her expression, but I also see the need. If she was going to leave me, she would have by now. "I ran into… uh, I ran into a friend and we have some catching up to do." She pauses as her friend speaks. "Claire, I'm okay, I promise."

"Let's go," I growl. My hand finds her hip and I pull her toward me, but this time she pushes me off her. She turns her back to me.

"Mustard," she whispers, and I tilt my head. What? But I'm now close enough to hear the other side of this phone conversation.

"I'm coming to get you," her friend says. I step closer to hear better.

"Claire, no. I'm not saying the code word because I'm not safe. I'm with a friend—"

"Put them on."

"No, I'm not—"

"Put them on or I'm calling the cops."

I snatch the phone from her hands, and Maren whips around, eyes flashing as I put the phone to my hear.

"She's with me."

There's a brief silence on the other end. Then, "Mac?"

I flex my jaw, if only to keep from grinning like a fucking idiot. Maren's obviously talked about me to her friend, which means she broke one of her own rules. I'm not as secret as she'd have me believe.

"Yeah."

"So listen, I know Maren is a big girl and can take care of her own," Claire says into the phone. "She could probably even kick your ass, though I hear you're a tank. But she's also my best friend. If you hurt her, I swear to god, I'll hunt you down and make you pay."

This time, my smirk breaks through. I hide it with a cough, shooting a side glance at Maren. Figures she's watching my every move.

I grunt my agreement, then hand it back to Maren. She glares at me, but I see a hint of curiosity in her eyes. I'm starting to wonder if she's actually angry, or if she's just using it as a front to keep me at arm's length. Then again, the fact that she even got that angry seeing me with someone else… again. Does she think she's already mine?

"Yes," she whispers into the phone, then it's her turn to hide a smile. I can hear Claire squealing through the phone, even though Maren has stepped a few feet away, her back to me. I move closer again, but this time it's not to listen in. I wrap my arms around her, then wait to see how she reacts.

"I'm not going to do that," Maren says to Claire. She turns remaining in my arms, her face inches from mine. I stand my ground, my eyes daring her to make a move. She doesn't, but she also doesn't step away. Instead, she matches my gaze, even with the phone attached to her ear.

"I'll leave my locations services on," she finally says, "but don't look for my body until tomorrow." Her hand has found my chest, and I am well aware of the pressure of her fingers, almost as if they're touching my skin. Her palm remains still, but her fingers trace a hypnotic circle. I keep my stance rigid, but inside, she's turning me to lava.

She finally hangs up, and I have completely forgotten why we are out here and not tangled in my sheets. We stare at each other, the electricity building between us until it feels like a goddamn inferno in my chest. I lick my lips, preparing to dip my head to her pretty mouth, when she slams her hands against my chest with such force that the current is broken.

"What the fuck, Maren."

"Who is she?" she demands.

And that's when it all comes back. The look of hurt on her face. The way she stormed out of that restaurant. How obvious it is that this woman cares about me more than she'll ever let on. I bite back a smirk, then resist the urge to flinch when she lands an icy glare on me. I'm not one to cower—I've been through too much shit to be afraid of anything—but damn if this girl doesn't have some serious sass. I'm half tempted to rile her up, just to see her in action. I don't, though.

"She's not who you think, I'll tell you that much."

"You know what I'm thinking, asshole?" She slams her hands against me again. I don't move, even though this tiny thing packs a punch. "I'm thinking I had the best fuck of my life with a guy who has me re-thinking everything I've ever thought about relationships, only to hear crickets."

"The best, huh?" I raise an eyebrow, challenging her to take it back. Her eyes remain like daggers, but there's another kind of heat brimming beneath that fiery gaze.

"You're missing the point. Why didn't you call?"

I see the slightest wince, as if she can't believe the words coming out of her mouth. I get the feeling that Maren isn't one who begs, or even gives second chances.

"You're the one who left me, Maren," I remind her. "I figured you didn't want me to bother you."

"Then I see you on a date," she says, completely ignoring anything I'm saying. "And not just any date, a date where you're presenting her with something in a little box, which leads me to believe this isn't just another one of your casual flings, but something more serious. Which would make me the other woman, and that's an incredibly shitty thing because I would never try to steal another woman's man."

"You're not."

"You're right, because I'm done, Mac. We had our fun, but I get to walk away while you get to explain to your girlfriend why you're here with me and not with her."

She starts to leave, but never gets that far. I push her back up against the wall, her hands pinned above her head. She could fight me, but she doesn't. Her breath comes out in hot, sweet pants, her heart racing against my chest.

"That woman is not my girlfriend," I growl. She starts to argue, but I press my mouth to hers, effectively shutting her up. "Are you going to listen?" I ask, still against her lips. She nods as much as she can with limited movement.

"She's not my girlfriend. She's Amanda Crawford, an estate jeweler," I continue. "She traveled from out of the area and met me at Breakers so she could see if the sapphire Cartier brooch I have is something her boss wants in his collection."

"You were…selling it to her?"

She relaxes a little, even though I can see she's still wary. I wait for her to ask questions I'm not prepared to answer. I can see she's curious, but also that she's holding back. There's this wall she wants to keep up, one I'm ready plow through and take what I want. But it's also keeping her from prying. If she doesn't pry, then I won't either, and the wall remains in place.

This time, the wall is my advantage.

"I need to get back in there," I say, and she immediately stiffens. "Hey." I lean down, looking her in the eyes, my hands holding her shoulders. "Come with me. I have to wrap up this sale," I pause, then look her up and down, hardening at the way her breath hitches. "Then I have some unfinished business to attend to."

She takes in a deep inhale, and I know she's thinking about our night together. I am too. The way her back arched while my mouth tasted every inch of her. The soft moan in the back of her throat as she pulled me closer. How her hips met me thrust for thrust.

Maren is calculated to a T. I saw it from the moment I first saw her, and now that she's in my orbit, I know it for sure. I could have let her have her way last night, but

I also knew she was treating me like any other fuck. Another wall. Her way of keeping me at arm's length. But she'll soon find out, I'm not any other fuck.

I told her this was casual. What a fucking lie.

We walk back to Breakers, but she draws the line at joining me and Ms. Crawford while we finish the transaction. I can feel Maren's eyes on me as I take my seat.

"Everything okay?" Amanda asks, sneaking a glance in Maren's direction.

"Yes," I say, not bothering to explain myself. To her credit, Amanda waited a good thirty minutes in this restaurant while I convinced Maren I wasn't fucking someone else. But then again, this brooch is worth waiting for. I pull it out of my jacket pocket and open the box, allowing her a closer look. Amanda leaves the box on the table and uses a magnifying glass to get a closer look. While she studies the piece, I peek in Maren's direction, who quickly averts her eyes. She takes a sudden interest in her phone, and I know she's dying to keep watching us. It must kill her to play it so uncool when I know she's used to being in control. She finally does look, and the embarrassed grin she flashes at me is enough to make me want to rush this sale so I can show Maren exactly what she does to me.

Amanda is now on the phone, and I tear my eyes

away from Maren as she talks with her boss. When she hangs up, she's smiling.

"We'll take it," she says, pulling an envelope from her purse. I open it, my face a damn glacier as I take in the amount on the check that once felt like Monopoly money. Even now, it's not a small number. $1.2 million for a piece of metal and some precious jewels. It just might be enough to undo some of the old man's sins.

Amanda and I both rise. She shakes my hand, sealing the deal, then leans forward and offers a small kiss on my cheek. When she leans back, there's something different in her eyes. A question. She glances at Maren, then back at me, and the corner of her mouth turns up.

"Maybe we can meet again sometime, when you're not…" she glances at Maren again, "Preoccupied." She offers a meaningful look. "I don't run."

I flex my jaw, knowing that Maren is seeing this entire exchange. I feel like an idiot for missing the signs.

"Goodbye, Amanda," I say, dismissing her proposition. She smiles again, but this time with unspoken understanding. There will not be another meeting. Not for business, nor for any other reason.

She leads the way from the restaurant, and from the back I can see the slight glance she shoots toward Maren. But my girl doesn't give her the time of day. She looks past Amanda, settling her wary gaze on me.

"Are you ready to go?" I guide her to her feet. She pauses, as if to mull something over. Then she lifts her hand and brushes her thumb over my cheek where Amanda kissed me.

"I never want to see another woman's lipstick on any part of your body," she says, and I can't help but laugh.

"You better wear lipstick tonight, because it's your red lips I want all over my body."

And goddamn, the look in her eyes rumbles through me and straight to my cock. She's like a drug, and I've barely had a taste. I need this woman in my bed tonight, and every night after.

"You should probably work on your persuasion skills," she teases, then slips her hand into mine before I lead her from the bar.

Once outside, she shivers as the cold air meets her bare arms. Her jacket is hanging over her purse, and she starts to unfold it when I stop her.

"Turn around," I command. Her eyes sparkle, and I have the feeling she's secretly enjoying when I order her around, as she complies without argument. I slide the sleeves over her arms, running my hand across her skin as I do, then rest at her collarbone. I lean forward, my lips brushing against her ear.

"Let's get out of here," I whisper. She nods and starts to turn, but she freezes as her eyes settle on a group of people across the way. Four guys and one girl.

"Lydia," she breathes.

Chapter Thirteen

Maren

Lydia was nine the last time I saw her in person, but I've seen her photo on Instagram enough times to know it's her. It also doesn't take a scientist to see she's blitzed out of her mind. She's clutching a bottle in a paper bag while stumbling in her platform boots, and I wonder if our father saw how short her skirt was when she left the house. He surely wouldn't approve of the guys hanging around her. But I'm not really worried about what my father would think, I'm worried about the position Lydia is in as I see the guys pass her the bottle again, catching eyes above her head.

Years ago, before I got sober, *I* was Lydia. I felt like the sexiest girl in the world as I hung out with some guys who were years older than me. We'd just done a few lines of coke, and they were awfully generous with a bottle of whiskey they were passing around. I don't remember much about that night, but I do know that when I woke up the next morning behind a dumpster near some apartments, my underwear was missing, there were bruises on my arms and thighs, and I had a deep pain in my groin that lasted for days. More than anger and fear, I felt completely stupid. I knew better. You don't live on the streets and not see stuff. I knew what happened to girls who let down their defenses. And I'd done just that—trusted a bunch of guys I barely knew only to be violated. I was so ashamed that I didn't give details when I got tested at the free clinic, and I was lucky I didn't get pregnant or any STDs.

Now I'm seeing the same scene unfold in front of me, but it's my sister, and these guys are purposely getting her drunk.

"Lydia!" I tear myself from Mac's arms as her name falls loudly from my mouth. She turns around as I stalk in her direction. For a moment, I see the lack of clarity as she tries to figure out who I am. And then it washes over her, followed by a sneer that too closely resembles a look I've seen on my father's face.

I don't wait for her to talk, instead I grab her arm and pull her away. She tries to fight me off, but her drunk ass can barely form a sentence.

"Who the fuck are you?" One of the guys takes a menacing step toward me, but Mac is between us in an instant, his hand like a vice around the guy's throat.

"Back off, fucker, or I'll beat the shit out of you. Then I'll call the cops for supplying a minor with alcohol. Fuck knows what else you were planning on doing with an underage girl."

He pushes hard, and the guy coughs and gasps for breath as soon as Mac releases him.

"We weren't doing nothing but hanging out," another guy mutters, but loud enough that Mac swings at him, catching him in the chin.

"Leave them alone," Lydia screams, finally finding words as the guys take off running, leaving her with us.

"Why, so they can finish getting you fucked up before they rape you?"

Lydia pulls away from me, rubbing at her arm as if I've done more harm to her than those bastards. "They're my friends. But I guess a whore like you wouldn't understand."

"Don't talk to her that way," Mac intervenes, his face twisted in an angry scowl as he shakes out his hand. "Who is this twit, anyway?"

"She's my sister."

"You are *not* my sister." Lydia stumbles, and I catch her before she falls. She yanks her arm from me again. "You're a fucking stranger who probably stalked me here so you can get money from me."

I know she's saying things to get under my skin. And it's working. Every word she throws at me, every sneer, is like a punch to the gut. I hear my father. I wonder what he's told her in the years I've been gone.

"Your sister is the bravest and strongest woman I know," Mac says, "and she just saved your ass from what those guys were going to do to you."

"They weren't going to do anything. We were just having some fun."

I bark out a laugh, "And Dad would have no problem seeing you like this?"

She doesn't have a chance to shoot me another sarcastic remark, because suddenly she's bent at the waist, puking all over the street. I jump back to avoid the splash zone, but then quickly maneuver around her so I can pull her hair back.

"I'll get the car," Mac says, and I look up, catching his eye. I'm overwhelmed at how grateful I am that he's here with me. As furious as I am with Lydia, reality is starting to catch up with me. Lydia wasn't lying when she called me a stranger. She doesn't know me; she only knows the picture my father has painted of me. Now I have to deliver her back to the lion's den and face my father's rejection once again.

"Thank you," I say, and Mac nods before trotting off

in the direction of the car.

By the time he returns, Lydia has puked half her weight on the street and is now leaning against a wall with her eyes closed, moaning periodically.

Mac pulls up in a Jaguar, panther black with silver details and shiny rims, which still smells like new leather when he opens the door. It's another reminder how different our worlds are, along with a stab in the gut that someone like him could not possibly be interested in someone like me.

Imagine if he knew I lived in the Beale Street apartments, with its mildew scent and dark spots on the ceiling. That it was a huge step up from my life before, that this is the progress I've made while he sleeps between thousand-dollar sheets. It's one thing for him to know where I came from. It's something else for him to know I've only come this far. If he knew I lived in that teardown apartment, he'd really know how different we were. My ego, more than anything, can't risk this.

"I'm sorry if she pukes in your car," I murmur as Mac lifts her up. Lydia keeps her eyes closed, moaning as he places her in the backseat. He buckles her in, but she slumps over, lying on the bench seat as if it were a bed.

"I'll let you help me clean it if she does," he says, followed by a wink. He opens the door for me and I slide into the passenger seat.

It's like an out of body experience as I direct Mac to

my parents' home. It feels both familiar and strange as I navigate through streets that grow more recognizable with each turn. Then we're on the same street, and my heart is pounding as he slows in front of the house I once called home.

"Breathe, Maren," Mac says, taking my hand and stroking the back of it.

The night I met Mac on the top of Torches, wearing the glass of wine I never drank, I revealed more about myself than I ever had to anyone. Beyond Claire, that is. There was something about Mac that made it easy to let my guard down, and before I knew it, I was telling him all about my fucked up past and how it cost me my family.

The way he's holding my hand now, I'm sure he can see the tempest brewing inside me. I hadn't even known I was holding my breath, or that I was crying. He wipes my tears with his thumb, then cups my face as he looks into my eyes.

For a moment, I'm tempted to ask him to come with me as I deliver my sister. But as much as I fear my father's wrath, it will be worse for Mac. There's no way my father will see anything but malice if some strange guy came in carrying his drunk daughter.

It has to be me.

"Wait here," I say, moving from Mac's protecting

hand. His jaw pulses, and he pauses like he's going to say something. But he finally nods.

I leave the safety of my seat, opening the back door. My sister is still slumped over, and she moans as I unbuckle her seatbelt.

"Lydia, you have to get up, I can't carry you." I tug at her until she finally pulls herself into a sitting position. When she opens her eyes, I can see it's a struggle.

"Maren?" Her voice is strained, and I'm worried she's going to be sick again.

"Let's get out of the car," I say, taking her arm and putting if over my shoulder. She stands, but I bear most of the weight. "Can you walk?"

She nods, taking a shuffling step forward. She murmurs something else, and I lean in to hear what she's saying.

"How's it feel?" she slurs, then takes another few steps. I cling to her to keep from falling as she stumbles.

"How's what feel?"

She laughs, dropping to the asphalt, probably skinning her unprotected knees.

"How's it feel to know that you fucked up so badly that Mom and Dad don't want you? That they pretend you're dead because they can't stand to know you exist."

It takes all my effort to not push her back down and cram her face into the street. I hear Mac's door slam shut, and I whirl around, losing Lydia in the process as I press my hands to his chest.

"It's fine, I got this."

"It's not fine. That little brat needs to learn a lesson."

"And you're going to teach it to her?" I ask, still holding him off.

"No," he says, shaking me off him. "But no one gets to talk to you that way, least of all a spoiled drunk kid. I don't care if she's your sister."

"And you'll stand down *because* she's my sister. This is *my* business, Mac. Not yours. I can handle my own."

Even though he's made it clear that no one gets to tell him what to do, this is where the line is drawn. He can run his alpha mouth all day long, and I will not back down.

The hardened look remains in his eyes, and he glares at Lydia, who is back on her ass on the ground not even bothering to get back up.

"Fine," he relents, "But I'm staying with you, and not in the car like some bitch."

"Fine," I spit back at him. But secretly, I'm glad. Just knowing he's there eases my nerves about facing my father again.

We get Lydia to the front steps, and I'm about to ring the doorbell, when she stops me with a flailing hand.

"No," she says. She looks at me, and this time I see the fear in her eyes. "He can't know."

After all this girl has said to me, I have half a mind to beat the door down and get him really angry before he opens it to find his drunk daughter. But something in her face stops me. Even though I owe her nothing, and I have every right to turn her in, I lower my hand.

"Give me your keys," I say, and she fishes around in her purse before finding them. "Not a peep. If I'm going to sneak you in, you're going to be dead silent, you hear me? Because if Dad catches me in there with you, being drunk will be the least of your issues."

Lydia won't be the one to pay—I will. Still, a new look of fear crosses her face, and she nods.

"I can try to make it to my room by myself," she slurs, but I shake my head.

"You can barely stand up, let alone walk. Now stop talking and let's get this over with."

"I'm still coming with you," Mac says. I nod, even though this feels like an impossible mission. But I also don't want to go in there alone.

I slide the key into the lock and turn it quietly. Then I ease the door open, holding my breath. I look at Lydia and nod, and we both make the first step into the house.

The smell in the house hits me all at once, an earthy scent I haven't smelled for years. There's the hint of whatever they had for dinner—my mom's Chile relleno, if I'm smelling it correctly. The porch light casts a soft glow on the living room, and it's apparent nothing has changed. It's like time has stood still, and I'm seventeen again, coming in after a night out. Pictures of Lydia line the entryway, starting from when she was little all the way up to her track photos from this year. Gone are any photos of me.

For Lydia's part, she manages to stay upright with each step. Mac stays close as we advance down the hall, one careful step at a time. Lydia nods to the door that used to be my room, and my heart aches as I open it. In the moonlight streaming through the bedroom window, I can see all my things are gone, replaced by hers. It's like I never lived here. Like I never existed.

Mac is in the room but turns his back as I undress my sister and get her into bed. Her breathing deepens as soon as she's tucked in, and I pause for just a moment to look her over. Asleep, her face is peaceful. She reminds me more of the girl I've seen on social media and less like the vile bitch I've just spent the last half hour with. I know my feelings toward her are changed forever. The mystery is gone. Maybe it's time to give up my family once and for all, to never look back.

A piece of me breaks, knowing this is the end of what I once wished for.

The journey back down the hall feels a thousand steps long. It's too quiet, and I hear each creak as we tiptoe back to the front door. This is different from when

I was a teen, when I used to sneak out of the house to meet a boyfriend or find trouble. Now, I'm the stranger. The intruder. I don't belong here, and I feel it with every step, every inhale, every touch of the wall as I find my way through the dark.

My hand reaches the doorknob, and I let out a deep exhale, turning the knob. But then the room is bathed in light, and I hear the unmistakable click of a gun behind us being cocked.

"Who are you and what the fuck are you doing in my house?"

Chapter Fourteen

Mac

"Turn around slowly," Maren's father orders.

I do, along with Maren, only to face the barrel of a gun directed at me.

"Dad! Stop! It's me!"

His face takes on a look of surprise. "Maren?" He lowers the weapon, but the shock in his expression quickly turns to rage.

"What are you doing here?" he hisses, "I almost killed you. Would that have been worth whatever you're stealing from us?"

"What? I'm not—"

"Don't lie to me, Maren. You think I don't know what you're doing? This is how you thank us? After all this time? After all we did for you?" He huffs out a laugh, shaking his head. "We gave you everything, and you threw it all away. And for what? A temporary high? How's that working for you, huh?"

He's still holding the gun. He could have put it down, but it remains in his hand, as if he thinks he needs it for protection. Maybe he sees me as a threat, but he's barely regarded me. His eyes remain trained on his daughter.

Something dark and winding unfurls in my belly, a surge of poison traveling to my clenched fists and pulsating in my jaw as I fight the urge to take down this guy who dares to look at Maren this way, to put her in this kind of danger. I have to keep reminding myself that no matter what, this is her father. But fuck this guy, because my restraint is hanging by a thread.

"Sir," I bite out through clenched teeth, "if you'll just let her explain."

I don't have a chance to finish because his gun is trained on me again. That thread of restraint snaps, and I grin, feeling the charge in me before I teach him a lesson. But before I can act, Maren jumps in front of me. Like she'll take a goddamn bullet for me.

"Get out of the way," I growl, placing my hands on her hips and pulling her aside. I stare down her father, mentally daring him to pull the trigger, and seeing in his eyes that he won't. He lowers the gun, but the tension remains in his face.

"Manny?"

I keep my eyes on Maren's father, but out of the corner of my eye I see a woman lingering in the hallway, likely Maren's mother.

"What's going on?" she asks.

"Stay in the room, Isabella," Manny orders. He's now focused on Maren, his eyes narrow and sharp. It makes me want to push her behind me before I wipe that stern look off his face. It's been so long since I've known what it's like to have a father. Not Benji, who treated our relationship like a business transaction. But my real father. I remember him, but sometimes it feels like I only remember a muted version of that man. Only bits and pieces. So there is a lot I've forgotten. But one thing I am absolutely certain of, I was never afraid of him. He never raised a hand, never his voice, and certainly not a gun.

Maren shared a little about her family situation that night at that rooftop bar. I knew she hadn't seen them in years, and that she went through some hard shit until she finally course corrected. I knew things were strained enough between her and her parents that she was no longer welcome in her childhood home. And the venomous way her sister treated her, even though she was drunk, made it clear that Maren's name had been dragged through the mud in this house.

But the look on her father's face makes it clear just how bad it really is. If I wasn't sure before, I am now.

"I won't call the cops," Manny says, as if he's showing mercy. "I should, but I won't. Just know that my job here is to protect my family, and I take that very seriously."

The way he uses the word *family* sparks the fire inside me. A look at Maren's face, and I can see it's a gut punch. If Manny thinks he needs to protect his family from his oldest daughter, then I will be the man Maren needs and protect her.

"Look, asshole, the only reason you should call the cops is because I'm going to kick your ass for speaking to your daughter this way. You don't even know why she's here, haven't even asked. She brought your—"

"No," Maren cuts in, turning from her dad and pushing her hand on my chest. "Let's just go."

I was about to rat out Lydia, to let Manny know that his perfect youngest daughter isn't as innocent as he thinks. The look on Maren's face is clear though. Keep Lydia's secret safe. Even after the way her sister treated her, even with the way her father is looking at her, Maren's holding fast to loyalty. She owes this family nothing. All they gave her was the blood in her veins, and yet she's willing to leave here without defending her character.

Fine, I'll keep her secrets. But I'll be damned if we leave before I give this shithead a piece of my mind.

I place my hand over Maren's, taking it from my

chest and folding it into my fist. It becomes my anchor to remember that, through everything, this is her father and I am not allowed to beat him to a pulp.

"We'll leave, but first you'll hear what I have to say. Maren won't tell you, so I will."

"Mac, please," Maren begs. I stop and squeeze her hand.

"I won't," I promise. *I won't tell on your fucked up sister.* I turn back to Manny. "Your daughter is an amazing woman. She's smart, and funny, and so full of heart. Her musical talent is off the charts, and she's going to be famous one day. But even if she isn't, she has so much she should be proud of. And if you'd get your head out of your ass, you'd be proud of her too. But you're too blind to see it. You see her in your home after all these years, and you automatically think she's stealing from you without even considering there might be another reason why."

I'm squeezing Maren's hand, but she's squeezing back just as tight. I glance at her, and I can see she's done. The look on her face is full of pain, even as she tries to keep her mask on. Her need to escape is stitched into every cell of her body.

"We're done," I murmur. She immediately turns, releasing my hand and racing through the open front door. I follow after her, hearing the door close behind us without a further word from her dad. I'm so pissed, I can barely see straight.

But Maren? She's volcanic. She tries to open the door to my car, then slams her hands on the windows when she discovers it's locked. I don't care if she breaks the windows. It's just an overpriced car.

I reach her side, then pull her into my arms. She struggles, pounds her hands against my chest, a rageful growl in her throat. I hold her tight, as if I can squeeze the fury from her veins.

"Get off me!" she screams, but I hold fast. Her struggle lessens, and then she's shaking. I smooth her hair, my hold lessening as I glide my hands over her back. When she pulls back, this time I let go. Her face is free of tears, her eyes dry. But the veins in her temples, and the way she's clenching her jaw, let me know how hard she's holding back.

"I just want to go home," she whispers.

I'm struck by the layers in her words. *Home.* The one her family barred her from? Or the one I took from her when I sold the apartments?

I feel like an asshole. I had no choice, but she'd never understand that. I now understand the depth of her pain over the concept of home. Her family denied her a home, so she picked herself up and made her own home. Then I come along and rip that away from her too.

"I'm so fucking angry, I could scream," she hisses

through clenched teeth.

I unlock the door and open it, pushing aside my guilt. Right now, the last thing she needs is for me to bow to my guilt. She doesn't need a confession, she needs a release.

"Get in," I order.

She glares at me, looking ready to fight me. But then she surprises me and does as she's told. Once I'm in the driver's seat, I peel away from the curb. Maren's eyes are glued to the window, and I realize she's watching her parents' house in the side mirror. I glance at the reflection in my rearview mirror, seeing the lights off at her parents' house—as if we were never there, as if they're sleeping soundly, safe from harm.

We don't speak as I drive, even as I take the interstate to King's Cove, away from the heart of Sunset Bay. She doesn't know it, but we're heading toward my home on the hill. I take the winding roads, the city getting further and further away as we're surrounded by darkness. The only light is from my headlights and the glow of the full moon reflecting on the ocean below. The only traffic would be from people who live up here, and at this late hour, the roads remain empty.

We pass my gated driveway, and I keep going. I long to bring her to my house, to show her where I live, to feel her body under the satin fabric of my sheets. I want to kiss away her hurt, to touch her in ways that will make her forget. But right now, I know this is not the release she's looking for.

I reach the turnout, the one that's miles from any home and offers an uninterrupted view of the ocean. It's not like we can see much at this time of night, but no one will hear us either. No one will hear *her*.

"What are we doing here?" she asks, breaking the silence. I say nothing. Instead, I unbuckle and get out of the car. She's already opening her door when I reach her side. It's windy enough that I feel protective as she takes a step closer to the cliff edge.

"Don't do anything stupid," I say, and she shoots me a weary look.

"You're the one who brought me here," she reminds me, her voice raised over the sound of crashing waves below. "Why, though?"

I gesture to the miles of ocean below us. "You wanted to scream, right? Here's your chance."

She hesitates for only a second. Then she turns, takes a deep breath, then empties everything she has into the screaming wind. There are no words, just an animalistic, guttural cry that carries with the tempest around us. I wrap my arms around her waist as she gives it everything, unloading years of hurt into the wind. Her tiny body shudders from sheer force, and she clutches my arms as she continues to scream—for the sister she saved, the home she was turned from, the ways she changed, and how her family would never know.

But *I* know, and I'll be damned if I ever let anyone make her feel that way again. Even if it means I have to keep my secrets, because the only other choice is to stay away from her, and I already know that's no longer an option.

Maren sinks to her knees, and I drop with her. She's sobbing now, and I scoop her into my arms, holding her as she buries her face in my chest. She clings to my shirt as she fully submits to the brokenness inside, no longer fighting. Maren, who is always so strong, who keeps her mask on tight. But in her vulnerability, I am struck by her true strength. She will walk away from this, I know. In this moment, though, I will be the pillar she can lean on so that she can truly feel. I cradle her head, kissing her tangled hair as I crush her against me. She pulls me in tighter, our bodies molded together like she can't get close enough.

And then her mouth is on mine, and she's kissing me with unbridled fire, sparked by tension and rage. She searches my mouth for solace, I search hers for absolution. She straddles me as I sit in the gravel against the car, my slacks and the thin fabric of her panties the only barrier between us. Her hot breath contrasts with the wind around us, and I clutch her ass, needing all of her—needing inside her.

My thoughts immediately go to the condom in the glovebox, and how far away it seems. But it's as if she's reading my mind.

"I'm on the pill," she breathes in my ear, and it's all the convincing I need. I unbuckle my belt, pull down the zipper, then nudge her panties to the side. She's dripping wet, her cunt hot and tight as I slip my fingers in. She groans, clenching around me, and I realize neither of us has this kind of patience. I need to feel her around me.

I free my cock, and hiss as she slides on me. My mouth greedily tastes hers as she clings to me, grinding down on me. Her skirt is hitched around her waist, her thighs gripping mine, and I know her knees are scraping against the rough ground. She doesn't let it slow her down, though. This is raw and animalistic, especially the way she growls as I hold her hips in place, pushing her down so I can reach the deepest part of her. I taste her tears mingled with sweat, and I lick every inch of her skin within my reach. We push and pull against each other, and it's unclear who's in control. For the record, I feel out of control as she grips the back of my neck, meeting me thrust for thrust as she rocks against me. Like I'm slipping into space and she's the only thing keeping me grounded.

Headlights flash from a passing car, but she never breaks rhythm. She grips me by the neck, squeezing slightly, and fuck if the threat of suffocation paired with the threat of being caught doesn't send me over the edge. I cry out against her mouth, her hips rocking over mine as we come together. She feels so fucking good, the bareness of her sliding over me as I throb inside her.

We stay connected once it's over, our foreheads touching as we recover, breathing hot, steamy breath into the cold night air. My hand remains on her hip, the other tangled in her hair. Despite the wind, she's covered in a thin sheen of sweat, and she grips my shoulders to keep herself upright.

I watch the transformation like I'm watching the seasons change color. For a moment, her face holds the hint of a smile as we both catch our breath. But then the realization slides over her. The expression on her face falls first, followed by the strength of her body. My spent cock is still inside her as she starts to pull away. But I keep a firm grip on her hip, preventing her from leaving. I can't bear the thought of leaving her body. Not yet. But I also see the way her mind has wandered, already gone from what just happened.

"Hey," I whisper, tilting her chin up so she's looking at me.

"Hey," she whispers back.

I don't miss the tear that slides down her cheek. I catch it with my thumb, then I brush that same thumb over her lips as she gasps out a sigh. This time when she shifts, I let her go. She rolls off me, adjusting her skirt before she sits in the gravel. I wrap my arm around her. She leans into me, burying her head into my side. I say nothing as she shatters. All I can do is be here for her.

I hope it's enough.

Chapter Fifteen

Maren

Whatever casual agreement we had before, tonight it's broken. I know this as Mac punches the gate code in at a driveway just down the street from where we were. He doesn't even ask to take me to his home, and I'm not arguing. Besides, I had no idea he lived this close. Ever since Nina introduced me to Naked Coffee Guy, the morning delight from our kitchen window, I thought he lived in her neighborhood. But of course he wouldn't. Why would he? Nina's house is nice, but it's not McMansion nice. And once Mac's house comes into view…

Fuck. The man is more loaded than I thought.

The house looks like it could have its own zip code with enough space to shelter a small school. For some reason, I think back to the days when I lived in my car as I'm about to enter this modern-day castle. My stomach does a slow roll as he parks in the driveway, and I'm not sure if it's nerves, excitement, or a warning that I'm about to puke.

"I don't feel so great," I manage to groan before I open my car door and dry heave on the asphalt. Thank goddess nothing comes up. I'm struck by the irony that his fancy Jag has been the setting for two puke events this evening. "The Huerta girls really know how to party, don't we?" I rasp out, capping it with a weak laugh as he reaches my side.

"You're exhausted." He takes my hand and helps me to my feet, then wraps an arm protectively around my waist. "And you've had an emotional evening. Let's get you to bed, all right?"

The way he says it, I know he has no ulterior motives, and I'm embarrassed that it's his wealth that's giving me a mild panic attack. The walk to the front door in the fresh ocean air helps ease my nerves, and once he ushers me inside, I'm feeling more myself. Drained, but no longer ready to spill the contents of my stomach across his tile floors.

Which are beautiful, by the way. I momentarily forget my aversion to wealth, along with my exhaustion, as I take a look around. A great room with ceilings that reach two stories high. A chandelier that has got to be twice as tall as Mac. A fireplace that takes up one wall, and floor-to-ceiling windows on another, overlooking the dark ocean outside. A second story that, when I crane my neck, reveals a wall of books and several closed doors. And the kitchen…

"You cook in this thing?" I ask, taking in the dozens of copper pans hanging above a massive center island, the grills and stove that line one wall to wall counter, the two refrigerators, the copper farm sink, the cabinets and pantry…the unreal amount of space. "I think I could fit my whole apartment in here." I say it before I have time to think, then I want to take back the words when I remember my apartment is probably reduced to dust by now.

Mac rubs the back of his neck, and I sense embarrassment. "What, you didn't choose this place?" I ask, offering a crooked smile.

"No, I chose it. But now that I live here, it does seem like an insane amount of space for just one person, and you haven't even seen the bedroom."

He leads the way upstairs and opens the door at the end of the hall. The size of his kitchen has nothing on the bedroom. His bed alone is about the size of my bedroom at Nina's house, which he sits on now, a smirk on his face.

"I know, it's obscene," he says.

"A little," I laugh. But I'm also in awe, especially as I peek through double doors to what I think is another room but ends up being a goddamn bedroom for his clothes. "Your closet could house a small classroom," I say, taking in the row of perfectly lined suits, the shelves of shoes, the dozens of drawers, with space to do a couple open arm spins in the center of the room.

Then there's the bathroom. My jaw drops at the shower alone, with nozzles at varying heights to get every body part clean…or something. I think of what a shower like that would have been like during my dry spells. I'd never have need for a man.

"Drought, be damned," I joke, not just referring to dry California. But something in my voice catches. I don't belong here, and just that realization alone invites my exhaustion to return. I should go home, forget all about this night, forget about my family, and forget about Mac.

"It's weird to me, too," he says, and reaches around me to turn on the water. I face him, trying to think up something to say to hide all these uncomfortable feelings I'm having. It's just money, I know this. But when you spent a whole year sleeping in your car, money has a different meaning to it.

"How is it weird for you? It's all yours. You earned this."

"Kind of." He starts removing my jacket, then my

boots, which I step out of while holding his shoulder. "I mean, I chose all of this, and I like it. But sometimes I feel like…"

"An imposter?" I guess. He smiles and nods.

"Yes, like an imposter." He slips my shirt over my head, then kisses the tip of my nose. "My paycheck paid for this, and thanks to my brokerage, I can afford to keep this lifestyle. I've built my business from the ground up, and it's very lucrative. But I never would have gotten here if it weren't for Benji. It's his name that helped bridge connections when I was first starting out. If it were just on my name, I'd…" He looks around, then laughs, "Well, I wouldn't be here, that's for sure.

I'm reminded once again that Mac isn't some out of touch rich guy. He's an orphan, much like I'm an addict. We may look different on the outside—him with his fancy suits and luxury car, me with my guitar and paid bills—but inside, that younger version of ourselves will always feel like the real truth.

Mac finishes undressing me, his hands sliding over my body like he knows me better than just a few days. His touch is gentle as he takes off each layer, then guides me under the spray. I feel water come at me from all directions, the scent of eucalyptus surrounding me as I close my eyes and lose myself to the therapeutic waters.

"It smells heavenly in here."

"It's the infusion system," he explains, "The scent comes through the water."

I hear the distinct sound of his zipper and open one eye as his expensive ass pants fall to the floor. His manhood stands at attention in all its glory. Goddamn, the man is well endowed. He joins me in the shower, and I raise my hands to his chest as I draw closer. But he captures my hands, stopping me at the pass.

"Just relax," he says, "let me care for you."

He turns me and I hear the click of the shampoo bottle cap. Then his hands are in my hair, kneading my scalp, making me weak in the knees as every part of my body relaxes under his touch. He takes his time, his fingers seeming to memorize every place he touches. A small moan escapes my lips, and I can feel his cock flick at my backside.

"Down boy," he mutters, making me laugh. I reach behind me and wrap my fingers around his shaft, and he utters a swift inhale before swatting my hand away. "There will be plenty of time for that later, but not tonight."

I groan in protest, but honestly, it's fine. I feel like I've been through the ringer tonight, and Mac's magic hands are lulling me into an ultra-sedated state.

He rinses my hair, then follows up with conditioner. His fingers work through my drenched locks, seeking every tangle. Each tug of my hair sends shivers throughout my body.

"Ever since I saw you, I've been dying to run my hands through your hair," he says.

"If I'd known it would feel like this, I would have showered with you that first night," I joke. I'm instantly reminded of the details from that night, of why I left so suddenly. I quickly push the thought from my head. He was just the agent. It's literally his job. It's not his fault some asshole decided to sell the place with absolutely no warning.

"Fuck, I knew I should have led with that," he teases back. He finishes rinsing my hair, then works at lathering my body. His hands touch every part of me, smoothing over my skin until I'm completely sudsy. Then he begins kneading my muscles, and my moan sounds almost orgasmic as it bounces off the tile.

"No, you should have led with this," I say, melting as he works out every kink in my body. He lingers at my core, his fingers glancing off my folds in a way that makes me feel like begging.

"Tomorrow," he whispers, and I bite my lip as he moves on to my hamstrings.

By the time he shuts off the water, I am complete mush. I stand still as he grabs a towel to dry my skin, then his own, and finishes with my hair. Then, before I know what's happening, he scoops me into his arms. I lay my head against his damp chest and feel his heart, counting the moments as he carries me to his bed. He lays me down gently on the silky sheets, and I sink into the most comfortable mattress I've ever laid upon. I had no idea beds could feel this way. I'm not sure I'll remember how to fall asleep in my own bed after experiencing luxury like this.

Mac turns off all the lights, then curls up behind me. The feel of his skin is so delicious, the way his body hugs mine, his arm draped over my waist, his legs tangled with mine. It's like I'm in a cocoon, which also includes a hard cock nestled between my thighs.

"Don't worry about him," he murmurs with a chuckle when I burrow against him. "He'll go to sleep soon, and so will I."

He nuzzles his face against the back of my neck, and I can feel myself sliding into sleep. For the first time in my life, I feel completely safe.

This is what it feels like to be cherished. As I fade from consciousness, I know I'll never be able to settle for less.

The light is streaming through the windows when I open my eyes a crack. It takes me a moment to gain my bearings, but the satin sheets are the first clue. I'm in Mac's bed. Alone.

I sit up and look around as if he'll come out of hiding.

He's not here, but the ocean is—like right there in his backyard.

I slip out of bed, pulling a sheet with me to cover my naked body, and head to the window. The view is incredible. I recall all the ways I kind of turned my nose up at his wealth, and this view makes me want to take it all back. I would sell my soul for this. He basically owns his own cliffside, and the ocean stretches as far as the eye can see. There's not even a need for me to cover up because there is no one else to see. So I drop the sheet and spread my arms wide, feeling free and easy with all this nature around me.

"Now, that's a sight," Mac says from behind me. I look over my shoulder and shake my behind at him, and he rumbles a growl in response.

"Careful girl, I just might pounce on you before you get your first sip of coffee."

Just the mention of coffee awakens all my senses. I inhale the rich aroma, along with the breakfast he has on a tray—bacon, eggs, sourdough toast, and a bowl of fresh berries.

Then I realize it's a hell of a lot later than I thought.

"Damnit, I slept in!" I start to scramble for my clothes, but he takes me by the wrist.

"Calm down, I already called you out."

I stop at that, pausing as I make sense of his words.

"You…called me out?"

"Yeah. You're feeling awfully sick, so sick you couldn't even make it to the phone. So I had to call your work for you and let them know you won't be making it today."

"But how?"

Mac hands me my coffee, and I hold it but don't sip. "I've been to your work, Maren, and they have a phone. So, I called it."

"And they accepted that?" I have not called out in ages. None of us do since there really isn't adequate coverage. Plus, the few times I have, Susan gave me such hell it wasn't even worth the hassle. "Who did you even speak with?"

"Someone named Nina."

Oh, that explains it.

"And she didn't ask where I was?"

He laughed. "No, but I don't think she believed me either. She told me she got this, and that you're to text her as soon as you're feeling up to it."

I dive for my phone, half expecting to see a dozen calls from Susan. But there's only one text, and it's from Nina.

Nina: Good for you, finally getting some dick. Hope it's good!

I grin, tuck the phone away, and I finally sip my coffee—rather, a latte—and it's fucking phenomenal.

"Hold on," I say, lowering my cup. "Why did you go to Insomniacs if your coffee tastes like this?" I take another sip, then shake my head. "Ours sucks compared this. What did you do, roast your beans in your own private roastery?"

He snorts into his own coffee, the usual black I remember from the other day. I can't help wondering how many shots of espresso are in there. Judging by the bulge in his gray sweatpants…I'd say four. "Sure, right after I picked them from the coffee tree." He finally gets in a sip, then nods. "Yeah, that's good shit. I have it special ordered, plus I have a built-in espresso machine in the kitchen."

I roll my eyes. "Of course you do. But that doesn't answer my question as to why you'd buy overpriced crap coffee when you have the real thing at home?"

"Because you were there."

"And you knew this, how?" I grab a piece of bacon and start nibbling at it as I wait for an answer. He has a kind of boyish grin on his face, as if he's just been caught in the cookie jar and is going to eat the cookie anyways.

"Because there was a little blue Honda outside with a hand sized dent on the hood. I matched it up to my hand, and the dent fit. So I had to go inside to see if my

Miss Charming was there."

Before I can react, he's swooped me back into his bed. "And you, my sweet thing, are driving me crazy with that hot little body of yours, all ready for the taking."

"But I haven't finished my breakfast!" I protest. He pulls away, then gives me a pointed look.

"Would you like to eat, or would you like to fuck and then eat?"

I take a long look at his muscular body, the way his chest tapers down to his lean belly, and a happy dusting of hair that leads to the bulge under his sweatpants. He has a delicious smirk on his bearded face, and it makes me want to lick him all over.

I don't answer him, but I do leap up and tackle him to the bed. This time, he doesn't play that whole alpha bullshit. We take turns taking each other, tearing up that huge, oversized bed as we explore each other the entire morning.

A few hours later—fully satiated on sex, coffee, and bacon—we lay in the tangled sheets while I lazily watch the ocean outside.

"You're probably so used to this," I say, unable to tear my eyes away.

"Not at all," he answers. I turn to face him, ready to learn more. We really don't know much about each other except for this crazy connection we can't avoid. He's given me his life story in bits and pieces, and I've held him at arm's length this entire time. But now I'm curious.

"You say this is all new to you. I know you were an orphan before, but surely this wasn't an overnight development. I mean, you've had to have lived a life of luxury for years now. You said Benji took you in at fifteen, right? And you're, what, thirty?"

"Thirty-five," he says, "So yeah, it's been twenty years since I've been a no-good thief."

I sit up, suddenly very interested.

"All right, Mac Dermot. Spill the beans. Tell me everything."

And he does—or at least, as much as he can in a short amount of time. I already knew that he lived in an orphanage then ran away. What I didn't know is that he cased and robbed houses to survive the streets.

"Back then I was this scrawny, toe-headed kid with a baby face who got caught up with a group of older boys ready to use me to their advantage. No one expected a thing. I'd go door-to-door selling magazine subscriptions, or so they thought. If a house looked interesting, we'd watch it for a few days, and if there was no obvious security system, we'd break in and grab what we wanted. It worked like a charm. That is until Benji."

Mac had gotten ballsy in the operation, since it was working so well. They all had pockets stuffed with money and a stash of other people's belongings still waiting to be sold. But Mac wanted more, and Benji's house on the top of the hill was his golden ticket.

"No one answered when we went to the front door. We watched it for an hour, and no one came. I got it in my head that it was abandoned, because it didn't make sense to me that someone who lived in a house like this would ever leave it. The other guys told me to keep waiting, that we should case it for a few days. But I didn't have a lot of patience and talked the guys into breaking in that day. We were inside for only ten minutes before someone's voice came on over the intercom, telling us to keep our hands where they could be seen until the cops got there. Those fuckers all ran, but I was too scared to leave."

"So what happened? Were you arrested?"

"Nah," he laughed, "no one called the cops. Instead it was Benji and a few of his bodyguards. They scared the shit out of me, though. The bodyguards were huge, especially to a twig of a kid like me. They pushed me around a little, threatened to break a few limbs, but then Benji called them off. He asked where the other guys were, then commended me for staying when I could have escaped. 'You have guts, kid,' he told me. He asked about my story, if I had parents or anything. Something in me said to tell this guy the truth, so I did. I admitted I was in the system, but I'd been on the run for the past two years.

I told him how I made my money. I also told him I was tired of running, which was the first time I ever admitted that to anyone."

Mac pauses, and I see something shift in his face—a shadow so brief, I almost miss it. "That's when he offered me a job and a place to live, and I've been under his wing ever since."

"So, all this is because of him? He gave this to you?"

Mac's expression darkens as he shoots me a sharp look. "I earned this on my own," he says.

"Sorry, I just—"

"No, I'm sorry," he says, taking my hand, "I'm not going to say that my connection to Benji hasn't opened doors. Without him, I'd probably have found adult ways to swindle people out of their money." He laughs then. "I guess I have, since I sell homes in this inflated housing market. But it's all legal, so there's that. But as far as my money goes, I earned it. I hit the books and got my license, I did my time as an agent and built my clientele, I invested in all the right things and learned the art of flipping houses, and I bought out a brokerage and built it up until it became what it is today. I used Benji's contacts to connect with the right people, but I did the work."

I believe him, but I'm having a hard time understanding how any of this is "new" to him, as he told me last night. "You've been with Benji for years, though."

"I lived in a small room in the back of his house, one meant for staff. I was a worker first, not a son, not even a ward. I was an employee. He made sure I went to school and graduated, but outside of school hours, I was working. I see now it was kind of a training regimen. He was keeping me in line by keeping me busy. I was too tired to get into trouble or to even fight it. I knew I couldn't fuck this up, because where else would I get this close to this kind of money?"

"You didn't think of stealing from him again?"

"Think of it? Sure. But I was too chicken shit to actually do it. I got to know his security detail really well and knew it was impenetrable. There was no way some smart-ass kid would be able to get past that. And for what? I had to work my ass off, but I also recognized there was future potential."

He looks around, then back at me. "I bought this house a few months ago. The car, it's also new. I'd been holding off for a while, even though I've been making good money. But when you grow up an orphan, that identity sticks to you. It felt fake to have things as nice as this when I also know there are kids like me still out there on the street, just wishing they could be here. But when you're rubbing shoulders with some of the richest people in this country, you have to be a part of the culture. Plus,

I've never had nice things, and suddenly I could afford them without anyone's help. So I bought a house, a car, and built up my wardrobe of rich fuck clothing, and now I'm playing the part."

I rub his chest, my hand brushing against his beard. His hand covers mine, and I clasp his fingers.

"I get it," I say, "I wasn't always this rich either." I look up and flash him a grin, and his eyes laugh with mine. "For real, though, you know my story. You met my dad." I lay my head against his chest, lulled by his heartbeat. His fingers caress mine, and I continue. "I was homeless for a year, drugged out of my mind. If someone had it, I was on it. I didn't have money, but there were other ways…" I pause, not sure he wants to hear this. But then I realize we're sharing truths here, and I might as well share mine. "I made my money through rich, old, horny men. You wouldn't believe what these old guys will pay for a young piece of ass. It's probably why I hate money so much, because these guys were willing to drop a few hundred for an hour as if it were nothing, and I was barely scraping by." I utter a sharp laugh. "Well, I was actually wasting it on blow. Food, though? Shelter? Not a priority. I'd sleep in the gutter if I could get a good high. I was lucky to have my car, and lucky I was never arrested. But some fucked up things happened to me out on the streets, stuff I'll never forget."

"So, what changed?" he asks.

I realize that he's still here. He's not repulsed by what I shared. I haven't even told Claire this much; afraid I'd shatter her vision of the world we live in. But Mac holds me as if I'm precious—fragile—as if he'll keep me safe.

I've always been my own savior. But for the first time, I wonder what it would be like to trust someone else with my life.

"Finn," I say, "my best friend's son and my unofficial nephew. When Claire got pregnant, she called me. I was coming down off a bender and had to fake sobriety really quick. But once I saw that kid, it's like the whole world opened up. I realized there was so much more to this life, and that if I wanted to be a part of this kid's world, I could not be the person I was. So I got help. I detoxed, entered a recovery program through state funds, moved into a sober house, got a job, and eventually moved into my own apartment."

I pause then, and I'm so tempted to tell him that I know he sold the building. I want to lay out all my feelings about it now, to just admit that this is why I disappeared that first night, and what I've struggled with ever since. I lift my head and look into his eyes, watching the sunlight dance off the gold flecks in his blue eyes.

"What are you thinking?" he asks, then kisses me lightly on my nose.

The words are on the tip of my tongue, but I can't

seem to say them. I realize it doesn't matter, that in the grand scheme of things, it isn't important. He played such a small part in me losing my home. Besides, look where I am now.

In Mac's bed. Happy and safe.

I am not in danger, nor would I ever be. I was never going to be homeless, as long as I have Nina and Claire in my life—and now Mac, if things are going the way I think they're going.

Definitely not casual.

"I'm thinking we need to get out of bed before I turn into a jellyfish and stay here forever."

"I like the stay here forever part," he teases. He whips the covers aside. "But I'd also like to get out of this house and go do something."

"Yeah, let's blow this dump." I nudge him out of bed, then follow him straight to the shower where we spend another forty-five minutes before we finally make it out the door.

Chapter Sixteen

Mac

We get in the car, and Maren buckles up before turning to me.

"Where to?" she asks.

I've been considering this ever since we stepped out of the shower. If I had my way, we'd be in bed all day. But breakfast is wearing off, and the fridge is limited on food. I like to keep some fresh ingredients in there at all times, which is why we lucked out on berries and breakfast foods. But there isn't much else to choose from since I've been staying at Benji's house the past few weeks.

"Well, I don't know about you, but I've worked up an appetite. Let's start with lunch, and then go from there. Any favorites?"

As she mulls over ideas, my guilt taps at my conscience. I haven't even checked in on Benji. He's probably fine, but yesterday's state of confusion was concerning. The nurse on shift would get a hold of me if he took a turn for the worse or was too difficult, but I still feel pulled to check in, especially after another night away.

"How about Sandpipers, that place that serves those huge cheeseburgers right on the beach?" Maren asks, breaking me from my thoughts. Just the mention makes my mouth water. It's also so different from what every other woman would have suggested. Most expect some fancy meal with a long wine list, only to order a salad and steal bites off my plate. The last date I had, I practically had to drag her to Hillside because all I wanted was a greasy burger and fries with a cold beer. Helena pouted the whole time, and picked at the salad she ordered when I refused to share my fries. It only took her an hour to realize I couldn't tear my eyes away from Maren on stage. Let's just say that when Helena threw her drink in my face before walking out, I only wondered what took her so long.

"That sounds like the perfect spot."

The place is packed when we get there, so we opt for a spot at the bar. I hesitate for a moment as I look at the beer menu on the wall.

"Go ahead," Maren says, nodding her head at the menu.

"It doesn't bother you? I don't have to drink around you, you know."

"So, if we end up hanging out a lot more than today, are you just going to give up drinking alcohol?"

"Sure," I say, not even hesitating. But at the same time, I realize what she's saying. If this thing we have going gets serious, I could be promising to be sober alongside her. I'd do it. But at the same time, I really enjoy unwinding at the end of a long day with a cold beer in my hand.

"Order whatever you want," she says, "I've been sober long enough that it doesn't bother me anymore."

I think back to the day I saw her on the rooftop. When she had that glass of wine in her hand. When I bumped into her because I already knew she didn't drink.

It was a terrible day for her, a day when she found out she was losing her apartment.

Because I was the one who sold the building.

"I'll have a burger with grilled onion and jack cheese, medium rare, and a Coke to drink," I say to the waitress.

Maren shoots me a look, then she glances over the menu.

"I'll have the same, but a Lagunitas IPA to drink."

My eyes immediately whip to hers as soon as the

words leave her mouth. The waitress takes our menus, while I figure out how to react here. It's not my business. Her sobriety is hers alone to manage, and any direction from me would be an infringement on what is supposed to be her choice. I already overstepped when I made her spill her wine. But right now, there is no reason for this. We've had a good day, despite the turmoil from yesterday. I think she's enjoying my company.

So what is she doing?

The waitress returns with our drinks, and my hand feels shaky as I pick up my soda. I try not to stare as she does the same with her beer.

"Mac," she says.

"Yeah?"

"Put down the soda."

I do, and she immediately picks it up, placing the glass of beer in front of me.

"For the record, I have always hated beer. I was always more of a tequila girl. Probably the Mexican in me."

I breathe a sigh of relief, then take a long sip of beer. Fuck, that's good. Half the glass is drained before I put it down, then I take her hands in mine.

"I just didn't want to make you uncomfortable," I say, "I know you said it was no big deal, but…"

"But what?" She slips her hands out of mine, then

sips my/her Coke, waiting for a real explanation.

I don't want to bring it up. I should bring it up. I should tell her about my role in her reason for being there that night. But looking at her, the way her eyes shine as she waits for my explanation, I just can't.

"That night at Torches," I finally say, swallowing the rest of it, "the wine."

Her face flushes, and I regret saying anything.

"It was a mistake," she says, "One I haven't made since I stopped drinking."

"But you almost did this time. If you can do it once, I don't want to be the reason you do again."

She reaches over and squeezes my hand.

"It was a bad night. It doesn't excuse what I almost did, especially when there will be other bad nights, I'm sure. In this instance, there were other steps I could have taken instead of ending up at a bar with a drink in my hand. But I can promise you that I am fine sitting with you while you enjoy a beer or two. I'm fine with soda, I actually prefer it." She takes another sip, and my cock twitches at the way her red mouth wrap around that straw. She finishes, then lightly licks the moisture from her lips.

"You're such a brat," I growl with a grin. She winks, then looks up as the waitress brings our burgers. Maren doesn't even hesitate. She picks up her dripping burger, almost the size of her head, and sinks her teeth in it.

"Fuck," she breathes, "That's better than sex."

"Doubtful." I do the same, and fuck yes, that burger is good. But sex with Maren will always be best.

Back in the car, I take a moment to check my phone. I felt it buzz in my pocket during our meal, but we were close to being done so I chose to wait. My mind has been on it ever since though, knowing it could be the nurse on shift.

Which it is. Fuck. I click the button to listen to the voicemail.

"Hi Mr. Dermot. This is Anna. Benji is fine, so don't worry (I breathe a sigh of relief), *but he's been combative. He keeps asking for you, and I was hoping you could come by if you have the time."*

I hang up the phone and pinch the space between my eyes as the guilt settles firmly in my stomach.

"Everything okay?" Maren asks.

I nod, forcing a smile. "Yeah. But before I do anything, I need to swing by Benji's."

The fact that I haven't been there in more than a day is unacceptable. He's nearing the end of his life, just inches from leaving this earth, and here I am chasing tail.

I also realize I cannot take Maren to Benji's house. It's bad enough she's with me, but I was just following orders—Benji's orders. It would be cruel to take her to meet the man who not only sold her home so it could be destroyed, but he's also responsible for everything that went wrong in that apartment. Rather, all the things he never took care of.

I owe Benji. She does not.

"Can I drop you off somewhere?" I ask.

Maren's mouth opens, and the silence sinks between us. She closes her mouth, and her eyes narrow.

"No, I'm fine." She reaches for the door handle, but I grab onto her wrist. "Let go of me," she growls, yanking her hand away, then she opens the door and steps out. I'm out of the car and at her side in seconds.

"It's Benji," I say. Her face softens for a fraction of a second but disappears under her icy stare. "He's in a state, and I really don't want to bring you around him while he's like this. From the nurse's tone, I have a feeling I'll be there the rest of the day."

This time when she softens, she stays that way. She smiles and shakes her head. "I'm being stupid," she says, "This isn't even supposed to be anything, and I keep acting like some possessive girlfr—" She catches herself before saying the word, though I'm still affected.

Girlfriend. What the fuck am I doing? I can't even tell her the goddamn truth—that I know she lost her home, that I already knew she was sober, that I have heard her songs long before she was on stage.

That the reason I know all of this is because I owned her apartment building, sold it without warning, then reduced it to rubble, knowing full well that she, along with all those families, would never be able to find a place that would match the rent they were paying.

"It's fine," I say, and I pretend I don't notice the flash of hurt that crosses her face. "Can I drive you somewhere?"

"Tell you what, Benji lives in Holland Heights, right?"

"How did you…oh." I laugh, remembering how she almost ran me over with her car when I was out for a run. The girl has amazing deduction skills. "Yeah, he does."

"Well, so do I. But I'm not letting you take me home; a girl needs her secrets after all. For now, it's where I live."

I want to argue, but I have no fucking right.

"So, where do I take you?"

"To Benji's house," she says. I start to protest, but she places her hand on my arm. "Not to go inside, I can walk home from there. We're wasting time. Didn't you say he's in a state?"

She's right, and I have been feeling pulled to get there ever since I heard the voicemail. But now I am plagued with conflict, especially at my reaction to Maren almost using the "G" word.

"Besides," she continues, "I should get home and freshen up in case any of my other dates want to take me out for a good time."

She squeals as I grab her around the waist and bring her into me. I capture her hands, and she grins, even as she's unable to move.

"Like hell you will," I say, then force a kiss on her. There really isn't much forcing going on, though. She matches my kiss with the same ferocity, bringing me back to what it felt like to hold her all night long. That surprises me more than anything. My dick is straining to attention, wanting a replay of this morning's fuck session. But my mind is on the feel of her body close to mine, how she looked while she was asleep, the sweet smell of her breath with every inhale.

If the situation were different, if I weren't such a liar, I'd tell Maren where she could shove this whole casual relationship. Fuck casual. If things were different, Maren would already be mine, and there would never be anyone else for either of us.

Chapter Seventeen

Maren

I know it killed Mac to drive me to Benji's house only for me to walk home. I don't really care if he knows where I live anymore. We've gone far beyond the boundaries of what was supposed to be casual, but there are still barriers between us. Which is why I'm keeping my living quarters private, and why I still haven't told him I know he's the agent who sold my home—and I probably never will.

At this point, it's more embarrassment than anything that keeps my mouth shut. The fact that I ever cared as strongly as I did in the first place. Now that I've had some space from that apartment, I've gained some perspective on what a dump that place was. The funky smells. The mold growing in the corners. All the things that stopped working. The maintenance guy used to be prompt whenever something broke down, but eventually all requests for maintenance went unanswered—even though I was fucking Brock, the goddamn apartment manager.

But also, I was embarrassed that I couldn't afford anything more than that. Waking up in Mac's mansion of a house really highlighted that for me, even staying in Nina's house. I mean, I already knew my house was a shithole compared to other people's homes, but now it's even more apparent.

I've never been one to care what people think of me. Fuck them if they can't handle what I'm about. So it's dumb that it suddenly matters with Mac. But it does. So, Mac doesn't need to know that I lived in an apartment that probably should have been torn down ages ago. And to keep my barrier intact, my current living situation can just remain a mystery.

I laugh as I walk home, Google Maps leading the way, knowing the unfairness of the situation. I not only know where he lives, but I now know the exact location of his benefactor's home—where he's apparently been staying for weeks instead of his fancy McMansion, judging by his morning strolls. I can stalk him whenever I want…or avoid him. I'm stuck between the two, knowing I'm falling for him a lot more than I should.

Isn't this the point when I usually kick them to the

curb? When I realize I'm starting to catch feelings?

But with Mac…

Last night—after a day of disaster—when it was apparent my family was no longer mine, he treated me with such care. He wasn't afraid of my tears. I never cry in front of anyone, but he was there for me in my lowest moment. The feral way we fucked on the side of the road, my knees probably scarred for life because of it. The gentle way he washed my hair. How he held me all night long in his massive bed.

I don't know if I'll ever be able to let him go, which means I've let this go on far too long. The thought of losing him scares me more than falling in love.

Now I have a full day ahead of me, thanks to Mac calling me out sick. It's kind of a waste since I won't be spending it with him, and while I get it, I can't help feeling a bit lost now that our plans fell through.

I hate that I feel lost, I hate that I'm even falling for him, and yet, I can't stop the reel of memories from last night that's on repeat in my mind. I'm not sure I want to.

The door is unlocked when I get home, which is so classic Nina. For someone who has a big house all her own, she sure is careless with it. But that's Nina for you.

I glance at the time on my phone. It's three hours into my shift, which means I have the house to myself for another—

"Last night's clothes, huh?"

I jump out of my skin at Nina's voice, and she laughs as she looks me up and down.

"What are you doing here? Why aren't you at work?"

"Headache," she shrugs, though the glint in her eye lets me know there is no headache.

"So who's running the shop?" I can feel a thread of obligation to turn myself around and head to Insomniacs, knowing that there definitely won't be enough coverage without both of us.

"Let Susan handle it for once," Nina says, flopping on the couch, then patting the pile of clothes beside her. "Spill," she says, "and leave nothing out."

"Spill what?" I ask, moving the clothes to the floor so I can actually sit. I kick off my boots, stalling to find a cover story as I feel her eyes bore into the side of my head.

"Spill why you're wearing the clothes I saw you leave the house in after work, and who you were with this whole time."

"I was with Claire, you know that," I lie, "Besides, why are you all of a sudden acting like my mom?"

"I'm not, but I do want some dirty details. Come on, Maren, it's not like you to have a slumber party at Claire's."

I contemplate playing it cool, keeping up this charade for…ever. But my body doesn't get the memo, starting with the grin on my face. I try to smother it, but she pulls my hand away.

"I knew it! Just tell me his name, how good he is in bed, how long his penis is…"

"Meh, names aren't important," I say, ignoring every other question she asked. But if I want to keep the details under wraps, I need a distraction. Like the truth. "I did run into my sister, though."

Nina's eyes widen, and she gestures for me to continue. Nina knows about my past, and that I no longer talk with my family. So I share about how I saw Lydia, drunk off her ass, surrounded by predators.

"How did you get her away?"

I hesitate for a moment, recalling the way Mac beat down two of the guys before they all took off.

"I can be scary when I want to be."

Nina stares for a moment, scrutinizing me. Then she nods.

"This is true. Hey, you want some coffee?"

Nina has just spent the whole morning in a coffee shop, and I'm still riding the high from that exquisite coffee at Mac's, plus everything that came with it. But I'm also feeling the drama of the past twenty-four hours pulling at my energy. It's either coffee or a long nap.

"That sounds great."

I follow her into the kitchen as she jabbers on about

the latest gossip, which is basically a rundown of our morning regulars because this is our life.

"Did you know Paper Guy has a boyfriend?" she asked, referring to the well-dressed guy who comes in every morning with a newspaper tucked under his arm. He always wears suspenders and a hat, which feels ironic since he's got to be younger than us. But it's the newspaper that really stood out, since no one under the age of thirty gets their news in print. Hence his nickname.

"And Strawberry Shortcake is back with that Scottish dude." This is the red-haired girl who came in once wearing a dress with giant strawberries on it. "But they don't live up north anymore. Apparently, they now live in Wisconsin."

"What's in Wisconsin?" I ask, only half listening as I look out the window. I can't help wondering what Mac is up to right now. Is he thinking of me? Does he miss me?

"Bees, I guess," she says, handing me my coffee, then peering out the window. "Oh wow! I thought he was a no show today."

I lean forward, my heart pounding at Mac's flawless half naked form making his way around the corner and up our street. Surely Nina can hear the thunder in my chest as Mac slows once he nears his house.

"Oh my god," she murmurs.

Mac pauses next to my car, then runs his hand over

the dent in the hood, as if he's running it over a warm body. My body. *Fuck.* I love how he touches my car.

And then it hits me. *He's touching my car.*

It's like a slo-mo roll when he lifts his gaze to the kitchen window where both Nina and I are peering out like dumbass schoolgirls. We immediately move out of view, but Nina's eyes are like saucers, and I can see she's slowly putting the pieces together.

It honestly never occurred to me that he'd recognize it. But why wouldn't he? It's how he found me at Insomniacs, and now he knows where I live.

Nina peeks back out, and I can't help but do the same. Mac is still there, and his face breaks into a grin upon seeing us. He points to the window and gives a slow nod, his crooked smile still in place. Then he turns and continues his walk. Meanwhile, my face is burning hot and probably a brilliant shade of scarlet.

"You slut," Nina laughs, pushing my shoulder. "Of course it would be you that lands Naked Coffee Guy."

"I don't know what you're talking about," I say, twisting my coffee cup in my hands. When I look at her, she has a look of awe on her face.

"Right, and you're also not wearing yesterday's clothes and don't look like you've been fucked sideways. You're banging him, aren't you?"

I say nothing, taking my coffee with me back to my

bedroom.

"Maren! You have to give me something. I need details!"

But I just chuckle as I close the door and lock it, considering an afternoon of remembering everything that happened last night with Mac…by myself.

Mac never shows up at my work the next day, even though I jump every time I hear the jingle of a new customer walking through the door. It's for the best, really. Nina spent all last night trying to get information from me, and she spends this shift doing the same. But I'm as closed up as the KFC recipe vault. I can only imagine how annoying she'd be if he showed his face.

He also doesn't text me, just like I don't text him. I'm not disappearing, but I also don't want to appear as eager as I feel. Still, it doesn't keep me from checking my phone every five minutes. But all in good fun, It feels like a game to see who will cave first.

The game stops being fun, though, when I reach the end of my shift and there's still no word from Mac. I mean, I could text him myself, but then I'd lose.

Losing would be worse than not hearing from him all day. Right?

Nina and I head to her car once the coffee shop is locked up. I regret not taking my own car as she continues peppering me with questions about Naked

Coffee Guy. Meanwhile, I'm keeping my eyes peeled, trying to appear casual and unbothered while searching for him.

I am the epitome of unchill, and I know I need to get a grip. Thank goddess for tonight's gig. If anything, it will serve as the perfect distraction for a few hours while I get lost in my music.

When I arrive at Hillside, I immediately head to Claire's table in the back where she's sharing a plate of fries with Finn. I haven't had a chance to fill her in about everything that happened—about Mac, but especially about the drama with my family. I feel terrible that Nina knows at least part of the story before her. That said, we have little ears listening to everything we say, so I give her the Cliff's Notes version.

"There's so much to unpack, I don't even know where to start," Claire says.

"Well, we can save the stuff about Mac for another time." I tilt my head in Finn's direction for emphasis, and she nods her approval.

"Good plan," she laughs, but then grows serious. "So, how about your family? I can't believe Lydia treated you that way after you saved her."

"It hurt," I admitted. I pull out my phone, flipping to her Instagram page and showing it to Claire. "I mean, I see her in these photos and she appears so nice and approachable. But when we came across her, she was not only drunk off her—" I pause, looking at Finn, who's looking back at me, waiting for me to say the word. "Butt," I say with a grin, shuffling his hair. "It seemed out of character for her. But she's also grown up hearing stories about me that you know weren't flattering. She probably thinks the worst of me, thanks to my father."

I glance away, then do a double take as I see a familiar face walk through the front entrance, looking around as if searching for someone.

Lydia.

"Speak of the devil," I say, nodding my head in my sister's direction. Claire gasps as she catches sight of Lydia, just as my sister's eyes land on us. She freezes, and I can see how uncomfortable she looks.

Good.

Lydia looks at her feet, unmoving, and as much as I want her to suffer, I also want to hear what she's going to say. So when she looks my way again, I give her the slightest of nods.

"We're going to see what Ethan's up to." Claire takes Finn's hand, coaxing him to his feet.

"I'm not done, Mom," Finn complains.

"Dad has more fries in the kitchen," she counters, pulling him with her. She glances back at me and mouths *be nice.* I roll my eyes but shoot her a small smile as if to say *I'll try.*

"Hey."

I turn my head slightly at Lydia's voice, noting her twisted hands and lowered eyes.

"Can I help you?" I ask, then turn back to the plate of cold fries as if they're the most interesting thing in the venue. I hear her sigh, and she moves around the table and sits across from me. She doesn't say anything, and when I finally look at her, I see the tears brimming her eyes. I exhale hard, shaking my head. I also hand her a napkin, which she uses to dab her eyes.

"How'd you know I was here?"

"I've seen you here before," she admits, "I was with some friends and you were playing, and I realized it was you. I heard there was live music tonight and hoped it would be you. And, well…"

She trails off, and I watch her for a moment. I see the bits of her I used to know, the shy kid who used to follow me around when I let her. But I also see the woman she's becoming…as long as she doesn't fuck it up.

"Did you survive the hangover?" I ask, and she releases a watery laugh.

"I felt like I got hit by a sledgehammer all day yesterday. Mom and Dad think I have the flu. Mom made me stay home from school again today, just in case."

"And they let you out of the house? Wow, times have

changed." I wave down one of the waitresses. "Hey, can I get a soda water with a splash of tonic and some lime?" I look at Lydia, then back at the waitress. "One for her, too."

"They haven't changed," Lydia says once the waitress is gone, "If anything, they're worse. They're on my back about everything. My grades. My friends. What colleges I'm signed up for. How I spend my free time. They won't even let me quit the track team. They say it will be good for my college application, but I think it's because it takes up so much of my time. They monitor me constantly. It's as if they think they can prevent me from getting in trouble by filling up my day and keeping tabs on me at all times."

"And yet, they had no idea where you were that night, and would probably flip their lids if they knew you were here with me right now. How'd you escape their surveillance?"

"I leave my phone at home," she admits, "As of right now, they think I'm still in bed because that's what my phone says. But if they looked closer at my bed, they'd find a mountain of clothes under my blankets, and my phone under my pillow on a snore loop." She offers a sheepish grin.

"A modern-day *Ferris Bueller*," I say and can't help but laugh.

"Who?" Lydia's face is twisted in confusion.

"Movie reference," I say, "Never mind. So, you snuck out the window. Do they still have the spiny cactus garden planted there?"

"Yup, but I know where to step and how to hide the evidence."

This time I belly laugh. When it was my room, I'd perfected the art of knowing exactly where to place my foot so I wouldn't get speared by the thorny plants, and then how to drown my prints clean.

"A glass of water?" I ask, which is exactly what I used to use. The waitress hands us our drinks, and I push Lydia's toward her. She takes a sip, then picks it up and mimics pouring it over imaginary footprints.

"Works like a charm."

She bites her lip and looks down at the table for a moment. When she glances at me again, it's with utter seriousness.

"I'm really sorry. I don't remember a lot from that night, but enough to know that you kept it secret from Mom and Dad. They would have killed me."

"Lydia, if I hadn't stepped in, you'd have a whole hell of a lot more to regret. Do you remember the guys you were hanging out with?"

She shrugs. "It was just Austin and a few of his friends. They're harmless."

"Harmless?" I laugh, "Hardly. Those guys were

getting you drunk on purpose. If you were paying attention, you'd have noticed none of them were drinking."

Lydia stares at me, blinking slow. Then she shakes her head. "You don't know that; they were just being nice."

I'm trying so hard to keep my cool, reminding myself that she's still just a kid. But I'm also seeing red at how naïve she is.

"You know what I saw, Lydia? I saw a bunch of predators getting a minor drunk. I saw the looks they were giving each other as you got more and more wasted, and I saw what would have happened if I hadn't stepped in. You know why?"

The look of annoyance stays on her face, but she waits for me to answer.

"Because it happened to me."

"I'm not you," Lydia says, but she shifts her eyes to the table.

"Right. Because only a drug addict deserves to get raped, right?" I push up from the table. Kid or no kid, Lydia's elitist attitude is going to make me punch something.

"No, Maren. That's not what I meant." She reaches across the table for my hand, but I yank it away. I also sit back down, because even though I'm pissed, I have a shred of resistance to cutting off ties with her completely.

"Here's the thing," I hiss at Lydia, "getting raped could happen to anyone, whether you're sober or drunk. But the best thing you can do when you're with people you don't know very well is to keep your wits about you, and always bring a friend. I'm not telling you that you can't drink, but just be smart about it."

Lydia lifts her soda water and studies it. Then she nods her head at mine.

"Do you still drink?" she asks.

"I've been sober for seven years and counting." I clink my glass with hers, then take a sip. "And I'm not one of those sober pushers either. I don't care if you drink. I just learned from experience that I don't have limits, so it's better if I don't mess with any of it."

"I had no idea." Lydia is quiet for a moment, then she shakes her head. "The things they've said about you..."

She trails off without giving specifics, and I can only imagine what she's been told. Part of me wants to push for more information, but I also know that anything she tells me will hurt even more than it already does. Besides, it won't change anything. Our parents hate me, and there's nothing I can do about it.

I shake my head like it doesn't matter, then push up from the table just as Claire and Finn approach. "I have to warm up for my set. But stay. You remember Claire, right?"

Lydia nods, holding out a hand. Claire leans in instead, giving her a big bear hug. I haven't even hugged my sister yet, but it's not like I'm much of a hugger anyway.

"And this is Finn, Claire's son. His dad owns the place, so order whatever you want and he'll pay for it."

"Maren!" Claire laughs, and I give her an evil grin.

"I'm kidding," I say, "Put it on my tab."

"I got it," Ethan says from behind us, sliding a hand around Claire's waist and kissing the top of her head.

"Ugh. If they start macking in front of you, you have my permission to leave." I reach over and squeeze Lydia's hand. "You'll stay though, right?"

Lydia nods and pulls on my hand, bringing me closer. Then she hugs me. It's awkward at first, and I don't know what to do with my hands except hold them straight down to my side. But then I tentatively reach for her and return the hug. I'm surprised at the tears that form in my eyes, and I do my best to sniff them away. When we finally release each other, her face is wet, and I'm wiping my makeup all over my sleeve.

"Great," I laugh. But I don't really care about my ruined face. The relief I feel at having Lydia back in my life makes me feel lighter than I have in years.

It feels like a different night as I perform each song in my set, and I know it has everything to do with Lydia being a part of the crowd. But it's more than that. This past week, it's like my whole universe has shifted in a way I've never experienced. I started out this week saying goodbye to my independence as I moved from my apartment into Nina's. But then I saw Mac, and despite all the ways I fought it, he made me fall for him. I learned how much I needed his kind of love, and I no longer care that he was the agent who sold the apartments. It's not like they were his, and it's not like he even knew. It doesn't even matter. I see now how many doors this whole change opened up. I never would have run into my sister, and I never would have known what it's like to fall in love.

Because that's what's happening. I'm falling in love, and instead of fighting it, I'm going to ride this all the way as if my heart can't get broken.

I carry these feelings through my whole set, pouring my heart into every word, every chord. When it's over, my smile shines through my tears as I leap from the stage and engulf my sister in a hug—our first in years—before we all go home for the night.

It's late when I finally pull up to the house, but I don't feel tired. I sit in my car for a moment, mentally reliving the events of tonight. I reach for my phone, wanting to share it with Mac, but then remembering that he hasn't texted me all day. I pause, my fingers aching to reach out to him, but my mind reminding me it's against the rules.

"What rules, though?" I say aloud, then laugh. Fuck the rules. I find his name, then send him a quick chat.

Me: I missed you today.

Then I hold my breath, waiting for a reply. I don't wait long. My face breaks into a smile as three dots appear. Then his text.

NCG: Then get out of the car, silly.

I quickly look toward the house and see a dark human shape sitting in the shadows on the porch. I throw open the door and run to him. He stands and catches me, kissing my mouth as if it wasn't just yesterday we were waking up together, but years ago.

"You didn't call me all day," I protest when we break apart.

"It was a hard day," he says, and my heart lurches.

"Benji?" I ask. He nods, but then shakes his head.

"He's okay, but he's going downhill. Today he was more agitated than usual, and I couldn't find it in me to leave him alone with the nurse. I came here as soon as he fell asleep."

I take a hard look at him, though the lights from the streetlamps make his features look pale.

"How long have you been here?" I ask.

"Just a few hours." He pecks me on the nose, but I jerk my head back and swat his shoulder.

"You knew I had a gig. You could have come."

"Yeah, but I needed to stay close. Just in case."

Just in case this is the end. I know that's what he means. I rest my head on his chest, realizing just how hard this must be for him. It's so much more important than some silly romance. Still, now that he's here, I don't want to let him go.

"Do you want to come in?"

He winces, then shakes his head. "I'd love to, but I can't. I probably should have been back a while ago, but I just had to see you. and I wanted to be here to ask you a very important question."

His tone is so serious, I look back up at him, studying his face for a clue.

"Maren, I'd like to take this relationship to the next level," he says. My expression must be giving me away, because he grins then closes my dropped jaw with a finger. "Relax, I just want to take you on a date. A real date, to make up for the day we lost yesterday. Can I?"

Chapter Eighteen

Maren

Mac didn't tell me where we are going. His only command was to wear something elegant and warm. So I slip on a slinky black dress I usually pair with combat boots, opting for a pair of stiletto heeled boots instead. Over my dress, I wear a black faux fur wrap that is deceivingly warm. I glam it up with dark eye makeup and candy apple red lips that make my pale skin appear that much more dramatic, and I wear my dark hair straight and long with fringe bangs in front. I know I hit the right notes when I open the door and Mac sucks in a hard breath.

"Damn, girl. Maybe we should stay in." He grabs me by the wrist and pulls me in his arms, his hand resting on the curve of my hip as he tilts his head in an attempt to taste my mouth. I turn, laughing as I push him away.

"You should know that it took a long time to look like this. So yes, we're going out, and no, you're not ruining the look by messing up my makeup."

His laugh is a hearty rumble, vibrating against my hands as he releases me. I take a moment to appreciate the man standing before me. He's in a different suit this time, a little less stuffy than the other one, and it hugs his frame in a way that has me recalling what's underneath. His beard is trimmed and shaped, his hair in casual curls over his forehead. I bite my painted lip, hoping that whatever we're doing, it will end with my naked body pressed against his. By the way he's looking at me, I can pretty much guarantee it.

When I turn for my purse, Nina is there, her eyes like saucers. I offer a crooked grin, knowing she's also picturing him with a lot less clothes, and maybe a coffee cup in his hand.

"Nina, this is Mac."

I don't get a chance to say anything else before she stumbles toward him in an effort to shake his…hand? Shlong? Mac catches her, and I see Nina turn a shade of pink her hair has never reached.

"I'm Nina, your biggest fan. Would you like some coffee?"

I groan as Mac glances at me quizzically.

"I'll explain later." I shoot Nina a stern-eyed glare, noting that she seems to have recovered. She's staring at Mac like he's a snack, but when she finally looks my way, she offers an angelic shrug.

"Have fun, you two," she says, patting Mac on the bicep, pausing, then looking at me with appreciation. "Lucky bitch," she hisses under her breath, but not too quiet for Mac to hear judging by the way he's holding in his grin.

"All right, what did your roommate mean," Mac asks once we're in his car, "Biggest fan? Is it my coffee order?"

I start to laugh, but then see he's dead serious. "You honestly have no idea?"

"Idea about what?"

"About the stir you've created in the neighborhood because of your daily walks. There's a whole topic dedicated to you on Nextdoor. There's even a TikTok that just passed four million views. Surely you know."

"I have no idea what you're talking about."

I turn in my seat, my mouth dropping. "Mac, what did you think would happen when you walk the neighborhood barefoot, wearing nothing but a pair of shorts? There are a lot of lonely housewives living here, and I guarantee they all set their alarms to see your morning stroll. Let's just say you have everyone's full attention at a very early hour."

He tilts his head at me with a smirk. "Do I have yours?"

I swat his arm, refusing to answer. He barks out a laugh, and I know he sees right through me.

"Seriously, though. Why walk barefoot? I know you own shoes, and that can't feel good."

"I'm used to it by now," he says, "You could say it's like a meditation. I do it after my run because it's grounding. It helps me feel like part of the earth."

I'm immediately brought back to that first night we met—our shoes off, the way he held me on a rooftop bar under a starry sky. We were stories above the earth, and yet I'd never felt more grounded.

We're standing on holy ground.

Which brings me back to our connection—the one he doesn't know. I quickly brush it aside.

We take the highway into the hills bordering Sunset Bay, and he lets me play DJ during the drive. As the scenery fades to black, our headlights casting twin beams into the night, I set the mood with a mix of my favorite artists. First it's retro Gwen Stefani with No Doubt that kicks off the vibe. Then Florence and the Machine, which always brings out my inner free spirit. Which is why when Paramore fills the car, I sing on full blast, letting my voice mingle with Hayley Williams. Mac stays silent, but he takes my hand, squeezing it when I belt out the chorus.

"Have you ever thought about doing this professionally?" he finally asks, and I duck my head with a grin.

"What, you don't like the Hillside concerts I hold?"

He gives me a sideways smirk. "Well, I'm sure you're great when you're not mocking me in front of a whole crowd."

I shoot him a dirty look, but then take his hand back. "Well, show up with another woman at any other one of my performances, and I'll sic the crowd on you."

He brings my hand to his lips, pressing gently. "There's no other woman but you, Maren," he says, his tone serious, "And I'd like to keep it that way."

I bite my lip and look out the window. My heart is bursting, but I don't want to tell him. I don't want to jinx this. For some reason, Mac Dermot likes me.

As for me? I don't even care that he was the one who sold my apartment, because if he hadn't, I wouldn't be sitting in his car, ready to go wherever he wants to take me.

"Well?"

I turn, tilt my head in confusion. Then I remember his question.

"Professionally," I repeat, "Of course I've thought of it. It's honestly all I've ever wanted. But it seems so far away. Between working all day and performing small gigs, I'm beat. I send out singles and I hear nothing back. Sometimes there's a nice form rejection letter, but mostly it's crickets. I don't know if I have much more to give because loving this music dream means I hate every other part of my life. And honestly, I'm tired of being disappointed."

My eyes fill with tears as I'm talking, and I discreetly swipe them away while looking back out the window. It's more than I've ever admitted to anyone, even Claire. I'm embarrassed by how much I want music to be my whole world. I don't need to be rich, but I'd like to be able to quit my job because music pays the bills and affords me a comfortable life. I'm tired of watching every damn penny, knowing that I'm just one disaster away from being back on the street. To be able to work on my music all day wouldn't even feel like working.

Just thinking about this while traveling in Mac's luxury Jaguar makes me feel even more embarrassed. Silly even. I've played music all my life and been more serious about it ever since I got sober. But I make double digits at every show, which is barely enough to afford a meal out. Thank goddess for my tips at Insomniacs, because it's the only way I've paid my bills.

"You're really good," Mac says, cutting into my thoughts. I wipe the last tear, offering a grateful smile, hoping he can't see my shiny eyes in the darkened car and that my makeup has stayed intact.

"Thanks," I say, and leave it at that. Because *good* is subjective, and I can be good all day long and still fail to get anywhere with this damn dream.

We finally reach our destination, which is basically a large parking lot lit by streetlamps with a dome-like stone building at the far end. It looks kind of like a…

"A cave?" I ask, peering closer. It's large—definitely man-made—and it offers a warm glow, though I can't see anything else inside. I turn to Mac, who still isn't saying a word about what we're embarking on. He gets out of the car and jogs to my side. I feel more grown up and elegant than ever as he opens my door and holds out his hand. Have I ever been on a date before? Looking back, I realize this could be the first. I didn't think I had many *firsts* left in my life.

I take Mac's hand, and he pulls me to my feet. Even in my heels, I have to look up at him, and I warm at the way his blue eyes watch me, as if he can see inside my soul. This is different. How have I never experienced this before, any of this? The sexual energy between us is electric, but it's more than that. I can see myself in the reflection of his iris, and it mirrors the connection I'm feeling with him…as if my whole being has been breathlessly on pause until Mac stepped into my life.

It is said that time is irrelevant, that everything that

has ever been or will be exists in a sphere without beginning or end. It's a complex theory I never understood until this moment now. In Mac's arms, my whole life making sense. I have always known this man. I just hadn't met him yet.

"Ready?" he asks. He's talking about whatever lies beyond the threshold of that cave. But he could also mean whatever is in store for us, whatever this is, and whatever will happen to my heart as a result.

"I don't even know what to be ready for."

He leads me to the cave, which is glowing from soft artificial lights, and we pause at the entrance so the attendant can scan the tickets from Mac's phone. I peer ahead of us, curious at a stairwell within the cave that appears to curve into the earth without giving anything away.

"Always looking ahead," Mac murmurs, his hand at my back as his lips brush the side of my ear. "Trust me?"

The warmth of his breath travels through me, bringing me back to the first night he said those words. On a night like this, under a scarlet sky lit by the city lights, barefoot and on top of the world via a rooftop bar—before I knew his role in losing my apartment. It seems like ages ago, including all the reasons I was once mad at him. I'm no longer mad. I'm grateful.

"I trust you."

He stays close as we walk down the stairwell, as if to protect me from hurtling to my death as I navigate the stairs in six-inch heels. I'm perfectly capable of walking down any stairs on stilts, and yet, I find comfort in letting someone else take charge in my safety and care.

The staircase winds deep into the underground, lit only by sconce candles drilled into the stone walls. The air feels cooler the deeper we go, and I pull my wrap closer with my free hand, hoping wherever we're headed will have some sort of heat source. I'm not prepared when we finally reach the bottom, and I discover that, yes, there will be heat.

We're met by a large circular room filled with hundreds, maybe thousands, of tiny flickering candles on the ground and walls, creating a comforting glow. Even more, the thousands of candles make the underground warm feel almost toasty.

I'm so distracted by the candles, it takes me a few moments to notice the darkened shape of people sitting in chairs, and then the small stage at the center of the room, also covered in candles. I know better than to ask Mac what to expect, and instead submit to the surprise. He leads me to our seats, two solitary chairs in a private alcove, and I wordlessly take in our surroundings and the holy silence from everyone else. We're all waiting to know what's going to happen. And yet, I am perfectly content in this moment, warmed by the ethereal glow of candlelight, and completely distanced from whatever is happening above us on the surface of the earth. Here in this underground cave, my hand resting in Mac's on his knee, nothing else exists.

Just when I think nothing could get better though, it does. We watch as men and women dressed in black file into the room, holding various stringed instruments. My heart swells as the silence in the glowing cave is replaced with a cacophony of sound from the orchestra's warm up. Then the dissonance becomes one long, drawn out note, reverberating off the cave walls before falling into silence. But only for a moment, because the orchestra begins playing, sweeping us all away with them through a symphony of sound that echoes within this underground chamber.

I take in a deep breath, the passion of the music hitting me with such force I can't stop my hot tears from streaming down my cheeks. Makeup be damned. But in the midst of my emotional response, I realize I know the song I'm hearing. I wait a few lines, wondering if I'm imagining what I'm hearing.

Holy shit. It's "Still Into You," by fucking Paramore, but played as an orchestra. I turn to Mac, eyes wide and then narrowed as I take in Mac's shit-eating grin. He hands me a program and I look at the headline.

Candlelight Concert: Stay the Night with Paramore.

It's a whole concert of Paramore music, all with stringed instruments. I'm suddenly so grateful Mac kept this a surprise. If he had told me we'd be listening to an orchestra covering Paramore music, I would've declined because there is no way I'd listen to Hayley Williams be reduced to fucking elevator music. But this is not elevator music. This is my soul on fire. This is a new way to breathe. This is everything.

Mac doesn't move next to me for the firsts few songs, allowing me the moment to absorb the reverberation of the strings, to feel the pulse of the cello within my heart without any distraction. But around the fourth song in, I feel his hand snaking up my thigh. I close my eyes, the music traveling through me as Mac's hand travels to the top of the slit in my skirt, then coaxes its way to my inner thigh. His finger brushes against the hem of my thong, and I sharply inhale. My breath feels shallow as he nudges the material aside and slides one finger across my slick folds, then another.

There's no one sitting right next to us, but if the people in front of us turned around, they would see what Mac is doing to me. They would know by the flush in my cheeks, even in the dimness of this candlelit room. They would know by my spread legs, Mac's hand buried between my thighs.

I fucking love this.

I lift my hips and Mac pulls my thong down, then

over my legs, and finally my stilettos. He looks at me then, bringing my panties to his face and inhaling. I watch his eyes close, as if he's savoring the most heavenly meal he's ever tasted.

No, I'm mistaken. Because next he takes his fingers, the ones that have been inside me, and he brings them to his tongue, delicately licking them in the same way I wish he was licking me.

"Mac," I whisper. That's when he plunges those same fingers, now moistened with his spit, into my waiting pussy, showing me no mercy as the orchestra reaches a crescendo. I silently release around him, feeling my juices pour over his hand as he thrusts into me. My body is on fire, and as much as I love that we're here, I also wish we weren't. I need him inside me, to take me completely. I want to come undone.

His hand, my orgasm, the orchestra. All of it slows at the same time, and I eventually come back to earth. My neck is damp with sweat, and the cool air of the cave teases my wanting nipples. Mac leans in as he withdraws his hand, his mouth landing on mine in a soft kiss. His fingers explore my lips, and I can taste myself mingled with the warm honey of his mouth. It's a recipe I could never grow tired of.

"How do you like the concert," Mac whispers into my ear. He leans back, and I bite my lip at how sexy he looks in this moment, desire dripping from his face. I tug his beard, then pull him closer until I have his ear.

"It's the most explosive thing I've ever experienced."

Chapter Nineteen

Mac

"So, I get why you wanted me all to yourself in a crowded darkened room," she says, squeezing my hand. I can still taste her pussy, and it's taking all I have not to drag her back to my place and fuck her senseless. But I also want a proper date with her. Respectable. One where I exhibit a little bit of restraint.

But the honey of her essence is a taste I'll never grow tired of, and I know I'll fuck her before this night is over.

Emerging from the dimly lit cave, the parking lot seems like a whole other world. I glance at her, and the grin on her face is contagious. She does a quick spin on the asphalt, using my hand to twirl her. "Paramore? How did you know?"

I know exactly when I knew. Years ago, in her

apartment. When I was invisible and she was everything. But I can't tell her that.

"You told me," I say, then remind her of the *second* first night we met…the night at the rooftop bar. "I'd never listened to Paramore, but after the way you gushed about the lead singer, Hayley whatshername, I looked up everything that band ever sang and listened to them nonstop."

"Hayley Williams," she says, "You did that, even though I walked out on you?"

"I did that *because* you walked out on me," I say, which is the truth, "It made me think of you." I pull her in under my arm then kiss her forehead. "I thought for sure you figured it out when you started singing in the car. It took everything in me not to ask you."

"Never in my life would I have figured this out," she assures me. "I wouldn't have taken you for a Paramore fan." She tilts her head up to mine. "What do you listen to, anyway?"

"Not Paramore, though I see why you're a fan. I'm into Radiohead, Muse, Pink Floyd, Nirvana, Foo Fighters… Bands like that."

"Solid retro choices." She grins, then pokes me in the ribs. "You should try some girl bands, though. Women kick ass in music too."

"I do," I say as we reach the car, "I spent a whole month listening to Paramore, and then there's this underground chick more people need to discover. Ever hear of Maren Huerta? She has a voice that won't quit, plays a mean guitar, and has a slamming body. I'd totally fuck her if she'd let me."

She hip checks me, then turns under my arm and pulls me close, her back against the car. I fall into her, my mouth landing on hers. The chill of the night is forgotten as I lose myself in the warmth of her kiss.

"She'd totally let you, especially after what you did to me in there," she murmurs against my mouth, her hand landing on my hardening cock. I can feel myself straining against my slacks, and I swear to god I want to take her right here, right now. But that's the exact moment her stomach rumbles, reminding me we still haven't had dinner.

"We should eat," I say, pushing off the car and taking her hand, "I know just the place."

The place is The Coastal Plate, which is more touristy and laid back than the stuffy restaurants I usually frequent. But Maren isn't one of those status-obsessed girls that keep landing in my path, and I have a feeling she's down for some real food, and The Coastal Plate has some choice options.

For me, it's a huge cheeseburger with avocado and bacon, ordered rare as fuck. For her, it's the salmon poke bowl with extra ginger.

"So," she says, folding her hands in front of her once the waiter leaves.

"So," I repeat, taking her hands in mine. Her hands are soft, her black as night fingernails shimmering as her fingers weave between mine. Her skin is a luscious ivory against mine, a rarity in this beach town. On her, it's elegant,—but it's also rebellious, as if she shuns the habits of all these sun worshippers.

"So, what's next?" she asks, "We're not casual, so you say. But what then? Are you my…"

I hear the word she falters on. *Boyfriend.* It's reminiscent of the other night, when she nearly slipped up and called herself my girlfriend. It worried me then, for all the right reasons. Tonight, I find myself not caring about anything but her.

But the word *boyfriend* also carries a lot of weight. I've never been that to anyone before. I've dated girls, some over the course of a few months. But the word *boyfriend* symbolizes something more. Exclusivity, sure. But also a kind of belonging—as in, she belongs to me, and I… I belong to her.

Boyfriend feels like too small of a word.

"Yours," I finish for her, "I am yours, and you are mine. It's that simple. If you want to call me your boyfriend, your lover, your man friend, whatever you want, I'm here for it. I don't care what you call me, as long as I get to be the one with your heart. Because Maren, I'm falling for you, and it's the most delicious feeling in the world."

I take her hand closer, locking eyes with her as I brush my lips across her delicate skin. Her eyes fill with tears, and she starts to pull away in an effort to brush them aside. I hold firm, pulling her closer and kissing her damp face, tasting the sweet salt of her.

"Damnit," she laughs, "I seriously never cry. At least, I never used to. But you keep saying all the right things."

"I mean every one of them."

She's quiet for a moment. "You have my heart," she finally murmurs, "You're the first one to have it." She pauses, closing her eyes against the collected moisture. When she opens them again, her coffee eyes sparkle with something new. "And I hope you'll be the last."

The reason The Coastal Plate is such a hit with tourists is because it turns into a night club after dinner hours. The first song that comes on is a mix of Nirvana's "Teen Spirit," and she insists we have to stay and dance.

"It's your song!" she laughs, grabbing my hand and pulling me to my feet. I take off my jacket, and she lays her wrap over the chair before we join the throng of dancers. When I pull her against me, the curves of her body molds against my own like we're parts of the same puzzle.

I'm hers, and she's mine.

The energy in the room is high, and we're here for it. I join her in belting out the lyrics, mesmerized by the throaty nature of her voice. We're surrounded by people screaming the song, but I hear only her. I taste only the sweat of her body. I breathe only the honeysuckle of her hair.

I'm brought back to the night on the rooftop, the feel of holiness that had me remove my shoes so I could soak it all in. But I don't need to do that now. It's like the whole Universe has twisted into alignment, and we're at the very center of it.

But then I feel Maren stiffen, and I'm catapulted back to reality. I turn to see what's captured her attention, and that's when I see him.

My brother.

Former manager of the Beale Street apartments, and Maren's former fuck buddy.

Brock's eyes are on Maren as some barely legal Barbie sucks on his lip ring. But then the tool pushes her away, his face breaking into a shit eating grin when he notices I'm the one with my arm around Maren's shoulders.

"Let's get out of here," I growl, but Brock is already moving in our direction.

I haven't seen this dipshit since I handed him his last

paycheck. We hadn't lived together in years, and I hardly considered him family. But because he was effectively out of work, I'd paid him a healthy severance on top of his salary. The fucker still had the audacity to throw Maren in my face.

"Too bad you never had a shot at #17," he'd said, referring to her apartment number as he tucked the paycheck in his wallet. "Probably the best fuck out of the whole building. I should have stepped aside to give you a taste, but that bitch is like a goddamn drug. You should see the way she takes my…"

"We're done here," I'd cut him off. But what I'd really wanted to do was cave his face in.

This fucker has been busting my balls from day-one—from the day he moved into Benji's house, to the day he was made office manager while I did Benji's grunt work. I flash back to the first day I saw him walk out of Maren's apartment at the exact time I started my shift. This fuckhead laughed in my face for not making a move, and then he swooped in. All for a good lay, he'd brag.

Now here he is, striding toward us looking like the cat who caught the canary.

This fuckhead could ruin everything.

"Maren, babe, where've you been?" Brock asks. He looks from Maren to me, and his grin widens. "Man, you don't waste any time, do you? I'm happy to see you haven't lost your touch. Well, good for you, going for the big dog."

"Can it, Brock." His name is out of my mouth before I can pull it back in, and I feel Maren shift beside me. I don't have to look to know that she's staring at me, probably wondering how I know his name. Well, she's about to get a shit load of information—things I should have told her a long time ago. Fucking coward. I should have said something sooner, and now it's all going to come crashing down.

"Don't get jealous, Brock," Maren says, slipping out from under my arm to put her hands on her hips, "You knew we weren't serious."

"Jealous?" Brock laughs, "Maren, I knew my place. You fucked me because you thought I had rent control, but the only one who could control it was this guy." He nods to me, his grin widening as I feel my stomach plummeting. "Guess you knew how to get housing. What's this guy doing for you now that he's not keeping your rent low? Did he put you up in the penthouse? Buy you your own house? Because Maren, that pussy is good, but goddamn if I'm amazed at the power you wield. Well done, babe."

The words are barely out of his mouth when my fist meets his jaw.

"Hey!" The little blonde chick squeals as she jumps

out of the way. I ignore her, landing one more punch in his gut. Brock grunts, dropping to his knees. He was never much of a fighter. It's kind of unfair for me to continue, but ask me if I care.

"Don't fucking talk to her," I say, kicking at him as he remains on the ground. A circle has formed around us, and I'm pretty sure we're about to get booted. "Don't even look at her."

"Hey, you got her, man," Brock says, then spits blood on the ground beside him. He gets to his feet but takes a few steps back out of swinging range. "That's what you wanted, right? Maren's golden pussy. It's yours. You won."

This time, I do look at Maren. There's confusion on her face as she studies both of us. I can see security carving their way through the crowd, and I'm fired up enough that I could take all of them on if they so much as touch me. But it's Maren's touch that brings me back down.

"Come on," she says quietly. When I peer down at her, there's a plea in her expression. I realize this must have been just as uncomfortable for her. I also know she must have a million questions I'm not ready to answer, but that she deserves to know.

"We're leaving," I say as the security guards reach us. I raise my hands as they push us toward the door, willing my adrenaline to subside so I don't sucker punch one of the guards. Maren grabs our jackets, and we make our way outside, followed by Brock and his girlfriend. "Come on, let's go," I murmur, my hand at her back as I try to guide her toward the car. It doesn't work, as she moves out of my reach and faces both of us, her hands on her hips.

"Not until you tell me what the fuck is going on." Maren narrows her eyes, staring us down as she waits for an explanation. My wonder is where to start. With the fact that Brock is my brother? That she and I have met before? Or how about the fact that I *owned* the apartments she was kicked out of—that I'm the one who fucked her out of housing?

Brock only laughs, then shakes his head.

"I have nothing else to say," he says, "See ya, bro." He tips his head at me, then nods his chin at Maren. "Maren, always a pleasure."

Even with Barbie's hand in his, he looks Maren up and down, a smirk as his eyes land on her chest before he walks away.

I start moving toward him, the heat rising in my chest as I clench my fists, but Maren grabs hold of my bicep and yanks me back. My whole body is aching to shake her off and go after him, but Maren holds on. I feel the sparks in my veins as I turn from Brock and glare down at Maren. I'm not mad at her, but I'm furious in general, and frustrated that I can't relieve it on Brock's puny ass.

But Maren's flashing eyes disarm me.

"You don't get to be mad," she says, "not now. Tell me what's going on, or I'll go find my own ride home."

My jaw pulses, but the fire is simmering. It's now or never. I try to come up with the words that will absolve me, the ones that will result in her leaving here with me. But when they don't come. I shake my head, closing my eyes as I take a deep breath.

"I should have told you," I say. I look past her, unable to look her in the eye.

"Told me what?"

"Maren." I take another breath, a step forward and reach for her hand. She doesn't pull away, but her hand remains limp in mine.

"Mac, out with it."

I wince, but finally blurt it out.

"The Beale Street apartments, I'm the one who sold them."

Maren exhales, and I can almost see the relief rolling over her like fog on the hillside. The reaction confuses me. "I know," she says.

"You do?" I feel the weight lifting from my shoulders as she smiles.

"Yeah, you were the broker. I already knew."

The weight returns. This is not going to be an easy

fix after all.

"I'm not done."

Maren studies me, and it's as if a light bulb goes off. I can practically see the clarity washing over her.

"What are you not telling me?"

I think of the way she looked when I saw her standing on that rooftop bar. The glass of wine in her hand, the wind blowing through her hair, the look of hopelessness on her face. The way it felt to know that I was the one who did that to her.

"That night we met," I begin, "it wasn't by accident. I saw you there, and I felt like shit because I knew *why* you were there and why that drink was in your hand, and that it was all my fault. I knew you didn't drink, and I bumped you so that you'd spill it. I was just going to walk away, but as soon as you turned around, I couldn't."

The cloud of confusion is swirling around her now. "You knew…me? You knew I didn't drink?"

Fuck. Fuck, fuck, fuck. I move toward her, but she pulls away, clutching her stomach. She's looking at me now like I'm a stranger, like I'm a predator.

"Please, let me just start from the beginning."

I do, starting with all those years ago around the time I started working for Benji, when she was one of his newest tenants.

"Benji, my guardian, owned your building; well, at the end, I did. But back then, it was Benji's, and I worked for him in maintenance."

She's digesting what I say, her eyes shifting as she tries to make sense of all of this.

"But it said Malcolm D. Anderson on the last lease I signed," she says, "I saw it, noticing it changed." Her eyes narrow. "You lied about your name?"

"My name is Mac Dermot, but my birth name is Malcolm Dermot Anderson." I pull my wallet out, flipping to my ID. She glances at the card as if she can't bear to look at it. But then her eyes widen, and she grabs the wallet from my hands.

"I knew you," she says, running her hand over the face on my ID. I'm clean shaven in the photo, and a lot leaner.

"You did.

"You worked maintenance," she continues. I nod.

"I did. It was kind of a family affair. Benji used me to do the manual labor because I could. He put Brock at the front desk because he wasn't worth a shit."

"And Brock was…"

"My brother." Her eyes widen, but I continue before she can speak. "My foster brother. He was a runaway, like me, and came to live with Benji and me a short time after I got there. He got the best of everything. The best room. The best job. Better pay. But all of that didn't matter as much as him getting you." I shake my head, biting back my jealousy. Maren didn't need this right now.

"He didn't have me," she says, rolling her eyes.

I look away. I want to tell her all of it, how I wanted her for years, and she was always out of reach. But when I look back at her, I can see this isn't the time.

"Tell me about the apartments," she says, "Tell me exactly how you came to own the building only to kick all of us to the curb with only thirty days to gather our lives and find somewhere else to live. Tell me how we were supposed to do that when there wasn't a place in town that would come close to matching the rent we were paying."

"I'm sorry." I hang my head, but she shoves me with open palms.

"Tell me! I'd love to know all the ways you screwed me out of a home just so you could line your pockets. Tell me, Mac, how many fancy cars do you own? How many suits? How many expensive watches?" She leans in close. "How many more Cartier brooches?"

"It's not like that," I say, but I might as well say nothing at all, because she's not buying it. "Benji bought the lot years ago," I start, "He's had this vision to make these high-end apartments, much like the ones he's made all over Southern California. But when it came time to build, he got involved with a few other projects that took up most of his time. So he took a bunch of shortcuts with the Beale Street Apartments. He hired the cheapest contractor he could find, bought his way through permits, and had that apartment building standing in just a couple months."

"That doesn't explain how you—"

"Hold on, I'm getting there," I interrupt, "Brock and I had been living with Benji a few years, doing odd jobs to earn our keep. This is what he did, apparently. He called it mentorship, but I now realize it was child labor."

The guilt gnaws at me for saying the words out loud. Benji, who kept me from a life in prison, who gave me a roof over my head and three squares a day. Benji, who gave me a steppingstone into a world of wealth I never would have known before.

But also Benji, who whipped Brock and me if we ever half-assed our work, or if we complained about being tired, or if we so much as looked at him wrong. Benji, who dictated our every move so that, even now as I clean up his mess while he lays dying in his home, I cannot speak against him without believing I am biting the hand that fed me.

Benji, who let me know that I was nothing without him—and I came to believe it, to the point that when he does finally die, I'm not sure if I will mourn or feel relief. Right now, I feel numb.

"I realized right away what a shitty build the Beale

Street Apartments were," I continued, "I was working maintenance while taking real estate courses, and we were taught to look for things that add value to an apartment. That's when I started to see the things Benji was ignoring." I peer at Maren. "Didn't you notice anything weird in your unit? Any smells? Dark patches?"

Her face gives away that she had.

"How about headaches?" I continue, and she looks at me sharply.

"That was connected?"

"It was black mold. It was deep in your walls, the ceiling, the floorboards. When I came to your apartment, I could tell right away. I couldn't do anything about it back then because my hands were tied. Benji wouldn't…" I stop, unable to throw him under the bus any more than I had. "That was only the start of what was wrong. Once I started my own brokerage and it began making money, I tried to buy the apartments off Benji just so I could fix what he wasn't. But he wouldn't sell. Then there was the lawsuit, and then…"

"Lawsuit?" Maren tilts her head and her eyes widen. "It was Molly's family, wasn't it? She was in and out of the hospital with that boy of hers. Then they moved without any notice. You paid them off, didn't you?"

I nod, eyes trained on the ground. It was probably the lowest moment of this whole nightmare. It was the air conditioner. Every time they ran the unit, they were spreading the mold around the house. I didn't learn about the extent of the issue until Benji slapped the lawsuit on my desk.

"Buy the apartments," he'd said, pausing only to cough from the forcefulness of this words. By this time, Benji knew he was terminal. But it took legal action for him to finally let go of the apartments. *"Buy them and take care of this mess."*

"I paid them off, then I bought the apartments from Benji," I tell Maren now, "Benji had an inspector in his back pocket who wouldn't turn us in, but he leveled with me on the true value of the place. He said the cost of fixing the issues would be more than I purchased the apartments for, which I was willing to pay. But then he pointed out that we were lucky to only have one lawsuit, that if we took the time to fix everything, the other tenants would become aware of the issues and we'd have more lawsuits on our hands."

"So you tore it down to save your ass," Maren says.

I exhale sharply, and I nod.

"That's a simple way to put it," I say.

"It's not that simple," she retorts, "After all, dozens of us had to scramble for new places to live while you slept cozy in your bed."

Hundreds, really. The Beale Street Apartments were only the last of Benji's properties to go.

"And to make things all the better," Maren continues, "you saw me at that bar and actually thought it would be a great idea to get to know me better."

"It's not like that—"

"Really? Because it seems that way. You see me there about to throw away my sobriety, and you knew exactly why I was drinking in the first place. So, what? Did you have a good laugh that night? Have you been laughing this whole time?"

"Maren, you know that's not true."

"I don't know what to believe anymore, Mac!"

I take her shoulders, and she struggles to be free, but I hold firm.

"Believe that I made a lot of missteps in all of this, and it's a lot more complicated than you think. But also believe that I am in love with you, and none of this has been a joke."

The words slip out of my mouth, and I'm surprised at how easy I say them. I'm also surprised that I mean them. I notice the hitch in her anger, as if I chipped my way into her stony heart. But the fire is still there, and I know I have a long way to go to regain her trust.

"If I could take it all back, I would," I continue, "but if I did, I don't know that we would have met, and for that alone, I'm glad it all happened."

I search her eyes, looking for something I can hold onto. All I see is rage. She yanks herself out of my reach.

"You're fucking delusional," she says, "Love me? How? Our whole relationship is built on lies. You could have told me everything from the beginning, starting with how we really knew each other."

"Right," I say. I huff a laugh. "You never even gave me the time of day. I came into your apartment to fix that leak under your sink, and you just strummed your guitar with Paramore on blast, ignoring me the whole time. So, why would I start with that?"

"Paramore," Maren whispers. She points an accusatory finger at me. "I didn't ignore you at all," she continues. "You asked me about the posters on my wall, and then stayed an hour after you fixed that leak to listen to 'Riot!' from beginning to end." She pauses, then gives me a curious look. "Did you...like me?"

"I was fucking crazy about you."

A half smile forms on her face, but she quickly brushes it away. She shakes her head, as if shaking away any kind of reasoning.

"Crazy about me? You didn't even know me!"

"I didn't have to. You made a big impression." I dare a step closer, and when she doesn't move away, I take another step. "But when I saw you at Torches, a glass of wine in your hand, I knew I was the one who put it there. When I realized you had no idea who I was, I couldn't bring myself to tell you because then everything would come out, and I'd never get the chance to know you."

"And when I left?"

"I thought you figured it out."

"I didn't," she says, "I mean, not exactly. I found out you were the agent who sold it. I didn't know you were the owner or anything else. That night, it was enough to know you had a part in it, and I didn't want to have anything to do with you."

"And yet, here we are." I offer a small smile and my hand.

She looks away, leaving my hand in the air. I pull it back in, feeling the cold return between us.

"I need time to think," she finally says. She pulls her wrap around her. The look on her face is…defeated. I realize there's nothing else to say. I may have lost her for good.

"Maren, I…"

She stops me with a hand on my chest. I can feel the warmth of her skin radiating through my shirt. When I look in her eyes, I can see them glistening in the glow of the streetlamp.

I cover her hand with mine and close my eyes. Then I nod.

"Let me drive you home."

Chapter Twenty

Mac

I wait long enough to see her disappear into her house. I want to wait longer—like forever—until she comes back out and forgives me. But that's not going to happen. Not now. Maybe not ever. So once the door closes behind her without even a glance back, I pull away and head to Benji's house.

But I don't go inside right away.

The truth is, I'm angry. I didn't ask for any of this, for my parents to die, for all the awful people who used the foster system like currency, or for Benji, who never quite promised me a real home, but allowed me the room for hope regardless.

He had been clear from the start—I was there to be useful and nothing more. He'd give me a home; I'd do whatever he asked.

It wasn't like he had me do anything illegal. Well, unless you count child labor as illegal. It started with odd jobs, like deliveries and washing his friends' cars. Then once he could trust I wasn't going to steal, I began cleaning and landscaping at different homes, always with one of his bodyguards keeping watch. It was how he kept tabs on me.

If I half-assed a job, I answered for it with a switch to my backside, always by him.

It wasn't the first time I was hit by a guardian. Past homes felt like living in a puppy mill, with as many as fifteen of us taking up every space in the house. They were always run by lazy assholes who thought fostering would give them the paycheck their nine-to-five wouldn't. What they didn't anticipate was that we needed to eat, have someplace to sleep, and have clothes that fit our growing bodies. Those of us old enough to sass did plenty of it, even though it resulted in regular beatings. It also led to missed meals, sometimes several days in a row. These assholes told us we were lucky. Our parents didn't want us, they said—no one wanted us.

The last official foster home I was in, there were four of us sharing a room with a single bunk bed. To be thirteen and having to share a bed with another boy was awkward, especially when I was stuck with Rory, a kid who couldn't keep his hands to himself. I'd end up on the floor just to avoid Rory's "accidental" touches. But one night, after spending the day mucking the horse barn, I was dog tired and the thought of another night on the floor made me want to punch a hole through the wall.

"It's your turn on the floor," I told Rory. But the kid wouldn't budge. We were matched in size, and I knew I couldn't force him to do anything without getting the attention of Mr. Perkins, our foster parent. "Fine," I relented when Rory stood his ground. "Then get to your side of the fucking bed and don't cross the line over to mine."

I awoke that night with Rory's hand on my dick, his body curled around mine from behind. I leapt out of bed, dragging him with me as he struggled against my strength. But I was too mad, the adrenaline tearing through my body as I straddled his body and pummeled his face with my closed fists. The other kids in the room woke to this, and one of them got Mr. Perkins who pulled me off Rory in a fit of rage. By the time I could find my words, Mr. Perkins already had my ass bare while he whipped it with a belt. If he heard my reasons for the fight, he didn't acknowledge them.

"You ungrateful sack of shit," Mr. Perkins growled, never letting up, even though I'd given in to the beating. "We give you everything, using every cent we have to care for you worthless boys. This is how you repay us, by bullying the other kids?" Never mind that Mr. Perkins got money for each of us, or that he used it to feed his gambling addiction. Never mind that Mrs. Perkins had her hair and nails done every week and came home every Friday with a new outfit for her Sunday brunch with the girls.

He left my ass riddled with raised purple welts before he marched me outside to get back to mucking the barn. It was two in the morning, but he stood there while I walked barefoot through shit, shoveling manure under the glow of a hanging utility light, and laying down hay until the sun eventually crested the hillside.

It was the last day I ever spent in foster care. That night, exhausted to the bone, my stomach curling in on itself from lack of food, I lay on the floor of the bedroom, listening to the sounds of the night. Rory had kept his distance the rest of the day, but I was not about to get back in that bed. I was more tired than I'd ever been in my life, but my eyes remained wide open. I waited until I heard the soft snores of my bunkmates, then I rolled to my knees, moving one leg in front of the other, as I shuffle-crawled to the door and eased it open.

The door to Mr. Perkins' room was cracked, probably to listen for any more fighting in our room. But through that open door, I could hear the deep rumble of his snore, followed by the much softer sighs from Mrs. Perkins.

I got to my feet and tiptoed down the hallway, waiting in between steps to see if I was discovered. I reached the living room and then the entry way where all our shoes were lined up on a bench, like it was a friendly schoolhouse and not a house that swindled the system. With cautious hands, I found my shoes and slid them out carefully. I hadn't grabbed anything else from my room. I realized my mistake as I opened the door and was met by a soft sprinkle of rare California rain.

Something brushed against my shins, and I jumped back banging the doorknob in the process. It was just the cat, who shot out of the house at my sudden move. Mrs. Perkins would be pissed when she found out. I wondered if she'd be madder at her indoor cat found outside in the rain, or the fact that one of their walking paychecks had run away. My bet was on the cat. Fosters were a dime a dozen, and they'd probably have my half of the bed filled by the end of the week.

As far as I could tell, everyone in the house was still asleep. I stood there like I was made of marble, my ears straining to make out every noise in the house and heard nothing that sounded like someone was about to discover me. Satisfied, I looked back at the rain outside. It was getting harder, and I was standing there in my threadbare pajama bottoms that fell a few inches above my ankles and a thin white undershirt. I hadn't even thought to grab socks. I definitely didn't have a jacket.

But Mr. Perkins did. It hung there above the shoe rack, underneath the sign that said "Live. Laugh. Love." It was the coat he used every morning to tend to the animals, and it smelled like it may have never seen the inside of a washing machine. But I grabbed it anyways, slipping the long sleeves over my arms before I tiptoed into the rain, my shoes in hand as I carefully closed the door.

That damn cat followed me as I ran across the field. I stopped halfway through to finally put my shoes on, wiping as much of the mud off my feet before sliding them on while the cat rubbed against my leg.

"Go hunt something while you have the chance," I grunted, kicking her off me. She responded by swiping at my leg, leaving a red gash in her wake. It wasn't the worst wound I'd received on that day, but it was enough to make me kick at her again, more forcefully this time. Fuck that cat. Fuck the farm. Fuck Mr. Perkins and fuck every other foster family that treated me like their goddamn slave. Most of all, fuck my caseworker—a tired old lady who should have retired twenty years ago, and who was oblivious to the state of the homes she placed me in.

I was done.

Now I sit here in my car, the memory of that night—and

the many nights after—racing through my head while I remain parked in front of Benji's house. The Perkins never found me. I'm not sure they even looked. I have no idea how they explained me away to my case manager, but I dropped off the radar as easy as twilight slips into dawn. I spent those first few days of freedom searching for ways to survive. I discovered restaurants waste a lot of food in the dumpsters out back. I scoured piles of clothing abandoned outside thrift stores at night. I slept away from streetlights and stayed in the shadows during the day. My only goal was to survive, though it was hard to remember why.

Then I met a group of guys on the street, the ones who taught me how to lift items from pockets, and later how to steal from homes. Being the youngest, I became the key to their operation. I'd ring the bell with a sign-up form in hand that I'd swiped off some other door-to-door marketer. Upon answering, I'd charm the man or woman of the house into buying a subscription to magazines they'd never get. The checks were useless, but some paid in cash. But a look inside their homes was priceless, my eyes memorizing what I could before they closed the door again. A few nights later, their personal items were in our possession.

Benji's house was different, though. I look up now at the massive home, recalling what it was like to enter that home for the first time. We hadn't cased the house properly before because it seemed like no one was ever home. For days we'd waited, watching for signs of life, and finally I decided the owners were on vacation or something, and it was now or never to ransack the place for things of value.

Of course, what happened next changed my life. I got caught, the other kids ran off, and I had a choice to make—keep running or see what Benji had to offer.

I stayed, and I soon discovered it was not going to be the cushy life I envisioned it would be. Benji worked me hard. Outside of school hours, I was working. And if I fucked up, he beat me for it.

But here's the difference with Benji; instead of telling me I was worthless, he told me I wasn't living up to my potential. He said I was smarter than that. He told me I could have so much more if I would stop being a product of my circumstance and start moving into my future. His form of discipline was unlike the abuse of my former foster homes, and more like old-fashioned discipline. He'd take a switch to me, but never struck with anger. It was always him and not one of his guards, and he used that time to drill values into me.

I was not a street kid.

I was not a victim in the foster system.

I was Malcolm Dermot Anderson, a teenage boy who was learning how to become a man.

And that was why I stayed—even through the endless work, even though our relationship was more business-like than anything else. Benji was not my father, and I was not his son. I grew to care for him because he'd saved me, but as hard as I tried to please him, there was no warmth that came from his direction. I bonded more easily with his security guards than I did with the cold, shrewd man.

I soon discovered why. For Benji, every relationship held currency. He attended parties and held poker nights at the house, but none of these people were his friends. Eventually, these gatherings became fewer and fewer. He spent most nights at the long formal dining table eating alone while I ate at the small table in the kitchen. When he talked on the phone, it was always with a raised voice, often ending with something thrown and shattered against the wall.

He was losing his connections, and we were running out of money.

That's why I was placed in charge of the housework and landscaping, because he had to fire the house staff. It's why he brought Brock in, yet another teen that needed a home in exchange for some manual labor. Years later, when he built those apartments as a last-ditch effort to regain his finances, it's why I handled all the maintenance and Brock managed the rest—because he had nothing left and we'd accept the shit wages he gave us on top of room and board.

What can I say about Brock, except he was a weasel from the start. That guy saw this as his golden ticket and worked it to his fullest advantage. Don't get me wrong, we were both tasked with more responsibility than most teenagers our age. I was a few years older than him though, and I had been through enough to know it wouldn't get better. Brock, on the other hand, came in after Benji had fired his last security guard. He knew where the blind spots were in the cameras around the house, and things would go missing without Benji ever noticing. I noticed, though. I kept quiet, but I took note.

When he stole Maren, knowing full well I was interested, it was just one more "thing" Brock decided to steal. It was the reason I knew that, if I wanted to finally be free, I needed to make a way on my own.

Ironically, Benji was the only one standing in my way and the thorn in my side once I finally made a name for myself. He taught me not to remain a victim of circumstance. But when I stepped into the future—away from him—I was told I could only go so far.

"Everything you are is because of me," he told me.

And it was true. It was one of Benji's last connections, a man who remembered me from one of the poker games, who set me up with a mentor once I got my real estate license. This mentorship evolved into a partnership, and eventually became the foundation of my business when he retired and I started my own brokerage.

Benji wanted me to stay on to help him with the apartments, especially when he had to sell off his other properties to pay the bills or to keep from getting sued. When it was apparent I was rising to the top while he was tumbling down, he reminded me again and again that if it weren't for him, I'd be in jail or dead.

Everything you are is because of me.

Which is why he's still insured and receiving top notch, round the clock care, why his mortgage continues to be paid, and why—when I realized those apartments were beyond repair—the title was transferred to me in case anyone else decided to sue.

I turn the car off, but still can't bring myself to go inside. In the depths of this cold, dark house is a man who is living his final days. His rapid decline lets me know we are reaching the end, and I'm not sure how I feel about it. On one hand, here was a man who gave me a home and security, allowing me to sleep at night without worrying about my safety. But on the other hand, his death will finally break my shackles. I am tied to this man, whether I want to be or not. He never showed me love, I'm not even sure he was capable of love, but he did care for me in a way no one else had outside my late parents.

My phone buzzes and I am glad for the excuse to spend a few more minutes outside. But when I see the name of the person calling, something in me knows.

"Mac, you need to come to the house."

Hattie's voice catches slightly, and something in my chest drops. It's like all the life goes out of my body, knowing the exact reason she's calling.

"I'm right outside." I hang up without another word. My body moves of its own accord, carrying me down the walkway and up the steps. The same steps I took at fifteen before I snuck in a side window. The steps I took every day after school, and then later after work at the apartments. The steps I took before I told him I'd enrolled in real estate classes, and then when I said I was quitting the apartments to pursue my career.

The steps I have taken just about every day this month as I've taken residence in my old room, the smallest in the house, while the man who raised me lies dying in the living room.

A house that once held parties and poker games, a full staff, and was the setting for every lesson I learned on the way to becoming a man.

The house is dark when I enter, as it's been since Benji's health declined. Hattie stands by the bed, her hands twisted in front of her as I approach. She moves aside when I get close, resting a hand on my shoulder.

"He loved you, you know," she says, and it takes everything in me not to break the silence with a sardonic laugh. She never knew Benji before he was sick, so how would she know about his feelings? She presses something into my hand, then murmurs she'll be in the other room, and to take as long as I need.

I stare at Benji. I take in the gray of his skin, and how it just hangs on his bones without any life left to animate it. His eyes are closed, but his mouth is open, and I eventually have to look away so that I'm not haunted by the vacancy in his face. His chest remains forever still now that he's released his final breath.

I wasn't here when he died. After all of this, all the nights I stayed, the days I checked his status in between appointments—after all of it, I had failed him in the end.

I open my hand, revealing a folded piece of paper with my name on it. I've seen Hattie's handwriting on Benji's charts long enough to recognize it as hers. Sure enough, when I open it, a note from her is on the top followed by the rest.

This note was dictated to Hattie Wilson on May 23, 2023, by Benjamin Wright when he was of sound mind and good spirits.

Dear Malcolm,

If you are reading this letter, it is because I've left this world for the next, wherever that might be. I realize a letter like this is poor timing, because the things I want to express are things I should have said a long time ago. Even now, the coward in me is waiting until my death to share how I feel about you. The only word I can think of is Pride. I am proud of you. You came to me at your lowest point in life. What you don't know is that I was also at my lowest point. I'd made several business decisions that cost me dearly. My wife left soon after, seeing the writing on the wall. When you walked into my house, I didn't see a thief, but an opportunity. And thus, I treated you that way every day since.

What I never told you was how much I cared for you. You see, while I was saving you, you were saving me too. You were there as everyone else left my life. Even now, when you have every right to walk away, you have stayed. I take this knowledge with me to the grave. I gave you everything I could to ensure your safety, but I never gave you the acceptance you needed to excel in life. I never gave you the love I know you needed more than anything at all.

I love you, Malcolm. You, and Brock too, were like sons to me. I just didn't know how to be a father. But somehow, in spite of me, you learned how to be a man. I couldn't be prouder.

Your friend in death,

Benji

I wipe the tears streaming down my face, tucking the letter into my jacket pocket. By the date, it was written almost a month ago. Part of me glowers at this realization, that he had ample time to tell me these words. The other part feels like a piece of resentment has chipped away, leaving room for healing.

On the table is another folded letter addressed to Brock, and I can't help wondering what he had to say to him. But I leave it alone. I don't want anything to get in the way of what the old man told me, including any words he had for his other "son."

I take Benji's hand in mine—his joints are already stiff, his skin cold to the touch—but I hold it, letting the iciness penetrate the warmth of my own hand.

"I've thought about what I was going to say when we finally reached this point," I utter into the stillness of the room. "For years, I have felt indebted to you, like there was no way I could ever repay you for what you've done for me. All I wanted…" My voice breaks, and I look away. It's hitting me how final all of this is, and the way I'm feeling is unlike anything I expected. "All I wanted was your acceptance," I finish, "Everything I did was for you. Even when I quit the apartments, my plan was to make enough money to get you out of this mess. But by the time I did, you…you were dying, and it was too late. The only thing I could do was clean up your mess so that your legacy wouldn't be tarnished."

I let go of Benji's hand, then pace the floor in front of his bed. The note seems to be burning a hole in my pocket, and it almost makes me want to swallow the words I'm about to say. But I don't.

"Thank you for leaving me something kind to remember you by," I finally say, stopping as I pat my pocket, "I take your words to heart, and I believe you meant them. But it doesn't take away the fact that since I entered your home, my role has been to be the crutch you needed while everything around you crumbled. I thought you were raising me to be successful, but really you were grooming me to be your champion, and damn, I've done a good job. I've been the perfect codependent, making sure you always had the appearance of perfection. No one noticed the kid who was doing the work of the staff you fired. It took a long time for anyone to notice your manipulations, and that's only because you lent me out like my services were a free gift. I did it because this—" I slam my hand against my chest pocket. "This is all I ever wanted to hear from you. Even when I paid off your tenant to drop the lawsuit, and when I urged you to sign the apartments over to me, it was all for you.

"Well, I'm done cleaning up your messes. Now that you're gone, everything you've worked for is gone, including your name. I cannot let you pass from this world into the next without being held accountable for your actions. The only condolence I can offer is that you aren't here to face the full repercussions for your actions, and there's a big chance I will. But for those families, I will do what's right, even if that means exposing health issues they may not even know they have, and that their living situation was the reason for it."

I take a deep breath, holding it as I study my benefactor one last time. Then, when my lungs feel like they're about to burst, I let the air out slowly.

This is the end. And I am done.

Chapter Twenty-One

Maren

Three weeks. That's how long it's been since I last saw Mac. Not that I'm counting. Not that I'm looking out my window every morning, hoping to see a glimpse of him.

Not that I care.

"You ruined it for all of us, you know." Nina, my empathetic roommate, bumps into me on her way to get coffee while I pretend I haven't been standing at the window for a half hour. "All you have to do is go beg him to take you back. Is that asking too much? Because those of us who haven't been getting it on the reg would like to see a little ab action again."

I haven't told Nina everything about Mac, like how he once knew me before he was hot and rich, or how he was actually brothers with my fuck buddy, or how he stopped me from giving up seven years of sobriety, or the hurt look in his eyes when he knew it was over.

I also didn't tell her about the lawsuit, because as mad as I am at him, I don't need Nina to feed the rumor mill and paint him as a slumlord.

But I did tell her how he not only sold the building, but he also owned it, thus making him the one who kicked all of us out with practically no notice. And for that, Nina should be on my side. After all, it's why I'm here, encroaching on her space.

However, Nina's allegiance lies with Mac's sculpted abs. But judging by my morning station at the window, the way I watch the door at Insomniacs, how many times I've come close to calling him or stopping at Benji's house, it appears I'm on Mac's side too.

I won't cave though. All it takes is thinking of how he covered up the mold issue, or how sick Molly's son had been. How sick *I* had been without even knowing it. He covered all of this up instead of just dealing with it, and then he gave us thirty days to find a new place, knowing full well none of us would ever find anything in that price range.

No, Mac and I don't belong together. His world is too different from mine. He has no idea what it's like to skip a meal because there is literally nothing to eat. He doesn't know what it's like to turn on the lights and nothing happens because the electric bill hasn't been paid. He's never had to sleep in his car with a screwdriver in his hand in case anyone wants to rob him, rape him, or kill him.

He has no idea about the impossibility of finding a new place to live in just thirty days when every other apartment is almost double what we were paying. Yes, we were all lucky to live in a place with such low rent. But when the floor dropped out from under us, we were all screwed.

Thank goddess Nina stepped up, because I can never go back to the streets again. There were things I did back then in an effort to survive that I will not do now. That I *can't* do now.

I am not that person anymore.

If I were forced to live on the streets again, with no place left to turn, I would not have survived. For all of that and more, I cannot forgive Mac.

In the meantime, I've been left with a lot of time on my hands. I've taken a break from performing at Hillside, which means I've been wandering Nina's house in the hours I'm not working at Insomniacs. Every room is now organized. No clothes are hanging in the kitchen, the living room has clear spaces to sit, and I even cleared out another bedroom which Nina immediately took over as her closet.

However, as grateful as Nina was for the organization help, she also told me I needed to find a new hobby to keep myself busy.

She was right. If I didn't distract myself with something soon, I was going to end up painting every wall and re-staining the hardwood floors. Or worse—calling Mac and telling him I missed him.

So a week ago, I posted an index card on the bulletin board at Insomniacs, offering to teach music to beginners. The day hadn't even ended before I got a call. Now, at any moment, my first student is going to walk through the door.

There is no word to describe the mixture of nerves and excitement I'm feeling.

On cue, the doorbell rings and the butterflies I'm feeling do swan dives in my belly. I've stared death in the literal face, but this feels scarier.

"You got this," Nina says, shaking me loose from my anxiety. It's a rare moment when Nina is supportive, and I flash her a grateful smile in response. Then I gather my wits, put on my best mask of confidence, and head to the door.

The lesson proves to be nothing to be afraid of. Dylan is a fast study, which I fully attribute to the fact that he's eleven. He soaks up everything I teach him, and by the time his mom comes to pick him up, he can play Bob

Marley's "Three Little Birds," a personal favorite of mine that only uses three of the chords he's memorized.

"Mom, you should hear Maren play," Dylan says once he's shown off what he can do. I feel my face heat up as his mom, Lacey, looks toward me. After a little coaxing, I finally play an acoustic version of Paramore's song, "You First," off their latest album. I only play a few lines, but it's enough to remember why I love performing, and that I actually miss it. When I look up, Dylan is beaming while Lacey looks a bit starstruck.

I am not one to ever feel embarrassed about performing in front of other people, and yet, I feel a little shy as I put my guitar away.

"You're really good," she says.

"I'm just having fun." I tuck a strand of hair behind my ear and stand. She fishes a check out of her purse, and I discreetly glance at it, then do my best to keep my eyes from bugging out of my face. It's five times the amount I quoted her.

"I'm pre-paying for the next month, if that's okay," Lacey says, and I nod as nonchalantly as I can. Inside, I'm squealing. "Also, if it's okay with you, I'd like to pass your name to someone I know in the business. I can't promise anything, but she's looking for new talent to work with, and I have a feeling you might be the perfect fit. Do you have any samples?"

Do I? Only a few hundred of them. In my room, I

have a whole box of thumb drives that hold music, photos, videos of my performances, and my contact information, plus links to my social media. I retrieve one, but as I'm placing it in Lacey's hand, I realize how meager it is.

"I don't have a website or anything," I say, "and I'm not on Spotify." I start to go on, but she waves me off.

"That just means you're truly undiscovered," she says. "Talent is talent. Let's just wait to see what my friend says, okay?"

An hour later I'm racing out the door to make it to Claire's house to hang with my favorite kid while my best friend enjoys a much-needed date with her fiancé. I can't seem to lose the permanent grin on my face, which hasn't quit since Dylan and his mom left. Lacey's words are swimming through my head. Even though she stressed that this was a long shot, it was still a shot. It was closer than anything I'd experienced in my life. I mean, what if it turned into an audition? A contract?

A fucking album and concert tour?

"Don't get ahead of yourself," I mutter, but the grin remains as I slide into my car and turn the key in the ignition. I plug in my phone, and of course Paramore comes on since that was the last thing I was listening to.

But my smile falters.

The song is "Ain't It Fun," a song I've heard at least a million times. Except, all I can think of is the orchestra version, surrounded by thousands of flickering lights, and my hand safely encased in Mac's.

I miss him, and now that I have this news, I want to share it with him. Even if it amounts to nothing, especially if it doesn't, I need him to anchor me, to be thrilled with me, to dream up the possibilities—and if it all falls apart, I want him there to pick up the pieces.

Because I have spent my whole life being my own savior, and I'm tired.

"I'll just drive there," I tell myself. The car is already heading in the direction of the house where Mac's been staying, as if I'm not the one in control. "If he's not there, I'll take it as a sign."

Please be there. Please be there.

I turn down one street, and then the next until I'm slowing in my approach to the house. Before I've even pulled up, I can already see I'm too late.

A "For Sale" sign hangs from a white post on the front lawn. There's been some landscaping since the last time I was here, and the house appears to have much more curb appeal. As if it's waiting for new owners.

Because no one lives here.

I park in the empty driveway, and even though I'm already late for work, I get out of my car. Peering in the windows, I see there is no furniture. The place is completely emptied out. It's like no one has lived here for years.

I wanted a sign, and I think I got it.

I bite my lip, feeling the hot sting of tears threatening to spill down my cheeks. I force them back, swallowing hard as I turn to the street. In the distance, a woman is pushing a jogging stroller as she runs, her ponytail bouncing with each step. At a nearby house, a teenage boy wears large headphones as he mows the lawn, making perfect lines in the grass. A young girl rides her bike up and down a driveway as her dad stands nearby.

My whole world is one big ending, but life goes on.

Ain't it fun?

I shake my head, a small laugh escaping my lips. I could go search out Mac's house on the hill. I think I remember the way. But why? This was a momentary lapse of reason. Mac is still Mac. And me? I'm still Maren. Long after this day, I'll still be doing what I need to do to survive. It's a different fight than the one I battled years ago. But it's a struggle, nonetheless.

And I'm here for it. Because I'm Maren Huerta, and I'm in charge of my own destiny. I have survived this long without Mac Dermot. I can survive forever.

Chapter Twenty-Two

Maren

"I can't believe you're leaving me in this shit hole."

Nina leans against the counter as I clean the espresso machine—for the last time. It's been two months since I started teaching music, and what was supposed to be a side gig, is now a full-time career. I have twelve private students that meet with me on a weekly basis, and a group lesson I hold every Saturday. After today, I will be able to double the number of private lessons, plus have the time I need to focus again on my music.

In my own home.

That's right, ladies and gentlemen, Maren Huerta has the keys to a house. A real house. One with a backyard and a fireplace and no shared walls. Okay, so the backyard is the size of my car, the fireplace plugs into the wall, and the rent is a small fortune. But it's a house. I have a family room where I plan to hold my lessons, a huge bedroom with room for all my guitars, and a large walk-in closet I'll fill with my old clothes, plus some hand-me-downs from Nina that I snagged on a donation run.

Let's just say, life is pretty sweet.

Even if I can't talk to… Nope, not going to even say his name. Life is sweet, the end.

Okay, fine. I'd be a liar if I said I didn't keep tabs on him. I mean, he's not exactly out of the public eye. He has a goddamn billboard that looks over the freeway running through the center of Sunset Bay, for fuck's sake. I've also stalked his social media, but all it shows are homes and businesses he's sold, and I'm pretty sure it's an influencer behind the house and key emojis.

So I'm keeping tabs, but there are no tabs to keep. At the very least, I know he's alive and breathing, and we're still not talking to each other.

My choice. This was my choice.

"Want me to grab some extra boxes from the back," Nina asks, snapping me out of my thoughts.

"Yeah, and grab the extra newspapers while you're at it," I say. I finish the cleaning job, and then look around the shop. Susan never showed up for my last day, but she did send me a card with a gift card in it, $15 for

Insomniacs. It's the thought that counts.

"Face it, you're going to be so bored when you're not waking up at godawful hours to make overpriced drinks for the work rush."

"Oh, definitely," I joke. But inside, I know I will. This is the only job I've ever had, and besides music, the only thing I know. While I'm moving in the right direction, a part of my identity is wrapped up in this place. Who will I be when I'm not a barista?

A musician.

I smile, then turn to Nina and engulf her in a completely uncharacteristic hug. Neither one of us is the touchy feely type, and she stiffens in my embrace. But then she reaches around and hugs me too. I even hear her sniff, and I pull back to make sure. She shakes her head, wiping at her moist eyes.

"I hate you," she says, then shakes out a laugh.

"I hate you too."

I'm going to miss living with Nina. I know—weird. But it's true. These past two months, she's kind of been my rock. Don't get me wrong, Claire is still my best friend, and Nina is still a bitch. But she also cleared a space in her home so I could hold music lessons. She stocked the freezer with Chunky Monkey ice cream—my favorite—because my mopey mood was bumming her out and I might as well get fat. She's even made me start performing again. Rather, she told me if I didn't get my ass off the couch and on a stage, she was going to put hair remover in my shampoo. But once I was on stage, she was sitting in the audience, cheering me on. She even sat with Claire, even though neither one of them is a fan of the other.

Plus, she's helping me move. I thought she'd balk at the request, but she's been actually helpful. Not the twirl her hair kind of helpful while I do all the work, but actually helping. I thought that maybe she was just in a hurry to get me out of her house, but she assured me she wasn't. In fact, she said she was going to miss me.

Okay, she didn't say it. But it was implied in the way she grumbled over who was going to make the coffee now that I was leaving.

We lock up the shop, then juggle boxes and a stack of the Sunset Times as we make our way to my car. I toss the newspapers on the backseat, then do a double take when I see a familiar building peeking from behind one of the sections. I brush the top newspaper out of the way, and there's my old apartment building, back when it was still standing. I drove by there a few weeks ago, and the place had been leveled as if it had never existed at all. But there it is in black and white. I can even see my apartment with my iconic black curtains, dating the picture to sometime before I moved out.

In big, bold letters, the headline reads "Late Tech Genius Discovered to be Penniless Slumlord."

"Are we going or what?" Nina asks. I rifle through the newspaper, then find an identical section. I toss it at her.

"Read this," I say, then climb next to her into the front seat.

> *In the early 2000s, Benjamin Wright left the tech world in favor of real estate. He began snatching up empty lots as quickly as they hit the market, with crews that would erect contemporary apartment buildings in mere weeks. By the end of 2005, he owned 13 apartment complexes that housed hundreds of families. His modern style attracted people from all over California and beyond, and some of his apartment buildings have been featured in magazine like Oceanside Homes and Savor California.*
>
> *Wright passed away this year, but not before he sold all his commercial properties to Southshore Management Group, a well-known Sunset Bay brokerage owned by Malcolm Dermot, who then flipped the real estate to DMD Construction. Each of these properties are now in various forms of demolition, which makes us wonder if Southshore Management Group and DMD Construction discovered what we have—that each of Wright's swiftly built homes are full of cut corners and structural flaws that have resulted in dangerous living conditions.*
>
> *An anonymous tip has led the Sunset Times to uncover*

a long list of violations that include missing permits, cases of black mold, cockroach and rat infestations, leaking ceilings, sewage backups, and missing weather stripping, plus years of neglect despite pleas from residents. The mounting violations have resulted in rapid deterioration of even the newest of Wright's buildings, from his tri-level fleet of beach homes in Santa Barbara to his modest apartment buildings in Sunset Bay.

The car is silent as we read, except for the occasional turning of pages. I barely breathe as I read through everything. How Benji made some bad business moves that cost him his fortune. How he cleverly hid his financial situation as he turned to real estate as his saving grace. He thought the rents would save him, but the upkeep proved to be too much—cracked pipes, roach infestations, roof leaks, molding carpets, faulty heating systems…

I think back to when Mac was working maintenance, and how everything kind of stopped one day. I couldn't even get my leaking faucet looked at. I would call only to be told to file a work order. But there were so many hoops to jump through, I'd end up watching a YouTube video and learn to fix things myself.

But how many other families weren't as handy? Like Molly, raising those kids on her own, with no one to turn to if something were wrong in the apartment. If they were paid off to leave quietly, I can only imagine what their apartment looked like.

It just makes me that much angrier at Mac for not only keeping this from me, but going along with this whole charade. The fact that he owned those buildings too and had the money to make repairs infuriates me. How elitist can you be to sit on your golden throne while your kingdom crumbles around you?

"Whoa," Nina murmurs. I turn, thinking she's heard my thoughts. But she's still reading, her hand at her mouth as her eyes move over the page. I go back to the article, searching until I land on the part she's at.

> *Earlier this year, Wright discovered he had Stage 4 cancer. When told he only had months to live, Wright contacted specialist after specialist but was turned down by everyone.*
>
> *"He was told the cancer was too far advanced for anything to make a difference," said Lily Thebault, his former assistant. "Besides, he didn't have the money to pay them."*
>
> *According to Thebault, this is when real estate broker Mac Dermot stepped in to help. "It was noble, what Malcolm was doing," Thebault said. But it wasn't an easy road in the beginning. "At first, Benji refused. He was too stubborn even though he was in danger of losing it all. But I think Benji realized he was running out of time. He finally sold everything but the house he died in, and the*

money helped fend off collectors and keep his name out of the news. Even more, it allowed him the freedom to die at home."

But Wright's purpose wasn't just for survival, Thebault believes. "I think he did this to wipe the slate clean. He knew the properties were falling apart, and he wanted his name off the deeds."

But the story may hold another deep layer. While there is nothing on paper that links Malcolm Dermot and Benjamin Wright beyond the sale of every one of Wright's properties, one former employee believed their relationship goes much deeper.

"He was like Mr. Wright's kid or something," said Alistair Brock, manager of the Beale Street apartments for the past three years.

"I heard they met when Mac tried to swindle Benji," Brock said. The Beale Street manager relayed a story Wright once told him about the young teen who broke into the real estate mogul's home. "Mac managed to get past the alarms, but missed the cameras, which led to a confrontation with Benji's security team."

The discovery led Mr. Wright to take the kid under his wing. "The way he said it, business and thievery often looked like the same thing, you just wear different suits," Brock said. "I don't want to start rumors, but let's just say that statement makes sense in all interpretations when it comes to both Mr. Wright and Mac Dermot."

> *We have tried contacting Mr. Dermot to validate his relationship with Benjamin Wright and determine how much he knew about the condition of the properties, but he has not been available for comment. Interviews with his former tenants have been unresponsive as well.*

Nice of Brock to throw his brother under the bus like that. I realize their foster status was as legal as everything else Benji touched—meaning that it was not official at all. There was nothing to tie Mac or Brock to Benji except for hearsay.

Reading this article also reminds me of the weird voicemail I'd received months ago. I hadn't recognized the name, and when they mentioned the Beale Street Apartments, I deleted the message, figuring it was an opportunist looking to take advantage of someone looking for a home. I only now realize it was probably a reporter. But honestly, what would I have told them? I want to put Beale Street behind me. I want to forget about Mac. I want to pretend Benji never existed.

I have a better life ahead of me.

"Do you think Mac was in on it?" Nina asks.

I nod, then pause, then shake my head. "I don't know," I finally say, "Part of me thinks he's capable of it, especially if he was trying to rob Mr. Wright." The moment the words leave my mouth, I want to shove them back in. I have a past, but I'm not the same person.

Just because Mac used to be a thief doesn't mean he'd actually be a part of Benji's slum tactics.

But he had to have known. How could he not? And this had to be a coverup. I obviously never knew him as well as I thought. He could absolutely be an accomplice in all of this, covering tracks so that no one would be the wiser. I mean, you can't see black mold in a torn down building.

I take the newspaper from Nina's hand and throw both of them in the backseat. "Let's just forget about Mac and all of this nonsense. I shouldn't have read it. None of it matters anymore anyway, right?"

I look over at Nina, needing her confirmation. She gives it in a slow nod.

"Yeah," she said, "Even if I still miss his abs, he's a fucking asshole."

Chapter Twenty-Three

Maren

Days have passed since I read the article, and I've tried to let it go. I'm in my own home, the tiny house still empty due to my lack of belongings. I've held the first of many music lessons in my family room and done my best to make this space my own. I've poured myself into my music, letting myself dream once again of this becoming so much bigger than the Hillside stage.

But I'm angry. Angry at Benji for fucking things up for so many people, only concerned about his own ass in the end. Angry at Mac for going along with Benji's schemes and covering it up for as long as he did. Angry for being such a fool that I trusted this man when he screwed me over so thoroughly.

And the more time that passes, the angrier I get.

Tell that to my dreams, though. Mac has haunted almost every one of them, but in surprising ways—his chest flush against mine, claiming my with his mouth, my legs wrapped around his waist as he lowers me to the bed…

How can I hate this man so much during the day only to dream of him like this every night?

This morning, it took a few moments to remember my anger as I touched my lips, the ghost-like feel of him still lingering all over my body.

I can't keep doing this.

Swigging one last gulp of coffee, I grab my keys and the blasted newspaper—which I've almost memorized at this point—then head out the door. I have no plan as I plug Mac's office into my phone, and I let Siri lead the way. It takes fifteen minutes as I fantasize about running into some high-end lawyer and suing Mac for all he's worth…or maybe just kicking him in the balls.

I park my car between two identical Teslas and get out to a parking lot full of luxury vehicles. The housing market is apparently booming for all the assholes who work for Southshore Management Group.

"Can I help you?" the receptionist asks as I breeze past her.

"He's expecting me," I clip out, though I have no idea where I'm going. Luckily, a convenient chart on the wall shares the names of all agents and their office number, and Mac's name is at the very top.

"Miss!" the receptionist calls, but I take the stairs to save time. Even in platform heels, I can be surprisingly fast. I'm rounding the corner before I even hear her feet hit the stairwell.

Mac's name is on the door, and I have to hand it to him for making it so easy for me to find him. I burst through the door, interrupting Mac in the middle of some sort of presentation with a young couple, the mother holding a baby in his arms.

"Be sure to change the locks when you get your new home," I warn the couple, fueled by their shocked faces. "And get a good inspector, this guy will sell you a slum before he steals anything of value."

"Mr. Dermot, I'm sorry." The receptionist pushes past me. "She ran up here before I could catch her."

"It's okay, Tara. I can handle this," Mac says. I smirk at the receptionist, who glares at me in return as she leaves the office.

Mac offers his clients a warm smile.

"James, Anita, can we postpone the tour? I'm afraid I have a pressing matter to attend to."

He says it so calmly, as if this kind of thing can be explained away, and apparently his clients buy it.

"It's okay," the man says, shaking Mac's hand as his wife side-eyes me, "You gave us a great list of things to work on before we sell the house, so we'll start tackling that. Call me later and we can schedule another time."

I move out of the way as the couple leaves, shutting the door behind them. Once alone, I glare at Mac as he leans against his desk, arms folded across his chest, an infuriating half grin on his face.

"This isn't funny," I say, striding forward to slam the newspaper on his desk, "Explain this."

Mac doesn't pick up the paper, but the smile drops from his face.

"Which part?" he asks, "The part where they make Benji sound like a heartless bastard who laughed his way to the bank? The part where my brother acted like some innocent bystander while my name is plastered all over that article?"

"No, the part where I'm supposed to feel warm and cozy about your guardian because he took in two foster kids who needed guidance, when all he sounds like to me is a self-absorbed asshole who probably wouldn't save his own mother out of inconvenience. I'm sorry, I know he just died, but Benjamin Wright was only worried about his legacy in the end. He had no concern for those of us he fucked over, and you did everything you could to support his mission, even after you knew me."

"I know." Mac's eyes drop to the ground. "I wish I could take all of it back, but this was in motion long before I knew you."

"Was this before you were just some maintenance guy covering up the deeper issues in my apartment? Or after we met at Torches when you sold my fucking home?"

"Maren, he had dementia long before he was diagnosed with terminal cancer."

My hands remain clenched, but the admission gives me pause.

When I was young, before Lydia was born, my father's mother used to live with us because she could no longer take care of herself. Even though she probably would have done better in a nursing home, my dad cleared out my mother's craft room and set his mom up in there. At night, I'd hear Abuela pacing the house, unable to sleep, banging pots and pans in the kitchen while my dad pleaded with her to go to sleep.

Then there was the night my grandmother left the house.

We didn't find out until morning—the latch my father had put out of her reach unclipped. He blamed my mother, but it could have been him. Hell, it could have been Abuela; she managed to get into more trouble than one old lady should be able to.

Lucky for all of us, our story had a happy ending. Late that evening, with dozens of people canvassing the neighborhood and posters everywhere, a McDonald's worker found her sitting in the restaurant, eating from an abandoned food tray.

My grandmother was moved into a nursing home by the next weekend, and by the next year, she'd passed away in her sleep.

I only have snippets of memories from before dementia took over. Afternoons when she'd let me roll the tortillas for dinner at her house. Overnight visits when she'd tell me fables and fairytales from memory. How she'd weave my long hair into beautiful double braids. The dresses she used to make me. How, even though she knew English, she only spoke to me in Spanish. How I couldn't speak Spanish, but I understood her every word, and together we'd share conversations in our native tongues, and it made perfect sense.

But the memories are like ghosts, ones I have to strain to recall. The grandmother I remember most is the one who couldn't be left alone. The one who forgot my name, and then my face, until she eventually forgot to speak at all.

I look at the newspaper, a younger picture of Benji on the front page under the "Slumlord" headline, his smiling mug next to my former home.

"How does dementia explain this," I say to Mac, gesturing to the headline on the newspaper.

"Because Benji was not always this man." He pinches

the place between his eyebrows, taking a deep breath. Then he sits in a chair near the desk, gesturing for me to do the same. I hesitate, but eventually sink into the chair next to him.

"I didn't know what was happening at first," he says, "Benji was always so careful with his company. So careful with money. When he took me in, it wasn't for any other reason but to help turn my life around. He gave me a house to live in, security, and real life skills. I learned to trust him with everything in me, something that did not come easy because everyone in my life had let me down. So when Benji started snatching up land and building all these properties, I trusted he knew what he was doing. When I discovered they had some serious issues beyond my skills, I trusted him when he said he had someone lined up to fix it. By the time I figured out that Benji had lost all his money and was up to his eyeballs in debt, it was too late. I never saw the early signs when I was under his wing, and I definitely didn't notice when I was working on my own career."

Mac's eyes become moist, and it's so out of character, I'm not sure what to do. I want to take his hand in mine, to comfort him, but I keep my hands folded in my lap.

"It got to the point that Benji owed more than his properties were worth, and the bank was ready to foreclose on his house and take his cars to make up for his debt. But Benji knew that once that happened, it would become front page news."

Mac laughs, flicking the paper on his desk. "Ironic, huh?"

I don't laugh with him.

"Look, I know you won't understand this, but Benji was everything to me. He took me in when I had no one. I should have seen his deterioration, and it's my biggest regret. When I finally figured out what was happening, I tried to step in and fix everything. But Benji is nothing if not proud, and he couldn't admit he was losing his mind, or that he was in over his head. His so-called friends started to disappear. His businesses started falling apart. He tried to hold on to everything as long as he could, but when the bank started calling though, he knew he had to do something. To keep his name intact, he made me buy everything I could, and start selling them off. The Beale Street Apartments were last, and it took the lawsuit to make it happen."

Mac looks at me then, taking a deep breath. "Maren, it was my decision to sell the properties, though my hands were tied about the speed at which everything took place. With the condition of those apartments, it had to be a demolition company. Only one company made an offer, and they required a 30-day close. We were out of time, and all I could think of was keeping Benji's name clear." He winces, rubbing the back of his head. "I know that sounds horrible, and believe me, I was thinking of all of you as I signed that paper. But I owe Benji my life, whether he's a good man or not, and in that moment, that was what mattered the most."

It's not exactly a surprise. I know why he did it. But still, hearing the words makes every muscle in my body go tight. I start to get up, but he lays a hand on mine to stop me. I stay.

"I know I could have handled it so much better. I should have waited. But with the threat of a lawsuit—"

"You mean Molly," I interrupt, taking my hand out from under his. He grimaces, then nods.

"It should never have gone that far." He rubs the back of his neck, shaking his head.

"What, your benefactor getting sued?"

"No," he says, looking at me, "That her kids were suffering. The oldest was starting to get nosebleeds, and they were all sick. Their doctor pinpointed it to black mold, and they started adding up all the issues with the apartment and got a lawyer." He stops, picks up the paper and drops it. "I don't need to recap it. I know you read the article. I paid her off under the stipulation that she move and not say anything as long as Benji was still breathing."

I eye the newspaper, realizing the timing of all of this. "Was she the one who leaked the story?"

At this he shakes his head and he lowers his eyes.

"Was it…you?"

"It was the least I could do. I promised Benji I would take care of everything. But he's gone, and the people he screwed over are still picking up the pieces."

"The least you could do—"

"There's more," he says, cutting me off, "That was just the start. Benji left everything to Brock and me. I can't do anything about Brock's portion of the estate, but I can with mine, along with the money from the items I've been selling off."

"The Cartier brooch," I murmur.

"Yes, that and a few other things. Anyone who lived in Benji's apartments over the past five years will receive a portion of this fund once we've finished the paperwork. You should be hearing from my lawyer soon, who will present you with a check."

I'm not sure what to say. I came in here ready to rip him a new one, and now all the fight is out of me. Still, accepting the money feels wrong. Even more, I can't help but feel like there's another motive here.

"What's the catch?"

He leans back, crossing his arms in front of him. "No fooling you, huh?"

I cross my own arms, waiting for his answer.

"Yes, it comes with the stipulation that no lawsuit can come of this. My lawyer was very thorough. But we also ensured every former tenant would be compensated generously."

I eye him carefully. "How generously."

"Unofficially?"

I nod.

"You're receiving back everything you paid into rent over the past five years. I wanted to offer more, but this was the best I could do."

I do quick math in my head, and my heart races at the number. It's more than a hundred grand.

"Everyone gets that?"

He nods.

"You understand that I still hate that man," I say, even though I'm having a hard time staying angry right now. A hundred grand feels life changing to me.

He takes my hand back, and I let him. "You have every right," he says, "Benji had his good qualities, but he sure fucked over a lot of people. Including me." He squeezes my hand. "And including you. If I could change anything, I would have gone back to the day I met you the first time, that day in your apartment. I would have told you to move. I would have opened my eyes to see that Benji wasn't in his right mind and needed me to take over. But then none of this would have happened. I wouldn't have met you again."

I look at our hands. How perfectly they fit together. How safe I feel with him touching me, despite everything.

"It's taking everything in me not to show you how sorry I am," he whispers, and he starts to pull me toward him. I place my hand over his, not to stop him, but also not to start anything. I don't know what I want.

The truth is, I miss him. I haven't stopped missing him. Even though I've spent the past few months questioning everything I knew about him, I can't deny the fact that my life has been missing something since the day I walked away from him. He makes me feel things I've never felt before. He drives me crazy. He makes me so mad. But right now, our hands clasped, our bodies turned toward each other, I realize I'm done fighting this. I'm done being mad.

What is there to even be mad about, anyway?

The whole situation is shitty. But when it comes down to it, where my life is now, I can't complain. If I hadn't lost my home, I'd still be working at Insomniacs. I wouldn't have started giving music lessons. I probably would have burnt out on my dream of making it as a musician. Maybe I would have stopped making music. I don't know. All I know is that now, my life looks a lot closer to what I want it to look like, and I know a big part of that is because I was forced out of my comfort zone.

"Show me?" I ask. The corner of his mouth twitches as he stands, and this time when he pulls me toward him,

I don't stop him. Our mouths meet in a tentative kiss, gentle at first, then all-consuming as he wraps his arms around me and picks me up in one swoop. He places me on the desk so that I'm sitting, and he rests his body between my spread legs, straining the tight skirt I put on this morning. But then he stops, pulling away from me.

"Do you want to take control?" he asks. It brings me back to the hotel room, when he turned the tables and dominated me. It had left me feeling raw and exposed. It also was the most intense thing I'd ever experienced.

I love being in control, but with Mac, I feel free with him calling the shots—in bed, that is. Out of bed, he has another thing coming.

"Take me," I say, "Do what you will with me. Tell me what you want me to do, and I'll do it. Maybe then, I'll think about forgiving you."

If I were an artist, I would paint the look that crosses his face so that I'd never forget. It's somewhere between cunning and famished, and I cannot stop squirming as he crosses the office to lock the door.

"What's your safe word?" he asks, turning to face me. The way he slowly rolls up his sleeves makes me breathless, knowing he's about to get down to business. His thick forearms are marked with rigid muscle and black and white tattoos, and I lick my lips in anticipation.

"Safe word?" I ask, a small smile teasing my lips.

"Don't play, Maren. I have so little restraint, it's not

even funny. If you don't have a way to put the brakes on, I'll obliterate you."

I bite my lip. My skin is on fire at the mere suggestion of his punishment. I want all of it.

"There are no brakes," I say.

"Maren."

"Mustard," I blurt out, laughing lightly at the absurdity of the word in this moment. But Mac isn't laughing.

"You have exactly five seconds to change your mind," he growls.

I don't move from the top of his desk. Instead, I watch him and wait for whatever happens next.

My clothes are off before I can blink, save for my heels. He has me positioned so that I face the desk, my hands splayed out in front of me, my ass up in the air. I can see across the city and out to the ocean from his floor to ceiling windows as he strips off his belt in one move, and then lands the leather strap against my flesh. It's hard enough to make me hiss, but not enough to mark me. I feel him hesitate, waiting for me to stop him. I won't. I push my ass toward him until he gives me a few more swats.

"I'm sorry," he then murmurs, running his hand over my heated skin, and then slapping his hand against the tender area. I groan, lowering my head, but not losing my position.

"I'm so fucking sorry." He traces a finger down my slit before sliding it in. I'm already slick, and I inch my heels further apart as he adds another finger, then another.

"Let me show you how sorry I am."

My knees buckle as he moves his fingers in and out of me, and I drop to my elbows on the desk to stabilize my body. Mac grabs a fistful of my hair and pulls my head back, and then his mouth is on mine. My pussy throbs around his hand as I fervently search his mouth, unable to get enough of this man.

Did I really think I was getting out of here without getting fucked? Silly, silly girl.

"Please," I whisper against his mouth. I feel his mouth curve into a smile, his whiskers like tiny electric bolts against my skin. The fact that I'm here, butt naked, while he remains fully clothed is wholly unfair.

"Stay where you are," he says, slipping his fingers from me as I whimper. He backs away, and I hear the thud of his shoes, the hiss of his zipper, and the sound of his clothes hitting the floor. When I glance over my shoulder, he is completely bare, his broad body positioning himself behind me. He pulls me flush against him, my back to his front. Then he runs his hand over my body. It's so intimate the way he's touching me, like he's memorizing every inch of my body. But then he turns me around to face him.

"I want to take my time with you," he says, brushing his lips over mine, "But I'm afraid if I don't fuck you, I'm going to lose my mind."

"Then what are you waiting for?"

The words are barely out of my mouth before he has me lying flat on the desk, his cock nudging my entrance.

And then he's inside me. He moves as if we're each other's air, as if we're only alive for this moment. The way he takes me is as if he's always owned me, and it's hard to remember why we were ever apart, why I would deny myself this.

Mac is anything but gentle in the way he fucks me. But his hands cradle the back of my head, his fingers tangled in my hair as he keeps my head and neck safe. Our breath comes hot and heavy, moving in unison with the pace of our bodies. I wrap my legs around him, my heels glancing off his back as he thrusts harder inside me. His beard brushes against my skin, sending electric shocks throughout my body.

I don't care that we're here in his office, where someone could knock on the door at any moment. Nor do I care that his office window faces another, and all anyone would have to do is look outside to see him taking me on his desk. I don't care about the papers falling to the ground, or how my rigid stance has also fallen to the wayside. All I care about is that I am finally as close to him as I can humanly get, and it still doesn't feel close enough.

"Don't lose me again," I whisper in between hungry kisses.

"Maren Huerta," he says, his mouth never leaving mine, "I am never letting you go."

The words should scare me. Anything close to this kind of claiming would have me running for the hills in the past. This time, I'm met with the most delicious orgasm stemming from his words and the way he's throbbing inside me, washing over my whole body, and leaving me clinging to him as I mewl against his chest. His movements slow to a purposed rhythm. I feel him swell before he growls into my hair, thrusting hard as he milks the orgasm for all it's worth.

When it's over, he collapses on top of me, our bodies shining with sweat. I taste the salt on his skin, feeling him still inside me and dreading the moment he slips out. He stays for a few minutes, as if he also doesn't want to part. But when he does, he lifts me into his arms, then carries me to the oversized leather chair in the corner. He sits, cradling me in his lap, smoothing his hand over my hair as I lay my head against his chest. I can feel the thrum of his heart, and I remain still as I listen to it slow from its racing pace.

I love the way my body feels against his. I love how

safe I feel in his arms. If he'll let me, I know I could fall in love with him.

"Do you forgive me?" he asks, still stroking my hair as if I need comfort. And I do. I need everything he has to give me. I need him.

"I forgive you."

Chapter Twenty-Four

Maren

Seven years ago

"So, are you a musician or something?"

I looked up from my guitar to regard the handyman in the kitchen. He's sipping the soda I just gave him, and I have been trying my hardest to keep my eyes from wandering over the tight fit of his jeans against his groin.

Damn dry spell. This was not a good mix when the maintenance guy was this hot. *Focus, Maren.*

"Something like that," I muttered, then went back to my strumming. I'd been working on a song for a few weeks, and the lyrics weren't coming to me. And the fact that this guy, Mitchel or Malcolm or whatever, was still here, distracting me from my mission was irritating the hell out of me. I had my first gig in a week at an outdoor bar and restaurant called Hillside, and I still needed to come up with a few more songs to make a full set list so that it didn't sound like a bad karaoke show of covers. I didn't have time for maintenance issues, even if I was anxious for him to fix that damn egg smell coming out of my faucet.

"What do you mean, what do you mean, what do mean…" I sang quietly from the couch, feeling shy because I hadn't really played for anyone else before, but had no choice if I wanted to be ready for the show.

"You're good," he said, and I looked up to see him right behind me.

The compliment hit me just right, soothing my inner critic that had been in rare form all morning.

"Thanks," I said. A strand of hair fell in my face as I ducked my head, and I tucked it behind my ear before going back to my strumming. The guy moved around my apartment as I continued to play with lyrics. He kept shining a flashlight in different areas, his smooth-shaven face furrowed in concentration.

"Hey, these dark spots up here need a professional to look at them," he said.

"Isn't that what you are?" I asked, then grinned at him with angelic eyes.

"Hardy-Har-Har. I'm going to mention it to the

manager, but you need to fill out a request, and then keep on your landlord until he brings a specialist out. Promise me you will."

I nodded, already forgetting what he said. "You make me want to believe," I sang under my breath. "But your…" I hummed a few bars, ignoring him as I finally settled on a melody I liked, even as I struggled with the lyrics.

"Your mouth tells two different tales," the handyman murmured.

I stopped playing and looked at him. "What?"

He shook his head. "Sorry. I was just…forget it."

"No, what did you say?"

He rubbed the back of his neck, grinning. I think his cheeks are getting pink. "Your mouth tells two different tales. You know, like the person is talking out both sides of their mouth. He's telling you things you want to believe, but it's not the truth."

I nod slowly, then pluck the chords and begin again, this time using his words to fill in the missing piece.

When you say these things to me
You make me want to believe
But your mouth tells two different tales
What do you mean, what do you mean, what do you mean?

My face broke into a wide grin. "Thank you! I've

been messing with this for weeks, and it was like this huge block was in the way." I was suddenly glad I had an issue this guy could fix. "I'm Maren, by the way."

"Malcolm," he replied. He looked around my apartment, but instead of focusing on maintenance issues, his gaze settled on the posters of my idols on the wall. "So, tell me about these ladies with guitars."

***

Today

"Thank you so much for coming." I strum a few bars on the guitar, then look back out at the Hillside crowd. It's hard to believe I've been doing this for seven years now, and while I still haven't found the fame and fortune I've been hoping for all my life, I realize just how much this stage means to me, and the crowd that comes with it.

In front of me are a group of locals that come to almost every show to sing along, making me feel like I'm a much bigger musician than I am. At a table in the back are a few of my music students and their parents, forcing me to keep this show clean and free of any "F" bombs, which is not that easy to do.

Then there's the table off to the side, always reserved for my people. My family. Claire and her son Finn, plus her fiancé and owner of this bar, Ethan. My former coworker and roommate, Nina, sporting a lovely shade of pink hair.

And Mac, his tan arms crossed in front of him as he watches me with a smile in his eyes. That man is going to be the end of me, I know.

Ever since the day in his office, we've been inseparable to the point that he asked me to move in with him just last week.

"No," I told him, not even hesitating. Even though he has an endless view of the ocean and a kitchen built for a chef, I love having my own place, where I can control the environment and how I live. I can play music until two in the morning and sleep in until ten—as all my lessons are in the afternoon and I no longer need to wake up early to make the residents of Sunset Bay their morning lattes.

That said, I did splurge on my own espresso machine for my house, because good coffee is non-negotiable.

Also, just because I have my own place does not mean I actually sleep alone. If Mac isn't sleeping over at my house, I'm sleeping at his.

And every morning after his run, he treats me to a bare-chested stroll through the neighborhood, the coffee I make him in his hand, and a shit eating grin on his face as I watch him from the window, ready to race him back to bed once he's done.

I pluck at a few chords, then my fingers move into a familiar rhythm. "This next song was written a few years back with the help of someone really special to me. It was originally written as a song about a lying sack of...." I pause, looking at Finn, whose French fry-stuffed mouth is hanging in a grin. "Someone who speaks out both sides of their mouth," I finish, winking at the kid, "But I've recently discovered there are many different sides to a story. Sometimes a lie is because the truth is too painful. Sometimes it's to protect the people we love." I look at Mac, offering him a crooked smile. "And sometimes it leads us to something better that we might have missed out on if we knew the truth too early."

Mac tilts his head at me, and I know he's wondering what I'm up to. I've been practicing this song for the past few weeks whenever he's been away at the office, so he has no idea what's coming.

"At any rate, this new song isn't about any of that, though that was its origin. Now, it's something a lot more fitting about how I feel about this special someone."

I wink at Mac, then I close my eyes, letting the music take over me.

I was a broken fool when you came to me
A vacant pool of despondency.
You were uncharted waters, an endless sea

That captured my heart in spite of me.

Your words are ones I've never heard
Born from places broken and blurred
But full of hope despite the pain
You unravel the lies I'm quick to claim.

You tell me I'm wanted, that no one compares
And you undo the hurts I've suffered for years
My heart has been crushed time and again
But I see a beginning where I once saw the end.

You tell me I'm wanted, that I'm not a mistake
You kiss my hurts and mend my heartache
All the ways that they broke me and tore me in two
You pull me together; you make everything new.

When you say these things to me
You make me want to believe
But the daggers pointed at me
Have become the end of me

When you say these things to me,
You shield me from their harm
Your mouth tells beautiful tales
I believe, I believe, I believe.

I end the song looking at Mac, fighting the tears

brimming my eyes. He touches his heart, then his lips, and then points to me. I do the same for him before swiping at my moist eyes.

"I'll be back in five," I say quickly into the mic, then set my guitar on the stand. He's there at the bottom of the stairs to the stage and engulfs me in a hug once I reach him.

"I think I remember that one a little differently," he laughs in my hair. It was only a few short months ago that I spat those lyrics from the stage, but a much more spiteful version.

"I think you've ruined the coldhearted bitch part of me." I press my lips to his, lingering before pulling back to look at him—at his crinkling blue eyes, the curve of his smile, his delicious long beard that I love running my fingers through. I do this now, but he captures my hand in his.

"Oh, she still exists," Mac says, "I have to punish her out of you."

"Promises, promises." I offer him a wicked grin before lightly biting his lip.

"Uh, Maren?"

The soft, familiar voice jolts me back to reality, and I turn to find Lydia—and behind my sister, my parents.

I move from Mac's arms to face them, and I find comfort in the way he touches my back, letting me know he's here. But still, a seed of unease grows inside me now that I'm facing my parents again. The last time I saw my father, he was pointing a gun at me, accusing me of being a thief.

The look on his face is different now. Humbled. He rests a hand on my sister's shoulder, and I recognize that he's depending on her strength in this moment.

"Hi Dad, hi Mom," I say. My mother's face crumbles, and she rushes forward, engulfing me in a hug.

"Mi amor," she says, "My Maren."

The ice melts in my heart, something breaking inside me as I'm shown the first form of love from her in years. But my arms stay at my sides, and I remain aware of Mac's touch still at my back. *I'm here,* it says, *I will always be here.*

"Isabella," my father murmurs, and my mom releases me with a shower of apologies. She looks to my dad, and he nods at me.

"Maren, you look good," he says.

I could take this moment to point out that I look no different than I have for years, he's just refused to see me. I could point out all the ways he hurt me. How they refused to let me come home. How they couldn't see that I'd changed. How they once told me they loved me, but proved their love was conditional.

"Thank you," I say, "You do, too."

I'm lying; they both look tired. Older. Full of

remorse. I wonder if they had as many sleepless nights as I have over the years.

"Your music, your singing, you're quite good," he continues, "But you always have been. I told your mother when you were young, that girl has talent. And look at you now."

I laugh, in spite of the heaviness that surrounds us. "Hardly. But the tips and free soda don't hurt."

My father looks at Lydia, then back to me. He squeezes her shoulder.

"I told him everything, Mare," my sister says. I offer a confused look. "About that night you saved me," she continues, "You were right about my so-called friends."

I jolt with alarm. "Did they—"

"No," she says quickly, "but this other girl at school wasn't so lucky. Ended up in the hospital. Her family pressed charges, and three guys I thought were my friends are now in juvie." She ducked her head. "I testified at the trial," she says, "I tried to think of what you would do, and I did it."

I fold my sister into a hug, clutching her tightly as my heart bursts with pride. In this moment, I know my love for her has never stopped. She's no longer the sweet adolescent I left behind, but she's a young woman who has a better path in store for her than I did at her age. And for that, I am so grateful.

"I told Dad he was wrong about you, too," she says, pulling away from me. She glances at our father. He closes his eyes briefly, but then speaks.

"Lydia says you've been clean for years."

I nod, my hands finding their way in front of me as I fiddle with my fingers. I've dreamed of this day for so long, but now that it's here, I don't know how to act. In my fantasies of this moment, I tell my father exactly what a bastard I think he is. But now in reality, I see the man who raised me, who had stern ways but also treated me with tenderness in my younger years. I see a man who was dealt a hand he didn't have the tools for. I realize now how human my parents are, and that while I was making mistakes, they were making their own. I say as much to them, knowing it's an olive branch I don't need to offer.

"We were afraid," my father returns, "It's no excuse. We should have sought help, put you in a program, done whatever we could to help you. I've always said, family comes first. But when faced with the ultimate test, I failed. I thought I needed to bar you from our home to keep us safe. But I failed to keep *you* safe in the process, and for that, I will forever be sorry."

My father is crying. I have never seen this man show weakness in his life, unless masked with anger. But now, his vulnerability reaches for me, pleads with me, and I answer the call. I move from Mac's reassuring touch and enter the uncertainty of my father's arms.

This isn't fixed. I know this, even as I pull away and smile at both my parents through my tears. Even as I tug Lydia to me again and she leans into me, her arm around my waist. This is a moment, a steppingstone toward healing. But we have a long way to go before any of this is mended completely. Maybe it will never be completely mended. Maybe it will just be different than before, more cautious. After all, I've changed—and they have too.

We have years and years to get to know each other and build a new kind of family.

I step back and take Mac's hand. "Mac, you know Lydia." I wink at her, and she rolls her eyes, probably thinking about how she puked by the side of his car. "And these are my parents, Manny and Isabella Huerta. Dad, Mom, this is Mac, my…" I pause, looking at him. I'm brought back to the night of the concert, when Mac told me I was his and he was mine, and it was as simple as that. Months later, here we are, and it's as simple as that.

"Mac is mine, and I am his," I finish, looking at him. He squeezes my hand, his eyes softening toward me before he turns to my father.

"It's nice to meet you under better circumstances this time." Mac's voice is tight, and I know it will take him a while to trust my dad. I don't even trust my dad. But in

Mac's face, I see his vow to keep me safe, and this is something I can believe in.

If I was fooling myself before, I can't now. I'm falling for him, this man who doesn't mince words, who has my back, who would move mountains for me.

"All right, all right, schmooze fest over," Nina says as she approaches, towing Claire and Finn behind her, followed by a woman I've never met before. "I'm sure you all have a lot of catching up to do, but this family reunion needs to wait. Maren, I'd like you to meet Phaedra Collins." My brassy ex-roommate gives a dramatic pause, eyebrows raised meaningfully. "A record producer with Starboard Sounds."

It takes everything in me to not melt into a pile of goo as I shake Phaedra's hand and offer a stumbling greeting. I'm very familiar with Starboard Sounds, and I recognize Phaedra Collins's name. Truth be told, Starboard is kind of a dream producer for me, but I've never sent them any samples. I told myself I was waiting until I'd recorded more songs and had more experience, but truthfully, I was afraid of blowing my shot too soon and never getting another chance. It was safer to never contact them than to seek their representation and be denied.

Now, Phaedra Collins stands before me, her business card extended in her hand.

"You know Lacey Tanner, right?" she asks as I take her card. I glance at it, just to make sure it's real. It is.

"Dylan's mom, right?" I look toward the table in the back, spotting Lacey talking with a few of the other music moms. She looks toward me and breaks into a wide grin, then gives a thumbs up.

"Right. Dylan is my nephew, and Lacey is my sister-in-law. She told me how you've been giving Dylan music lessons, and I'm impressed with what he's learned in such a short time."

"Dylan makes it easy," I say, "The talent is all his, I just help him tap into it."

"Well, whatever you're doing, it's working. And what you're doing on stage, that's more than incredible. You write your own songs and music?"

I nod. "I play covers too. It helps the crowd to know a few songs to get them warmed up."

"I can't believe I haven't heard you before. But Lacey gave me your sample, and I've been playing it on repeat ever since. I don't know where you're at with your music, but if you want to take it further, I'd love to be the one in your corner."

I look to Nina, whose beaming smile is as bright as the afternoon sun. I look at Mac, who appears to be waiting for my answer.

"Hija," my mother breathes, and I'm more than grateful my family is here for this. They missed so much of my life, but now they get to see a brand-new beginning, one that could change everything.

"Are you asking me to sign with you?" I ask, just to be sure.

"Well, there's a lot of paperwork before we make it official, but yes. I want you to be a part of Starboard Sounds, and I personally want to be the one that helps steer your music career into the spotlight, where it deserves to be. Maren, you're a star."

Inside, I'm dying. Literally dying. Like, my heart could fall out of my chest at any moment, it's beating so fast. But on the outside, I rein it in with a smile and try not to gush too much as I shake her hand.

"Yes. Absolutely," I say, and laugh as everyone around me cheers. My people. Everyone who means something to me.

"You did it, baby," Mac says, once everyone has gone back to their seats and I'm back at the stage. I've taken a much longer break than anticipated, definitely longer than five minutes. But under the circumstances, it's fine. It's more than fine.

Mac presses his lips to mine. "I'm so proud of you, and it's so much more than record labels and stage presence and even how you handled your father. I'm proud of who you are and how you make me feel being around you and how fucking strong you are." He pauses, taking my face in his hands as he looks into my eyes.

"Maren Huerta, I love you. I think I've always loved you. But in this moment, I love you more than ever, and though it's hard to imagine, I know I'll love you more every day you let me love you."

I place my hands over his, the emotion in his eyes and in his words mirrored in my own heart. Those three words are so little compared to what I'm feeling now, but I say them anyway. "I love you, too. Once we can finally get out of here, I plan to show you how much I love you all night long."

Mac growls, then nips my lip with his teeth. If we didn't have a whole crowd watching us, I know he'd smack my butt. But he restrains himself. I on the other hand, do not, and land my hand firmly on the stiff denim covering his fine ass. "Later, gator," I say, and he shakes his head at me.

"What the fuck am I going to do with you?" he asks.

Months ago, on a rooftop bar under a maroon sky, Mac held my face and asked me the same question, and I never got the chance to give him an answer. This time is different.

"Love me," I say.

"Forever."

On stage, I look out at the crowd. Night has fallen, but the place is lit up by stringed lights like we're at a country barn dance. Everything looks different now, and I realize this could be one of my last shows here on this tiny stage. Once I sign with Starboard Sounds, anything could happen. I could be in the recording studio instead of freezing my ass off playing for a local outdoor bar. I could be on tour, singing for tens of thousands instead of mere dozens.

But for now, I'm singing for my people. My family. For Sunset Bay.

"Growing up, all my heroes were female rock stars—Hayley Williams from Paramore, Shirley Manson from Garbage, Chrissie Hyde from The Pretenders, and Stevie Knicks from a little band called Fleetwood Mac. I'd like to start this next set with one of my favorite Fleetwood Mac songs, as it holds special meaning for me, especially tonight. If you know the song, I'd love if you sang along.

I launch into "Landslide," looking at my father who is now sitting next to Mac as I sing about a daughter growing up and spreading her wings, preparing to leave her family.

I never got to experience a traditional way of leaving the nest. But like the song, time made me bolder, allowing me the strength I needed for each step of the mountain I was climbing.

My father mouths the words with me, tears forming tiny rivers down his cheeks. All the love I have for him, along with all the love I know we'll recover, shines out as we sing together.

My father is my past, and now he's my present. But then I look to Mac, who is my future—and as the song comes to a close, I know this man is my forever. My love, my burly man, my beautiful Naked Coffee Guy.

And no landslide could ever bring us down.

Editor's Note and Acknowledgements

There's so much I could say about Mac and Maren, and there just isn't enough space. Let's just say that before there was *Sunset Bay*, there was Maren. She was the whole reason I wrote this series. I came up with a half dozen storylines, trying to get her story just right. But nothing was working. I knew she was this kickass musician who refused to take anyone's shit. But every time I tried to write about her, I just couldn't do her justice.

Luckily, it made more sense to write Claire's story first. Maren became this awesome side character who always told the truth and never strayed from being herself. Through Claire's story, I got to know Maren even more. And when I was finally able to sit down to write her story, Maren took my computer and wrote her own damn story.

I mean, would you expect anything less?

This book was originally going to be single POV, but I realized something was missing. The story needed Mac's voice. The challenge? I hadn't dug deep enough into Mac's side of things to really know him. But oh man, once he started coming through the pages, I just couldn't escape him. Who'd want to, anyways?

I absolutely fell in love with Mac and Maren. These are two characters who believe they're different from each other, but their broken pasts make them more similar than they realize. I have not loved two characters more since Sonny and Cricket (IYKYK).

Oh, and then there's Nina. Who knew she was so funny?! Stay tuned for *Savior Complex*, because Nina's story is next.

Here are a few secrets from Naked Coffee Guy:

This book was born from a viral TikTok video of a real-life Naked Coffee Guy, teasing his whole neighborhood with his nearly naked barefoot stroll. A huge thank you to Amy Davis who caught the whole thing on video and posted it, and to the OG NCG, Daniel Levy, who served as great inspiration for a whole freaking book.

The scene on the rooftop bar was inspired by the song "Maroon" by Taylor Swift. Using TS songs is becoming somewhat of a theme in my books, and I'm not sorry.

Those who have read all my books will recognize a nod toward TWO of them in this story. Did you find them?

The playlist I shared in the front of this novel is made up of all of Maren's favorite artists. And they are all female because Maren insisted.

THANK YOU

Naked Coffee Guy wouldn't be possible without the following people.

First, my heartfelt thanks goes to Sarah Villanueva, my treasured editor. This is the third book we've worked on together, and I am so grateful we get to work together! I can't wait to do it all again.

To Summer McLerran, my firstborn daughter, my friend, and who this book is dedicated to for all the ways she's been there through Maren's story. She is absolutely Maren's biggest fan. Also, Summer is getting ready to release her debut novel. Watch out, because soon you'll see Summer Raine McLerran's name everywhere.

To Helga Breyfogle, who reads more than anyone I know, speaks Bookstagram fluently, and who has been instrumental in making sure I hit all the right romance notes (and slaps my hand when I don't).

To Lucas Dillon, my son who doesn't read romance, but never fails to cheer me on, and cracks all of us up when he "narrates" my books.

To my family, who is not allowed to read this book.

And all my love and gratitude to my husband Shawn. Everything I write about love is because I know it with you. Thank you for always being my biggest supporter, for believing in my dreams, and for loving me with all your heart. *I am yours, and you are mine. It's that simple.*

Coming in 2024

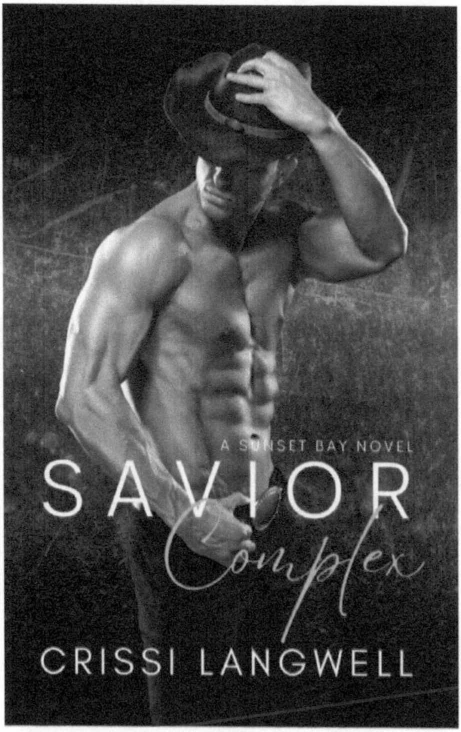

Savior Complex

Nina's Story

Sunset Bay, Book 3

Sign up for the first peek at
crissilangwell.com/subscribe

Books by Crissi Langwell

ROMANCE

Masquerade Mistake ~ Sunset Bay 1

Naked Coffee Guy ~ Sunset Bay 2

Savior Complex ~ Sunset Bay 3 (Coming 2024)

For the Birds

Numbered

Come Here, Cupcake

OTHER BOOKS BY CRISSI LANGWELL

Loving the Wind: The Story of Tiger Lily & Peter Pan

The Road to Hope ~ Hope Series 1

Hope at the Crossroads ~ Hope Series 2

Hope for the Broken Girl ~ Hope Series 3

A Symphony of Cicadas ~ Forever After 1

Forever Thirteen ~ Forever After 2

About Crissi Langwell

Crissi Langwell writes stories that come from the heart, from romantic love stories to magical fairytales that happen worlds away. She pulls her inspiration from the ocean and breathes freely among redwoods. She lives in Northern California with her husband and their blended family of three young adult kids, and a spoiled and sassy cat. Find her at crissilangwell.com.

www.ingramcontent.com/pod-product-compliance
Lightning Source LLC
Chambersburg PA
CBHW032236010726
47494CB00002B/512
9781961240025